# CLIENT N° 5

## JOY FULCHER

OMNIFIC PUBLISHING
LOS ANGELES

Omnific Publishing
1901 Avenue of the Stars, 2nd floor
Los Angeles, CA 90067
www.omnificpublishing.com

First Omnific eBook edition, x 2013
First Omnific trade paperback edition, x 2013

The characters and events in this book are fictitious.
Any similarity to real persons, living or dead,
is coincidental and not intended by the author.

Library of Congress Cataloguing-in-Publication Data

Fulcher, Joy.
   Client N° 5 / Joy Fulcher – 1st ed.
   ISBN: 978-1-623420-60-4
   1. Prostitution — Fiction. 2. Erotica — Fiction.
   3. Contemporary Romance — Fiction. 4. New York City — Fiction. I. Title

10 9 8 7 6 5 4 3 2 1

Cover Design by Micha Stone and Amy Brokaw
Interior Book Design by Coreen Montagna

Printed in the United States of America

# CHAPTER ONE

He thrust inside me with a grunt and I closed my eyes. In the blackness of my mind he wasn't an overweight, balding accountant who smelled of stale tobacco. He was tall, handsome, and gentle. God, I couldn't even remember the last time I'd *made love* instead of fucked. Maybe I never had.

"Ugh! You're so tight, sweetheart."

Didn't this guy have anything more original? I smiled sweetly at him as he pounded into me with his stubby cock. In all honestly, I could barely feel it. I'd already seen three clients that night and had only managed to get aroused with one of them. He hadn't even made me come in the end, but that was nothing new.

"Ride me!" the guy groaned, flipping us over.

I straddled his large belly and leaned back, giving him a nice view of my body. His eyes practically rolled back in his head. Men were so predictable.

Up and down. He moaned. Up and down. He smacked my ass. Up and down. I fought a yawn.

My hair fell in long brunette waves over my shoulder, and his hand reached up and tugged on the ends. It wasn't painful, but it motivated me to keep going. I was a professional and always wanted to make sure my clients were satisfied. But I was also exhausted and ready for bed—for sleeping, not fucking.

I glanced at the glowing red numbers on the alarm clock. I'd been there for twenty-six minutes. Technically, clients got to have me for an hour, but if I could finish them off before their time was up, they were usually happy to let me go. Happy dick, happy man.

I placed my hands on his chest and leaned forward, shoving my breasts in his face and slamming myself down on his toothpick. His grunting increased, of course, and I did what I had to do to push him over the edge.

"Oh, God, yes. Fuck me with your hard cock," I moaned breathily.

He grabbed my hips and pulled me down harder, over and over in a quick rhythm.

"So close!" He scrunched up his eyes.

"Ugh! I'm coming!" I screamed, even though I wasn't. I knew it was over the top, but it was what he wanted to hear and what he was paying me for.

He let out a long, loud groan and sunk into the mattress. His hands fell from my body, and I continued to slowly swirl my hips over him, milking him until I knew he was done.

"You're amazing," he sighed.

I swung my leg up and over his beer gut and fell next to him on the mattress.

"I aim to please. Is there anything else I can do for you, sexy?"

He chuckled and shook his head, still lost in the after-bliss of his orgasm. That was the key. If I let him recover, he would probably ask for round two. But if I could get out while he was still leaking cum, I'd be on my way home by the time he wanted more.

I smiled and gave him a playful wink before standing up and pulling on my bra and panties. He watched me with a satisfied smirk, the condom still hanging from his now-limp cock.

"Can I call you when I come back into town next month?"

"Sure. You have the agency's number." I didn't want to confirm that he'd get me again. More than likely he'd get one of the other girls. I tried not to have regular clients because things could turn messy.

Dressed and with his money safely in my purse, I went to the door and opened it. I looked back over my shoulder and, just before walking out, I gave him a wink and said, "You rocked my world."

I exhaled in relief as I heard the door click shut behind me and hurried toward the elevator. If I could get inside before he came into the hallway looking for me, I was home-free and on my way to bed. The elevator doors slid open, and I walked in, smiling at the middle-aged man who looked me up and down. If I'd tried, I could have probably gotten another job out of it, but I'd just done my fourth guy of the night and that was my limit. I usually only took on three.

I walked through the lobby and gave a small wave of acknowledgment to the girl behind the reception desk. She knew what I'd just done.

The street was deserted as I headed back to my apartment. Horns honked in the distance. New York City—the city that truly never slept. My cell phone rang loudly, echoing off the brownstones of lower Manhattan as I pulled it out of my bag.

"I'm on my way home now, Todd," I said, knowing who it would be. Who else would call a prostitute at two in the morning except her boss?

"Ally, I have a new client for you. Very rich, only in town for the night."

"Sorry, I can't take it. Maybe Jamie is finished with Mr. Spank Me."

Todd and I had a short relationship in college—meaning we'd fucked a few times and still spoke to each other afterward. He'd studied business management at NYU and always claimed that I was the best fuck he'd ever had, joking many times that I should go pro because of my awesome "pussy skills." After he'd graduated and started his own escort business, he'd offered me a job. Two years later, I was his best-selling girl.

"No can do, cherry pie. I promised him my number one girl, and that's *you*. How long will it take you to get uptown?"

"I've already done four guys tonight, Todd. I'm tired."

"I won't take a commission on this one. Just do it. For me? Please, Ally?"

*No commission?* Todd always got a commission. Fifty percent. Seven hundred dollars per hour. Three-fifty for me and three-fifty for Todd. It was like a law. Todd's law and one that had never been broken before. The client must have been a big deal for Todd to forfeit his cut.

"He's paying double because it's such short notice," he added, trying to entice me.

So I could earn fourteen hundred for just one more client. I could get uptown by three, stay with the guy until four (if he was lucky) and be home in bed by five with a wad of cash in my hand. That could work.

"Okay, give me the details."

"He's in room fourteen-oh-three at The Plaza. His name is Scott Walker."

I stared up at the imposing building. In two years, I'd never been invited to this hotel by a client. I'd been to nice hotels, sure, but never *The Plaza*. A rich guy in a fancy hotel hiring a prostitute — how quaint. I only hoped he didn't expect some *Pretty Woman* happy ending because I wasn't *that* girl. I wasn't going to giggle like a stupid schoolgirl at the sight of something shiny, and I certainly wasn't going to fall in love with him. It always amused me when people thought prostitutes chose their profession to meet men. Either that or they thought we were all drug addicts in need of a fix. I wasn't that girl, either. I loved my work and loved sex. Basically, I got paid to do something I loved. Everyone should be so lucky.

And yet, despite loving my work, *this* was something out of my comfort zone. I knew I wasn't dressed appropriately but there wasn't anything I could do about it. The prostitutes that worked The Plaza were so well-dressed that you'd never pick them just by looking. They were savvier than that, turned out in their finery, with jewels dripping and labels bragging.

I, on the other hand, in my short skirt and "fuck me" pumps, was obviously not in their league. After a deep breath and a little internal cheerleading, I walked purposefully through the lobby, straight into the elevator, and pressed the button for the fourteenth floor. Staring at myself in the mirrored doors on the ride up, I fixed my makeup, wiping the smudged mascara and touching up my lips. I scrunched my hair and smoothed the top before fluffing it over my shoulders in an attempt to look seductive. If I wasn't going to pull off high-class, I would at least try not to look trashy.

There was nothing I could do about my clothes, but most of my job was done naked, and I knew my body wouldn't disappoint. My best friend and roommate, Jamie, just had her breasts done. Hers looked good and they felt soft—I'd squeezed them—but I was happy with my C-cup, and I believed that guys liked natural better.

I counted the doors along the hallway and stopped in front of Mr. Walker's room before I shook my hair back over my shoulders and knocked.

"Just a minute!" he called from inside.

A few seconds later, the door was opened by a young guy, probably in his late twenties, with unruly blond hair and stubble covering his jaw. He was shirtless, and while not overly muscular, he was hard and lean in a sexy way. His suit pants hung low on his hips, hinting at what was hidden beneath. His piercing blue eyes stared at me, and he smiled.

"You must be Ally. Please come in."

He held the door open and stepped back to grant me access to his room. *Room* wasn't really the right word. *Suite* was more accurate. The sitting room was the size of my whole apartment.

"Would you like a drink? Champagne?" he offered.

"Thanks." I placed my purse down on one of the sofas.

It was time for me to turn on my charm—after all, I *was* getting paid. I sat down and crossed my legs, bobbing one foot up and down. Mr. Walker handed me a glass of champagne, and I took a sip. It was crisp and delicious and probably cost more than he was paying me.

"So, what brings you to New York?" I asked.

I'd learned that clients were one of three types of guy: Either they jumped on you as soon as you walked in the door, fumbled and stuttered because they were so nervous, or they wanted to pretend it was a real date. That last one required conversation. As he hadn't stuttered or jumped me yet, I assumed he wanted to talk.

"I come weekly for work. My company has an office here, and I fly up for our Sunday board meetings. I usually fly in and out on the same day, but I missed the last flight tonight and was forced to stay." He gave a little shrug.

"And where is home?"

I downed the rest of the bubbly liquid. It really was delicious. He smiled and refilled my glass. I didn't usually drink at work, but as he was my last client of the night, I thought I could have one drink. I wouldn't touch the top-off. I rested the full glass on the coffee table and turned my full attention to the client.

"I'm from Miami."

"I've never been there, but I've heard it's nice. Beaches, sun, bikinis…"

"That pretty much sums it up." He laughed.

Mr. Walker was the most attractive client I'd had in a long time. In another world, in another life, I might have been interested in him. He was watching me as he drank his champagne, and while his stare didn't make me uncomfortable, it felt predatory—like he was considering how best to devour me. The cave-girl part of my genetics liked it.

"I have an early flight and I'll need to leave the hotel at about six. I'd like you to stay until then. I will, of course, pay for the extra time."

He slid an envelope across the table toward me. I didn't need to pick it up to guess that there was several thousand dollars inside.

"Of course." There went my plan to be asleep within an hour, but, for the money, I could sleep all day.

He sat on the couch opposite me and sipped his champagne.

"So, how long have you done this, ah, work?"

I cleared my throat. "A few years."

He nodded. "What does a normal client like? I mean, what should I ask for?"

I smirked. "Have you ever used a prostitute before, Mr. Walker?"

"Please, call me Scott. No, I haven't, and I never thought I would."

"There's nothing to be ashamed of. Sexual desire is a normal part of being human."

His eyes darted to my body and back to my face.

"Think of me like a restaurant. You *could* stay home and cook for yourself, or you could pay a chef to cook the food and clean up after you. This is no different. I offer a service."

His shoulders dropped and he let out a breath. "I suppose you're right."

He stood and held his hand out. I placed my fingers in his palm and he tugged gently, encouraging me to stand before leading me into the bedroom.

"I'm just going to have a shower. Make yourself at home," he said.

The bathroom door closed and I sat on the bed, unsure what to do. I was out of my depth. I'd been here for fifteen minutes already and was still fully dressed. Usually I'd be throat deep in balls by this point.

The sound of water running came from the other room and I briefly toyed with the idea of joining him in the shower, but decided that if he'd wanted that, he wouldn't have closed the door. Instead I sat on the bed, fully dressed, and waited.

He appeared with wet hair and a smirk, wrapped in a fluffy white robe. "You don't look at home. In fact, you look like you couldn't be less comfortable if you tried. Come here."

I stood and walked across the room to him, kicking myself for not bringing my game. I was an excellent prostitute. I could suck the cum from a cock like a vacuum, but I had no idea how to act like a lady.

"I'm sorry," I said. "I'll just go to the bathroom and I'll be right out."

"All right." He gave me a warm smile. "Relax. We can just talk for a while if you like."

"I'm fine."

I practically ran into the bathroom and closed the door. I splashed water on my face and stared into the mirror. A sad, lonely girl with too much makeup around her blue eyes stared back at me.

"You can do this!" The girl looking back at me didn't appear convinced. "Suck it up."

He wasn't expecting anything from me that I hadn't already given to four other guys that night. Was I so broken that I didn't know how to be treated nicely? That thought bothered me more than it should have.

I steeled my resolve and walked back out into the bedroom. He was in bed with the blanket pulled up to his waist, smiling at me.

"Shall we begin?" he asked. The unsure man who had seemed so reluctant was gone, and in his place sat a confident man with desire in his eyes.

# CHAPTER TWO

I started toward the bed, but he held his hand up to stop me.

"Undress."

His voice was husky as he gave me that predatory look again. He'd only spoken a single word, and yet it sent shivers up my spine. It also set my nerves to rest now that I was back on familiar ground. Stripping was something that many clients asked for. No matter how cultured or rich, when it came down to it, all men were the same. They all wanted tits and ass.

My fingers found the top button of my blouse, and I undid it, moving quickly to the next.

"Slowly," he said, settling back to enjoy the show.

He appeared to be composed, but the quick rise and fall of his chest made me wonder if maybe he was as nervous as I was.

I took a deep breath and stretched my fingers, trying to calm myself down. I never got nervous at work. I was attractive, I was amazing at sex, and I'd never had an unsatisfied customer. Mr. Walker wouldn't be any different. As soon as he wet his cock in me, he would become as easily pleased as the rest of them. I knew I was right, and the thought reassured me. It gave me power.

I winked, putting on my work persona, and licked my bottom lip.

I released the second button and then the third, allowing the blouse to gape open and show my bra. He shifted on the bed, pulling the blankets down slightly and showing the slightest hint of hair above his groin. He was already naked.

Once all the buttons were undone, I let the shirt slip from my shoulders to the floor. My hands reached behind and unzipped the back of my skirt. I glanced up at my audience and smiled when I saw I had his undivided attention. I twirled around and wiggled my ass. Guys liked it when I was playful. I looked back over my shoulder to make sure he was enjoying the show. He laughed and spun his finger in a circle, requesting me to turn so he could see my body.

"You're a little skinny, but well proportioned," he said as if I were a horse he was considering purchasing.

"I'm not a drug addict if that's what you're worried about," I said defensively.

He laughed again. Was he so relaxed that he found this amusing, or was it a nervous chuckle? I wished I could read his mind.

"It was only an observation, Ally, not a criticism. You're beautiful."

I froze. A client had never called me beautiful before. I'd been called hot, sexy, gorgeous, fuck-worthy…but never *beautiful*.

Mr. Walker was watching me again with his lustful stare, so I got back to work, pushing my discomfort away. My hands ran up and down my body, cupping and squeezing my breasts mechanically. I licked my lips again, and he frowned.

"Is something wrong?" I asked, standing up straight and allowing my arms to drop to my sides.

"You're acting how you think I want you to. Just be yourself. You are much sexier than some made-up slut."

I was shocked. My mouth dropped open, and we stared at each other. I wasn't sure if he'd called me a slut or not, but either way, he wasn't enjoying the show.

"What would you like?" I asked.

"Undress how you would for a boyfriend. I'm not paying you to be a stripper. You're mine until six a.m. Act like you're mine."

Ugh! He wanted a girlfriend. I usually avoided the girlfriend experience because it often included kissing, and that was something

I never did with paying customers. My lips were for real dates only. But Mr. Walker had been nothing but nice to me and was paying a shitload of money for this. I could bend the rules a little.

I nodded, walked across to the bed, and sat down. I took his hand and used it to cup my breast. His fingers were smooth, like someone who'd only ever known desk work. He slipped his fingers under the lace of my bra and flicked my nipple. A spark of electricity ignited under my skin.

His fingers trailed along my shoulder and up my throat, leaving a shiver in their wake. I reached behind and unclasped the bra, letting it fall into my lap as he took me in.

"Beautiful," he whispered. There was that word again.

He leaned toward me, lips puckered, and I pulled back. I was prepared to bend the rules but not break them completely.

"I don't kiss clients."

He cocked his head to the side. "At all?"

I shook my head.

"All right," he said, not pushing my boundaries. Instead, he combed his fingers through my hair and let them glide slowly over my shoulders.

His cock was hard, peeking out from under the blanket. Sliding my hand down his chest, I gently ran my fingers over the hard flesh of his belly and under the bedspread, grasping him firmly. He hissed at the contact, and fire burned from behind his blue eyes.

"Lean back," I whispered. He obeyed.

I kneeled over him, pulled the blanket down, and licked my way across his body. His balls were safely cupped in my hand, and I gently rolled them between my fingers. My tongue traveled lower on his stomach, and it struck me how turned on I was. I hardly ever felt this aroused with clients.

My other hand stroked his length in a slow rhythm. Not enough to cause him to start thrusting in my hand, but enough to keep him hard and to give little waves of pleasure. His hooded eyes told me I was doing a good job.

"Do you want me to suck your cock?" I murmured.

I knew I was taking a risk. Some guys loved the dirty talk, and others just wanted you to shut up and be a silent vagina. I'd had experiences in the past where I'd tried to talk dirty to a shy guy—he'd freaked out and canceled the appointment. I was actually enjoying this job and didn't want it to end early.

"Yes," he hissed.

Bingo! Risk had paid off.

I smiled, looking up through my lashes, and licked his dick from root to tip. Mr. Walker's eyes closed, and he tipped his head back against the headboard.

This was what I was good at, and it felt safe to be in known territory again.

His hands found my hair as I sucked the tip into my mouth and swirled my tongue around. Pushing my head down, I took all of him in, and he let out a soft grunt. I sucked and licked his balls, taking each gently into my mouth.

Normally when I gave a blow job to a client, it was mechanical. Suck the cock. Lick the balls. Suck some more. Spit. Easy. But tonight, with Mr. Walker, I *wanted* to give him pleasure. I *wanted* to make it last.

I mouthed the head, stroking the shaft with my hand.

"Enough," he gasped, putting his hand on my shoulder and gently pushing my away.

I was confused. Wasn't he enjoying it? Insecurity swelled up inside me like a serpent and twined its way around my heart. Rejection was something I did not handle well.

His hands grasped my shoulders and lifted me to meet his eyes. He leaned forward, and I froze, thinking he was going to try to kiss me, but just before his lips touched mine, he diverted and kissed my jaw and then down my throat.

He quickly flipped us so I was lying on my back and he was over me. His mouth found my right breast, and he licked and nibbled on the nipple while he massaged the other with his hand.

"So beautiful," he whispered.

On one hand, I was a little freaked out. He was acting as if we knew each other, as if this was a tender moment between lovers, but the other part of me thought I could get used to being treated so well. My other clients could take a page from his book.

His hand slipped down my stomach and into my panties. He spread my lips and fingered my clit lightly. It was exquisite, and I let the pleasure swallow me up.

"I want you inside me," I moaned.

Surprisingly, I wasn't lying. It was a line I spat out frequently, but I never meant it…until now.

"I'm more than happy to oblige." He chuckled and rolled away.

I found I was saddened to have lost contact with him and watched as he made his way back to the bed with a small foil wrapper in his hand.

Fury washed over me. I was so angry at myself. How could I have let things get so far without thinking of protection? I was the condom queen. In fact, I'd never had sex without a condom, with clients or actual boyfriends. I wasn't taking any risks. And here I'd just begged a client, a perfect stranger, to be inside me, and I hadn't had a condom ready. Luckily, he was prepared.

"Allow me," I said, kneeling up and taking the wrapper from him.

He sat back on the bed and watched as I stroked his cock and ripped the foil open with my teeth. I held the rubber between my lips and slowly rolled it over him with my mouth—a trick I was well practiced at.

His cautious eyes reinforced the idea that maybe he wasn't as confident as he was acting, but when I was done, the vulnerable look disappeared.

"Come here." He pulled me into his arms.

He removed my panties and hovered over me for a moment, looking into my eyes until I felt like I couldn't breathe. When I was in the second grade, I'd been hit in the chest by a baseball. For a terrifying few seconds, I'd been unable to take a breath. Staring into his eyes, the sensation was the same.

Slowly, agonizingly slowly, he entered me. Once he was sheathed, he rested his elbows by my head and let his weight push me into the mattress.

"How extensive is your no kissing rule?" he asked, his mouth inches from my ear.

"No lips." I breathed deeply, trying to keep my voice level as he pulled out and then pushed back into me.

My body convulsed. He gave me a crooked smile and started rocking back and forth, sliding in and out with a delightfully pleasurable stroke.

"Shame," he said, his mouth hovering just above mine.

In that moment, I reconsidered my rule. Surely it wouldn't hurt to kiss this one client. I just wouldn't do it again. A one-off. Before I could lift my head and meet his lips, he moved down to kiss my jaw and throat. He sucked my earlobe and trailed kisses over my cheeks and forehead, all without breaking the rhythm of his hips.

I wrapped my legs around his ass, pulling him closer and meeting his thrusts. Gradually, everything sped up. We moved together with more urgency, both breathing heavily.

"It feels so good," I gasped.

He grunted his agreement and rested his forehead on my shoulder, pumping harder. The sensations inside my body were something I hadn't felt in a very long time. I could feel my orgasm building, and it was astonishing. I never had orgasms with clients. It was always about their pleasure, not my own.

"God, yes!" I groaned, scratching at his back, trying to do anything I could to pull him closer.

"I want to watch you," he mumbled in my ear.

Seamlessly, as if we were one body, we rolled so I was straddling him. I rode him with all the energy I had. Up and down, back and forth. Harder. Faster. *God.*

His hands were everywhere: grasping at my bouncing breasts, guiding my hips, stroking along my throat. His touch left fire wherever it traveled and I never wanted him to stop, even if it burned me alive.

"Fuck, Ally," he said. "So fucking good."

I was almost ready to explode. I *needed* to explode. Suddenly it wasn't about Mr. Walker anymore. All I could think about was the amazing pleasure coursing through my body. His eyes were locked on mine and I was lost in their color. Blue and pleasure. That was all that existed.

I was close and I wanted it so much. I leaned back, bracing myself on his legs with my hands and bucked my hips as fast as I could. He must have enjoyed the view of his cock sliding in and out of me because his gaze drifted down to the point where we were joined.

I tilted my head back, letting my hair dangle onto his legs, and enjoyed the ripples that threatened to crash over me.

"Yes!" I moaned softly.

Suddenly I was on my back again. and Mr. Walker was pumping into me with abandon. It was wild, primal thrusting that shook every muscle in my body. He held me close, and his soft grunts were only just audible.

Remembering that tonight wasn't about my pleasure, I threw my whole self into it and clenched my muscles around his cock, making myself as tight as possible.

It did the trick. He let out a loud groan and increased his speed, as eager to get to the finish line as I was.

"Oh, God, yes!" I exclaimed. "I'm coming!"

And it was the truth. Wave after wave of hot blood rushed through my body, carrying pleasure instead of oxygen and infusing every cell with release.

"Yes, yes," he gasped and pushed in as far as he could go, holding himself steady inside me as he filled the condom.

We lay, breathing heavily and entwined, for several minutes before he pressed a kiss to my forehead and rolled off me.

# CHAPTER THREE

I awoke with a start, looked around the luxurious room, and remembered where I was. I must have fallen asleep. Shit! I never slept with clients. Clients were for fucking; home was for sleeping. I'd never crossed that line before. I'd just been so relaxed after the orgasm—the first I'd had in a long time—and Mr. Walker's arms had been so warm as he'd held me. Another no-no.

Mr. Walker!

I jumped out of bed and glanced around the room. There was no sign of him. The bathrobe he'd worn was hanging neatly over the back of the desk chair. The bathroom door was open, and it was dark inside.

I grabbed his discarded robe and pulled it on over my naked body. Even though he'd gotten a good look at me while we fucked, I felt modest in the light of day. The alarm clock on the nightstand said it was just after nine thirty a.m. He was long gone.

My clothes were still pooled on the floor outside the bathroom door, and I quickly put them on. Now to do the "walk-of-shame" through the lobby. I hated that. Most of the time it was the middle of the night and only the staff saw me, but I had a feeling that the lobby would be full of rich elitists just dying to look down their professionally sculpted noses at me.

There was a note on the dining table next to a large fruit platter and a selection of bagels and pastries.

> *Ally,*
>
> *Thanks for a wonderful rendezvous.*
> *Scott*

It was a simple, polite note, but it made me cringe. He'd treated me like a date, not a prostitute. Next to the note was the envelope he'd passed me the night before, and it looked decidedly thicker than it had been before our *rendezvous.*

Flicking through the bills inside, I counted five thousand dollars. Much more than the agreed upon price. I just couldn't figure him out. I enjoyed a good puzzle, but Mr. Walker was a mess of contradictions. He'd treated me as if I was a person, not a vagina, and yet he paid me like a whore.

I grabbed a bagel and left the room with the envelope safely in my handbag. I considered giving Todd his fee after all, seeing as I'd been overpaid, but decided against it. He'd said he didn't want the commission, and I was about to earn every penny by walking through the lobby.

I was right. Every head turned and stared at me as I strode across the marble floor. My heels clicked and echoed as everyone fell silent. I tried to walk quickly, but the doors to the outside world seemed to get farther away. The sour expressions on the ladies' faces were expected, but I had to smirk when a few of the men looked at me with hunger rather than disgust.

If getting five grand for a few hours was normal for this hotel then maybe I could buy some fancy clothes and come back. No, I couldn't do that to Todd. I was his promo girl. His headliner. His business was based on selling *me.* The other girls were hired to supplement the jobs I couldn't take. I wasn't about to go behind his back.

My cell rang and I fished it out of my bag. It was my brother.

"Hey, Zach. What's up?"

"Not much. Just wanted to see if you could make it over today. Todd is eager to see you."

His tone implied something that I knew wasn't there. Todd and I naturally spent a lot of time together in business meetings and the like, but my brother assumed we were secretly dating. My life was so complicated. Zach and Todd had been roommates in college and got along so well that they still chose to live together. This made my life hell, of course. My brother didn't know what I did for a living, so having him living with my boss? Yeah, it was a mess.

"Sure. Let me just have a shower and I'll be over soon."

"Where are you? I can hear traffic."

"I just have the window open," I lied.

I jumped in a taxi. There was no need to walk or take the train when I had a huge payload in my purse. I flicked through the bills, counting them several times as we headed downtown. Five thousand would make a nice addition to my savings account.

I wasn't deluded enough to think that I could do this work forever. Prostitution was hugely based on looks, at least the high-end escort business that I was in. No drugs, no violence. Just sex. In fifteen or twenty years I'd be out of work, and I planned to make sure that I was well set up by then. I paid my bills, I bought what I needed for work, and I skimped on everything else. All the extra cash I earned went into investments that would eventually buy me an apartment. Rent was killer in New York, and I knew I wouldn't be able to afford it when I wasn't working.

So, I lived like a pauper despite making a king's salary and saved everything I could. It wasn't like I could walk into a bank and get a mortgage with the job I had, and there was no way I would fuck a bank manager for a loan. I had standards. A lot of people would probably laugh at that coming from a hooker, but it was true.

When I'd first decided to take Todd's job offer, I made myself a set of guidelines. No drugs, *ever*. That would be a never-ending spiral that I'd never get out of. Also, my services were only for paying clients. I was a professional. I didn't see dentists walking into Macy's and cleaning people's teeth instead of paying for the clothes they bought. In the two years I'd been working, I had never crossed those boundaries.

The taxi pulled up outside my building and I handed him a twenty, telling him to keep the change. After a quick shower to wash off the five guys from last night, I dressed in jeans and a Justin Bieber T-shirt just to annoy my brother.

Zach and Todd lived a block from me, and it was only a quick walk around the corner. I let myself into their apartment without knocking and sat on the couch.

"You've got to be kidding me!" Zach groaned when he walked into the room and saw my choice of fashion.

I laughed. In actuality, I wasn't a fan of The Beebs, but it was fun to make my brother squirm.

"And you *like* her?" Zach asked Todd as my boss came into the living area.

"What can I say? Your sister does have the mad pussy skills." Todd smiled wide, showing a row of bright white teeth.

"Gross. Shut up, both of you!" Zach cringed.

Todd stood behind the couch and swung his arm around my shoulder.

"Come with me, little one," he said just loud enough for Zach to hear.

I felt bad for my brother. He knew that Todd and I had slept together in college, and as much as it grossed him out, I honestly thought the idea of his sister and his best friend being together was appealing to him. If only he knew the truth.

Todd closed his bedroom door and threw himself onto the bed.

"Do I get some of that awesome puss today?" he asked, winking.

"Shut up!"

Both us knew that we wouldn't sleep together again. That part of our history was in the past, but he still liked to joke about it.

"Tell me about last night," he said, pulling a lock-box out from under his bed.

"It was fine. Mr. Toothpick wants to book next time he comes to town. I say you assign Kimberly to him."

I handed over Todd's share of cash for the first four guys of the night. He counted it quickly and locked it away. Neither of us talked about the lack of commission for Client Number Five.

"Why Kimberly?"

I shrugged. "Because I actually like the other girls."

Todd laughed. "And how was your fifth client?"

I ran my hand through my hair and twirled the end around my finger. "Number five was great."

"He's my cousin, you know," Todd said, smirking.

"*What?* Why didn't you tell me?" I was furious. I preferred to stay anonymous, and if Todd knew the clients personally then that just flew right out the window.

"Calm down, cherry pie. Let me explain."

I folded my arms across my chest, prepared to listen.

"He comes into town weekly for business. Last night he missed his flight, and he called to see if I wanted to have a late dinner. I was busy and couldn't make it but said that I could hook him up with a hot lady."

I rolled my eyes.

"He wasn't interested at first but I kept going on and on about how amazing you are, and he finally agreed."

"You're an ass," was all I had to say in reply.

"An ass you love."

I scoffed.

"And I love your ass in return."

"Oh *please*." I shook my head, making Todd grin.

"So, can I start booking you in for five a night?"

"No way. Three is still what I prefer. Four, only if one of the other girls can't take him. Five was too many. I fell asleep with your cousin last night because I was so exhausted."

Todd raised his eyebrows. He knew I had strict boundaries.

"Okay, okay. I wish you had a twin. Seriously, I could sell two of you ten times a night and still not meet all the bookings."

"Maybe we need another girl. Jamie is completely booked, and I know that Kimberly and Nicole are getting close, too. I could ask around and find someone if you'd like."

"Good idea. I'm also thinking of bringing a guy in. There are horny ladies in this city, too."

"As long as it's not my brother then I think it's a great idea."

Todd laughed. "Zach would never do it. He's too much of a romantic. How are you guys so different?"

"I believe in romance. I just think it's rare. Men only want sex."

"You bet we do!" He wiggled his eyebrows, and I shook my head at him.

"When did you last get laid?" I asked.

"Kimberly gave me a blow job last week because she'd spent part of my commission by accident and didn't have enough to give me. It was her idea. I didn't force it." He held his hands up defensively.

I glared at him. When he first asked me to join the business, I agreed on the condition that I would never have to pay him with sex, just a share of the payment from the client.

"I *swear* it was her idea."

"And you just couldn't resist having your cock sucked by a pretty girl."

"Hell no. There was no way I was going to turn that down. I upped her hourly rate after that. She has some skills."

I raised one eyebrow.

"Not as good as your skills…which I'd love a reminder of."

I patted his head. "Don't get your hopes up."

I turned and left the room.

"Oh, they're up, baby! Just like my cock whenever I see you," he yelled so I could hear him when I got to the living room.

Zach grimaced as he overheard Todd. I slouched next to him on the couch and rested my head on his shoulder.

"What are you doing tomorrow?" he asked.

I yawned and put my hand over my mouth. "I'm going to try to sleep all day."

"That's not fun! Mom called and asked if I wanted to come over for dinner. Want to go?"

"Yeah, sounds good." There was nothing like Mom's cooking, and I hadn't been to see her in a few weeks.

"Okay, I'll pick you up at five and we'll head over. Do you…want to bring Todd?"

I laughed. "Why? He's your friend. If you want to bring him, you can."

Zach looked down at me with a pitiful look. "I know."

"You know?"

"I *know!*" he said again in an over-exaggerated tone.

I patted his shoulder and stood up. "You *wish* you knew. But I'm afraid you're way off base with that one."

My brother rolled his eyes. "Whatever you say, but I'm not stupid."

"I think eating a whole roll of toilet paper might constitute stupidity," I said, smiling.

"Hey! I was *three* years old when that happened. You weren't even born yet, so shut up!"

"Dad called you Toilet Boy for years!" I was laughing now, I couldn't help it. The look on Zach's face was priceless.

He opened his mouth to reply but was cut off when Todd appeared in the doorway. "Now, now, children. Let's play nice," Todd said with a grin. He always enjoyed it when Zach and I fell into one of our childish spats.

I put my hands up in defeat. "It's okay. I'm going home anyway. See you at five tomorrow, *Toilet Boy.*"

My phone buzzed with a text from Todd just as I got home.

I need you tonight for an audition.
You get to test out the new guy. -T

Todd always took a "test drive" of the new girls before he hired them. He said he needed to know what he was selling, and it's his job to make sure his girls are of high quality. Yeah, he really hated his work.

He wasn't willing to test out the new guy, though. That job fell to me as the most senior girl. I'd have sex with the guy and say if he was any good or not. It sounded easy.

Jamie said she wanted to come and watch, which was fine with me. I'd done threesomes with her for clients. Plus, we lived together. Jamie and I had no secrets.

I knocked on Todd's apartment door, and he opened it almost immediately.

"Welcome, ladies! I'd like you to meet Adam. This is Ally, and this is Jamie. They're my two top girls," he said.

Adam's eyes lit up when he looked at Jamie, and I couldn't blame him. She was a walking Barbie Doll. Flowing blond hair, huge boobs, and a tiny waist. A guy's wet dream. She charged her clients almost as much as I did.

"Zach out?" I asked, double-checking that the coast was clear.

"He's on a date," Todd assured me.

Jamie and I stepped into the living room. I went to sit on the couch but Todd stopped me.

"Let's go to the bedroom shall we?" he asked, excited.

I knew why. What guy wouldn't be overjoyed at having a live sex show on his own bed?

Todd and Jamie made themselves comfortable on the loveseat in Todd's room. I sat down on the bed and started to take off my shoes.

"I don't want to give too much direction, just act how you would if Ally was a client," Todd said.

Adam nodded and smiled at me. I had to admit that he was attractive. He had broad shoulders and a cute, kind of goofy smile. He embodied the tall, dark, and handsome stereotype. The ladies would love him. I just hoped he was good in the sack.

Guys who were good looking often didn't put any effort into sex because they didn't have to prove anything. Some of the best sex I'd had was with average guys. Except for Mr. Walker. Talk about the whole package!

Adam had removed his clothes and stood in just his underwear.

"Let me undress you," he said.

I nodded and held my arms up over my head, allowing him to remove my shirt. Soon all our clothes were on the floor, and we were horizontal on the bed. Good so far.

"Do you want me to eat her out?" Adam called over his shoulder.

"Sure," said Todd, sounding a little too eager. I glanced over and saw that his cock was rock hard and tenting his pants. We hadn't even gotten things started yet.

Adam snaked his way down my body and sucked my nipples. Then he smiled up at me. "You're really hot."

"Thanks. So are you."

His hand found its way between my legs, and he pushed two fingers inside me. It felt kind of mechanical, but I didn't want to judge him too quickly. Maybe he was nervous.

"Have you ever had sex in front of people before?" I whispered.

He shook his head. Poor guy. I pulled him back up to face level and ran my fingers through his hair.

"Don't look at them. It's just you and me here. Remember, women want love, not just sex. When I go to work, I'm just a vagina to make a guy come. When you go to work, you'll need to be more than just a cock. Make me feel like you love me."

My words were reminiscent of what Mr. Walker had said to me the night before. Why couldn't I get him out of my head? I pushed thoughts of Client Number Five away.

Adam's eyes darkened and he leaned in to kiss me, but I turned my head at the last second and his lips landed on my cheek.

"I don't kiss."

He nodded but didn't remove his lips from my skin. They nibbled down my throat, between the valley of my breasts, around my belly button, and down my right hip. It was arousing, and I was pleased that he was making me wet. More than most guys had done recently. Except for Mister Five.

His tongue was firm on my clit and strong enough to sink inside me over and over. It wasn't earth-shattering, but it was good.

I rolled my head to the side and saw that Todd had given up any pretense of being professional. He had his cock out and was rubbing it slowly, eyes glued on my swaying tits.

"That's good," I said to the man between my legs. "Now fuck me."

Adam slid up my body and positioned himself at my entrance. I could tell he was big, bigger than most guys I'd been with. Bigger than Client Number Five.

"Stop!" I grabbed a condom from the bedside table and waved it in his face. "Don't *ever* service a client without one of these. I don't care if she tells you she's clean and on birth control. Don't take the risk."

Adam nodded and quickly slipped it on with one hand before bracing himself over me again.

He pushed in and grunted, "Fuck."

He pulled my legs up and hooked my knees over his shoulders, not that he needed the leverage to get deeper.

I couldn't find anything to fault him on. His cock was like magic, stretching me and filling me over and over again as he thrust frantically. He worked a little too fast for my taste, but he could leave his appointment early if he wanted to follow my trick.

The pleasure built quickly inside me, and I was surprised when I heard a woman moaning and realized it was *me.* I very rarely made natural sex noises; they were usually put-on and over-acted for the client's benefit.

"Fuck yeah," Adam gasped.

His face was turning red and his eyes were bulging, and I knew he was close. But the test was going to be if he could hold off until I—his client—had come. After all, he wouldn't be paid for his own orgasms, only the client's.

A glance over at our audience made me laugh. Todd wasn't even watching us anymore—his eyes were closed as Jamie sucked his dick. He thrust hard into her mouth, adding added to my arousal.

"Give him a fuck, Jamie," I said.

"Yes, please!" Todd said.

Jamie stood up and shrugged her shoulders, tugged her skirt up and pulled her panties to the side, then sat straight down on his cock. Todd groaned loudly.

I turned my attention back to Adam. His rhythm hadn't waivered while I was distracted, and he pounded relentlessly into me. I was starting to think he was a jack rabbit. In. Out. In. Out. In. Out. No variation in speed or pressure. But all of a sudden he swiveled his hips and pressed his thumb down hard on my clit.

Stars exploded behind my eyes, and I screamed.

I couldn't catch my breath. Just as one wave of pleasure subsided, another washed over me. What had he *done?*

Knowing that I came, Adam finally allowed himself to orgasm, roaring in my ear and collapsing on top of me.

Todd was still grunting happily in the corner. Jamie was mewling softly and holding her tits as she rode him. They had to be close. I'd seen them both come before, so I knew the signs.

Once we were all satisfied, we fumbled for our clothes and then went to sit in the living room. It was less awkward talking about what had happened when we weren't sitting in the wet spot on the bed.

"Ally, your appraisal?" Todd asked, suddenly all business again now that his balls were empty.

"He was fine. Really good." I glanced at Adam, and he gave me a wink.

"Did you orgasm?" Todd asked. "How was the rhythm? If you were a client, would you pay four hundred dollars for him?"

"I did. For a minute I wasn't sure if I would but then — what did you do at the end?"

Adam only smiled, showing perfect teeth.

"It was all very good. I'd pay for that," I concluded.

Todd grinned and held out his hand to shake Adam's. "You're hired."

As Jamie and I walked back to our apartment, I thought about the fact that I'd had two orgasms in less than twenty-four hours. Adam *had* been good, but he didn't compare to Client Number Five.

And as much as I hated it, there was a part of me that was sad I wouldn't see Scott Walker again.

# CHAPTER FOUR



I stared at the text from Zach and grabbed my handbag off the counter. Jamie was in the shower getting ready for work, so I stuck my head into the steam-filled room.

"I'm going now. Have a good night."

"Have fun!" she said.

I ran down the stairs and out onto the street, then climbed into the back seat of the taxi waiting at the curb. I settled in next to my brother as we pulled out into the traffic.

"Hey," I said.

Zach's expression was serious. "We need to talk."

"Okay," I said cautiously.

It was always in the back of my mind that Zach would find out that I didn't actually work in a mail room. I was so lucky that he hadn't figured out that I worked for Todd yet. I was sure he knew we were hiding something, but I was pretty confident that his assumptions were wrong. If he had guessed right, Todd was probably nursing a black eye right now.

"I think it's time we talked about you and Todd."

I chewed my lip while I waited for him to continue. It was better to let him talk than to accidently give something away. I hated lying to my brother, and my stomach churned as the silence stretched on. We were close, and apart from Jamie, he was my best friend. But there were some things that would only hurt him if the truth came out; my job was one of them.

"You're not going to say anything?" he asked.

"There's nothing to say."

He sighed and ran a hand through his hair.

"Before I left, Todd asked me what time you'd be home tonight and said to get you to call him."

I knew what that meant. Todd had a job for me after I got home from Mom's.

"Maybe he wants to complain about what an ass you are and he knows I'm the only one who understands."

"Come on, Ally. I'm trying to have a serious conversation here." He was exasperated, and I knew I couldn't joke my way out of this conversation. "I like Todd. He's a great guy. But he's not *boyfriend* material. Not for you."

"Zach—"

"No, let me finish. You know what his business is. He *sells* women as sexual objects. He doesn't respect those girls. What makes you think he'll respect you or treat you better than them?"

I let out a breath, hating what I was going to have to say. Lying to Zach was the only part of my job I detested. It was obvious that he was only looking out for me like a big brother should, so I made a snap decision. Maybe it was better for him to believe Todd and I were dating.

"Okay, fine. Todd and I have a thing going." The lie tasted like bile in my throat, but I was sure it tasted better than the truth would. "Don't worry about it, though," I added, seeing his expression cloud over. "I'm a big girl, and I won't let myself be treated like crap."

"How long has it being going on?"

I knew my brother well enough to see that he was fighting to stay calm. To avoid piling more lies on top of each other, I had to make Zach want to stop this conversation.

"Seriously? You want all the details? Do you want me to tell you how big his cock is, too?"

Zach grimaced. "Okay, fine. But if I find out that he's not treating you right, I'm stepping in. I don't care if he is my best friend. That guy will get the beating of his life."

I reached over and patted his hand. "Thanks, big bro, but I can handle myself."

Zach nodded slightly and turned to stare out the window. I took out my phone and sent Todd a warning text. It was only fair.

> Just a heads up. Zach thinks we're dating.
> Let him believe it, it's easier than the truth.
> Just watch your back because he's not happy about it. -A

He replied instantly and I shook my head at his response.

> So we get to make out all the time?
> I'm in! BTW—11pm, client named Paul. -T

> In your dreams! And, yes, I'll take the client. -A

"Are you guys texting now?" Zach asked, glancing over at me.

"Yeah. Just making kinky plans for tonight."

"Ugh! Gross."

"Don't ask questions you don't want the answers to," I teased.

The rest of the ride to New Jersey was spent in silence, and I watched the city disappear as we headed into suburbia.

"Ride me!" Pony Boy screamed.

I swatted him with the leather crop. He'd presented it to me when I'd arrived at his hotel room.

Pony Boy was also known as Paul. He was young. Most of my clients were in their thirties or forties, but Paul was only nineteen. He liked to pretend to be a horse and have girls treat him as such. Apparently the girls at NYU didn't find this particular fetish sexy, so he was forced to outsource.

I turned around and rode him reverse cowgirl, swinging my arm above my head like I was wielding a lasso. He loved it.

I was glad I was facing away from him when he *neighed* as he came. Giggling wasn't professional, but this was fucking funny.

No orgasm for me. Again.

We lay together for a while and I stroked Paul's hair.

"How are your classes going?" I asked.

I didn't feel the need to get out of the room like I did with some other clients. I was happy to give Paul his full hour. He was my only job of the night, and I wasn't in any rush to get home. Plus, he was a sweet kid.

"Pretty good. The subjects are easy this semester."

"What about girls? Are there any you like?"

He blushed. "There is this one girl. But there is no way that she'd be into…*this*."

He took the riding crop from me and wacked his own belly hard, leaving a red mark.

"You never know," I said hopefully. "I'd suggest you ease her into it, but there's nothing scary about what you enjoy. I think she could handle it."

He smiled. "You're the best, Ally."

I moved off the bed and started to put my clothes back on. It made me uncomfortable when clients treated me like a person. I was just supposed to be a vagina for them.

"Can I book you again in a few weeks? I'll need to save up some more cash."

I handed him Todd's business card.

"Just call the agency and Todd will send over whoever he has available."

"Can't I book you?" he asked, looking upset.

"Sorry, I can't guarantee it."

That meant *no!* I could tell he was getting attached to me, and I wasn't a substitute for a real girlfriend. I was a quick fuck, nothing more. I made a mental note to arrange for Nicole to take his next appointment. She was really good with the clingy ones.

The receptionist in the hotel lobby waved me over as I walked by. Awesome. I was about to get bitched out by some little snob. It wouldn't be the first time.

"Hi," she said.

I just stared at her. She was short, and I hated to admit that she was pretty, but she was. Her tight, compact body would drive guys wild. Her rack was decent. Not huge, but enough. Her hair was an asymmetrical bob dyed in thick red streaks over pitch black. It was daring, but she pulled it off.

"I wanted to ask you a question," she said.

"Shoot."

"Well, um…Are you a…I mean, your job…is it—"

Poor thing was so uptight she couldn't even say the word. "A hooker? You betcha!"

I gave her a toothy grin, and she blushed.

"How would someone, just a random person, get into that kind of work?"

What. The. Fuck. That was the last question I'd been expecting.

"You interested?" I asked, raising an eyebrow. She'd certainly be hot enough—*if* she pulled the stick out of her ass.

"*Me?* I guess I've thought about it from time to time but…I don't know."

Her bright red cheeks and fidgety fingers told me otherwise.

"Look—" I glanced at her name badge "—Amy, if you're interested, just tell me. If not, then I'll be on my way."

Todd had said he was looking for a new girl. If she could drop the shy act she could be good. Actually, the shy act would probably work for a lot of guys. She had innocence.

Her eyes widened, taken aback by my bluntness. *Way to make a first impression on a possible work colleague, Ally.* I gave her what I hoped was a friendly smile and made sure my voice was softer when I spoke next.

"Look, honey, I know it's embarrassing to start out with, but if you're serious then I can help you. You just have to say the word."

"I don't know if I'm serious, but I *am* curious."

"Curiosity is healthy." I gave her a more genuine smile, and she seemed to relax. "Why don't we get together and you can ask me whatever questions you have, and I'll tell you about my work?"

"Monday is my next day off."

"Let's have lunch. There's a little diner just around the corner from here."

"I know it," she said.

"Great. I'll see you there at one p.m. on Monday."

"Thank you," she replied. She had a little gleam in her eye as I turned to walk away.

I caught a taxi home and let myself into the apartment. On the couch, Todd's new guy, Adam, was balls deep in my roommate.

"Oh fuck!" he grunted, thrusting into Jamie.

"Sorry!" I said, covering my eyes and running past them to my bedroom.

I put on some loud music to drown out their noise and lay on the bed. I was exhausted and ready to go to sleep, but knew that it wouldn't happen with all the groaning going on just outside my door.

I flicked through a magazine, and when the noise finally stopped and the front door closed, I sighed in relief and turned off the stereo. There was a knock on my door.

"Come in, Jamie," I called.

She wouldn't care that I was just wearing panties and a bra, and she was wearing half that, just panties.

"Sorry I walked in," I said.

"Oh shut up! You should have joined us," she replied, sitting on the end of my bed.

Her new boobs bounced once and then hugged tightly to her chest. Perfection.

"I only do threesomes when I'm getting paid."

"What if I asked really, really nicely?" she said, batting her eyelashes and making kissy faces.

"Is there a reason you came in other than to show me your newest assets?"

"Oh! Right. Todd called. He said he couldn't get you on your cell and he wants you to call him back. He sounded happy."

"Thanks. I'll call him in the morning. I'm beat."

"I think he wants you to call him now. He seemed eager to talk to you."

I sighed. "Fine. Thanks for letting me know." She stood up to leave. "Your tits look awesome by the way."

She grinned before closing the door behind her.

I called Todd.

"Well, if it isn't my favorite girl," he answered.

"You wanted to talk to me?"

"Is that any way to speak to your boyfriend?" His voice was teasing and I knew that he was going to milk this lie to Zach for all it was worth.

"*Todd!*"

"Straight down to business, huh?"

"Well, did you want to chit-chat first?" I asked.

"I would, actually."

I knew he was just playing with me but this could go on for a while if I didn't humor him. "What would you like to talk about?"

"What are you wearing?"

I groaned internally but knew what he wanted to hear. "Nothing," I said in a seductive voice.

"And that's why you're my favorite! Okay, now down to business. I got a call from my cousin today."

*Client Number Five!* I sat up on the bed and clutched the phone to my ear.

"Did he enjoy my services?" I asked, trying to sound like I didn't care.

"He did. Said he'd like to book you again this weekend. He wants you for the whole night though, no other clients."

I hesitated. "Maybe you should give him to Nicole. I don't do repeats. You know that."

"Come on, Ally. He wants you for the *whole night*. Do you realize how much cash that is?"

I wanted to take the job. I would be guaranteed at least one more orgasm, and he paid well. My bank balance could use the boost.

"I can't do it, Todd."

Mister Five was a risk. I'd already let several of my boundaries go on our first meeting, and I wasn't about to break another one of my rules. *No repeat clients. No exceptions.*

"He specifically asked for you again. He won't take another girl. It's you or nothing. He's under the spell of your puss, and I can't blame the poor guy. Just do it."

"No. I'm not doing it. I'll do anyone else. Not him."

I wasn't sure why I was so adamant that I didn't want to see him again. It had been an amazing experience that I hadn't been able to stop thinking about all week. And *that* was why I couldn't go there again.

"I don't have anyone else for you. In fact, you've got the rest of the week off. All your appointments have canceled."

"Don't be an ass," I said, knowing that he was punishing me. "You know I need to work."

"All right, I do have one job for you."

I knew where this was going, and let out a sigh.

"Seven p.m. Sunday. The lobby of The Plaza. Wear something nice, because you'll be having dinner."

"Todd!" I said, exasperated.

"Take it or leave it, Ally."

I pouted like a child and mumbled, "Fine! I'll take it."

"Good girl. Oh, and look at that—I'm getting flooded with emails as we speak. All your appointments for the week are back on."

"So it's all or nothing?"

"That's right, cherry pie."

"Don't call me that!" I whined.

Todd gave me that nickname because he said I was the all-around perfect American girl—sweet and delicious as cherry pie. The name had stuck.

We hung up, and I flopped back down on the bed.

In three days I'd be spending the evening with Client Number Five again.

Fuck.

"Yo, Ally! Jamie! Lookin' good, girls!" the guy behind the counter called out as we walked into the gym.

"You're such a sweet talker, Jeremy," Jamie said, wiggling her hips. She loved the attention.

Jamie and I swiped our membership cards through the scanner and made our way to the cardio room. The walls were lined with mirrors, and there was a bank of televisions suspended from the ceiling. Each one was showing a different program and had a sign underneath with the tune-in frequency.

I pulled my MP3 player out, set the internal radio to the middle television which was showing *American Idol,* and put the buds in my ear. It would be good to run to music. I jogged for fifteen minutes, and once I'd built up a good sweat on the treadmill, I moved on to the step machine. It was important to have a tight ass when that was what most clients were looking at for the majority of your time with them.

Jamie was running on a nearby cross-trainer, singing along with her iPod.

An hour and a half later, when we were both gasping for breath but flushed with endorphins, we stripped down and sat in the sauna. Jamie and I were so used to being naked in front of each other that if the sauna was empty, like today, we were happy to go *au naturel.*

"I could live in here. I love the way my skin feels after all the toxins are steamed away." Jamie sighed.

"Not me. I only get in here because I love the feeling of jumping into the pool when I come out. The hot-to-cold makes me feel really refreshed."

"You don't want to stop your heart though. I saw on TV that a huge change in temperature can put your body into shock or something."

"I don't think a sauna is going to give me a heart attack." I rolled my eyes.

She shrugged and wiped a damp cloth over her bare stomach. "Your choice. Speaking of choices, have you thought about the boob job yet? I think you'd look so sexy with a double-D."

I shrugged my shoulders. "It's something I might think about in a few years, but right now my girls are still perky."

"But guys love them big." She squeezed hers for emphasis.

"I don't care what guys love."

Jamie laughed. "You're such a man hater. Have you ever thought about, you know…?" She put her fingers to her mouth and poked her tongue through them.

"Oh God, Jamie. What is wrong with you?" I threw my face towel at her.

"I'm happy to practice with you if you want to test out your orientation."

"Thanks, I think I'll give it a miss." I rolled my eyes and folded my arms over my chest.

Jamie was all about sex. She'd always been like that, and since she'd started working for Todd, she'd only gotten worse. But I also knew her as the sweet girl who visited her grandmother every weekend, even though she didn't remember who Jamie was. I knew the girl who was happy to cover my share of the rent the month that I got pneumonia and could barely work. I knew the girl who sold her car when she moved to New York and gave all the money to Alzheimer's research in her grandma's name. But she was also the girl with the fake boobs and the bleached-blond hair who fucked guys for money.

"We should have Thai food for dinner tonight, don't you think?" she asked, rubbing her knee.

"Sounds good."

We wrapped ourselves in towels and left the sauna. Jamie went to have a shower while I went to the swimming pool. There was no one around, so I didn't bother to change into my bathing suit; I wouldn't be in the water long.

One of the best things about working nights was that I could go to the gym while everyone else was at work. There were usually some people around, but it was never packed like in the evenings.

I dropped my towel by the edge of the water and dove in. The cool water soaked my hot skin as I broke the surface, sending a shiver through me. It was bliss.

# CHAPTER FIVE

I stepped into the lobby of The Plaza, feeling much more confident than the last time I'd been there. I'd spent a big chunk of the payment that Mr. Walker had given me last weekend on a gorgeous dress and shoes. I wanted to look the part.

Men in suits tipped their heads to me as I walked by. They were staring in awe now, not from disgust or lust. As far as any of them knew, I was one of them. A wealthy heiress perhaps, or a foreign model in town for a photo shoot. Either way, I appeared rich, and that was all they cared about.

Scott Walker was leaning against a marble pillar, smiling at me as I walked across the vast room.

"You look lovely, Ally," he said as I approached.

I'd paid special attention to my hair, allowing it to fall down my back in long waves. My makeup was less intense than I would usually wear, but still enough to make me see someone in the mirror who wasn't little Alison Mitchell.

"It's good to see you again, Mr. Walker."

"Scott, please," he said.

He looked down at me with warm, smiling eyes and I had to look away.

"Shall we go?" he asked.

I nodded, took his offered arm, and we walked out into the night.

Once seated in the restaurant — one I'd never been to because I could barely afford the starters — he ordered a bottle of champagne and turned to me. "I'm so happy you agreed to meet with me again. I thought about you a lot over the past week," he said.

His voice was warm and sincere and made no reference to that fact that he was paying me to spend time with him.

"It's my pleasure, Mr. — Scott."

He smiled. "Try to relax, and don't think about later tonight. Let's just have dinner."

The champagne arrived, and the waiter poured our glasses. I recognized the crisp taste as the same champagne we'd had in his hotel room.

"So, what do you do?" he asked and then froze.

I laughed. It was a normal question that you'd ask someone. I just didn't have a normal answer.

"I mean…aside from work," he elaborated.

"There's not much to tell, really. I work a lot."

"Do you have any hobbies?" he pressed.

I shifted uncomfortably on the seat. I really tried to avoid telling clients too much about my personal life. It wasn't professional.

"I like to read."

His eyes lit up. "I'm in the publishing business. I own a publishing house in town. That's why I'm here."

"But you live in Florida. How does that work?"

"I used to live in New York, but once the house was established and I didn't need to watch over it every day, I decided to move south for the lifestyle. I love the warm weather. I fly back for board meetings, but we do most of our work via email or voice conference. It works well."

"Can I ask which publishing company you own?"

He smiled. "Montgomery Books. It's a boutique house, but we're successful."

"I've heard of it." I had a few of their books on my bookshelf at home, but I wasn't going to mention that.

Our first course arrived, and I realized that we hadn't even ordered. After the waiter had walked away Scott said, "It's a set menu. I'm sure you'll enjoy it."

As we ate our salmon, I started to relax. We talked mostly about him and his life because that was what I was most comfortable with. I learned that he had a younger sister and had grown up in Miami. New York had never felt like home to him so he'd moved as soon as he could.

I asked a lot of questions to keep the conversation topics off me. We had similar taste in movies and music. He hadn't had a girlfriend for almost a year. His ex, Susanne, had cheated on him, and he'd been hesitant to start a new relationship. I steered us away from that topic—it was too close to memories of my own that I didn't want brought up.

I had other questions that I wanted to ask, but they weren't the kind that could be voiced in public. They would have to wait.

The conversation flowed so easily that I was surprised when the waiter cleared our dessert plates. Scott put several hundred dollar bills in the leather folder that the waiter dropped off, and then he pulled out my chair.

We walked, hand-in-hand, to Central Park and took a carriage ride. I'd never had such an extensive job. Usually it was into the room, suck his cock, let him jack-rabbit away, and then get out of there as quickly as I could. This was the whole-date experience.

It didn't even feel like I was working, and I had to keep reminding myself that I was.

I noticed that our carriage driver was wearing ear buds. He was probably listening to music, so I took the opportunity to ask what I couldn't voice at dinner.

"Last time we saw each other, you said you'd never used a prostitute before."

Scott coughed lightly and ran his hands over his thighs. "That's true. I never thought I would, either. When my cousin suggested it I was horrified—no offense."

"What made you change your mind? You didn't seem horrified when I got there. Nervous, maybe, but not put off."

A deep blush rose over his throat and he coughed. "It's been a long time since I've dated anyone and…"

"You were horny."

He gave me a guilty nod. I smiled, trying to show him that he didn't have to be ashamed.

"I'm assuming you enjoyed yourself, because you booked me again."

"The reason I asked Todd if I could see you again wasn't because you were good in bed."

"I wasn't good?" I asked, half teasing and half fishing for a compliment. I took pride in my work and never wanted to leave a client unsatisfied.

"No! You were great. I meant that wasn't why I asked to see you again. Yes, the sex was phenomenal and I can't wait to do it again, but I haven't been able to stop thinking about you, and I wanted to get to know you better."

My hand flinched away from his automatically.

"Maybe that's not how things are done in your profession. Maybe it should have been 'Wham! Bam! Thank you, ma'am!' But that's not the kind of person I am."

"That's exactly the kind of person I am," I said matter-of-factly.

He scrunched up his brow. "Are you really?"

I laughed. "You don't know me. That night last week when we met? I'd just had four other clients before you."

He cleared his throat. "I agree that is a lot of…experience…but it doesn't define who you are." His eyes went wide and a blush crept over his cheeks. "Did I leave enough money?"

"Actually, you overpaid."

We both sat awkwardly for the rest of the ride, and I mentally kicked myself for bringing up the topic in the first place. The walk back to the hotel was silent, but he held my hand the whole way. He had the same hotel suite.

As soon as I walked through the door, my eyes fell to the envelope sitting in plain sight on the table. He'd been prepared.

"That's for you," he said, pointing to the envelope.

"Thank you."

This was so uncomfortable. I didn't usually feel bad taking money from a client. I was providing a service, and in return, I got paid. It was a business transaction. I just happened to work naked. But with Scott, I didn't feel like I was working. It didn't feel right taking money when I was actually enjoying myself.

"I thought we might sit and talk for a while. Would you like a drink?" He turned to a fully stocked bar by the balcony.

I froze. *More talking?*

"Okay," I said.

"What would you like?" He waved his arms wide at the selections of bottles.

"I'd like to suck your cock."

He cleared his throat and continued over to the bar. "Maybe later," he said dismissively.

I sat down on the couch, defeated and trying frantically to think up more things to talk about. I'd used all my regular material at dinner and talking wasn't something I had to do a lot of. I was way out of my depth.

He carried over two drinks and handed me one. I'd had a glass of champagne at dinner that would usually have been my limit while working, but I had a feeling I was going to need another drink to get me through the night.

I sculled the drink, and vodka burned all the way down my throat. Scott raised his eyebrows when I put the empty glass down on the side table. His was still full.

I wiggled around on the chair and adjusted my dress, hoping to show some cleavage. I would have to heat things up in a more subtle way.

"What would you like to talk about?" I asked.

"We spent most of the night talking about me. I still don't know anything about you."

That was the way I liked it. Instead of telling him that, I asked, "What would you like to know?"

"Do you have a boyfriend?"

I laughed and made sure to shake my shoulders to give my assets a little bounce.

"With *this* job? No. I don't think any guy could handle dating someone who does what I do. It wouldn't be fair to either of us."

"But if you met someone, someone you might care about…what would you do?"

I shifted in my seat. The questions were already starting to get personal, and we'd only just started.

"I don't think I'll ever have to worry about that. I'm not in the market for a relationship."

Scott pondered my words and took a sip of his drink. "Often when you're not looking is when you find what you didn't know you were looking for."

I didn't like where this conversation was headed. Time to put on the brakes.

"Look, Scott, I've, for the most part, enjoyed our night. But we both know what you've paid me to do. There's no shame in it. You don't have to pretend this is anything more than it is."

"And what is this to you?" he asked.

"My job." I knew it was harsh but it was the truth. "You pay me for sex."

"Is sex a requirement? Am I obligated to have sex with you?"

That pulled me up short. I frowned. "Well, no. Technically you've paid for my time, not the sex. I've just never had a client *not* want to have sex."

"I never said I didn't want to have sex. You're a very attractive woman, and I had hoped our evening would end in the bedroom, but I didn't want that to be the whole night."

"I'm sorry. I don't understand what's happening here. If you wanted to get to know someone, why call a prostitute? There are millions of women in the city sitting in bars, waiting to meet men exactly like you."

He sighed and put down his half-full glass next to my empty one.

"I've asked myself that question a million times over the past week. When I booked you, I thought it was going to be just for that night. I had no future ideas about us. But then I got home and I kept thinking about you. Of course I thought about the sex too, but it was more than that. I thought about *you*."

I bit my tongue to stop myself from saying that I'd been thinking about him, too. Telling him that would only encourage his behavior, and that was the last thing I needed. My warning bells were sounding, and I had to get out of there. I stood up and looked down at him.

"I'm a prostitute. So, as lovely as this has been, if we're not going to have sex, then I'm going to have to leave. I'll only take the money that I've earned so far. I'm sorry, but I'm just not into playing games."

Scott stood and held out a hand, palm up.

"Ally, please don't go. I'm sorry if I crossed a line. Perhaps we could find a middle ground? I *do* like games. Maybe we could play Truth or Dare?"

I cocked an eyebrow. "The game teenagers play?"

"Why not? And to make it more *your* kind of game, we'll have a little wager. If a person refuses to answer a truth or complete a dare, they have to remove an item of clothing. The first person to be completely naked has to give the other person oral sex."

I laughed. It actually sounded like fun. Perhaps it was something I could use in the future with my shier clients. I wasn't at all worried about having to answer truths; I would pick dare every time. There was no way I was going to give him any information I didn't want to.

"Will you stay?" His eyes pleaded with me, and I couldn't resist.

"I'll stay."

We both sat cross-legged on the floor of the bedroom, facing each other.

"You can go first," I offered.

"Okay. Truth."

My plan was to avoid his questions and dare him to do a multitude of sexy things, determined to heat this night up if it was the last thing I did.

"What is a sexual fantasy that you've never done but would like to?"

He smirked. "Sex in a hot tub. Your turn."

"Dare."

He rolled his eyes. Damn. He was onto me.

"I dare you…" He paused to think for a second, and then a victorious grin broke out over his face. "I dare you to tell me something about yourself that nobody else knows."

My jaw dropped open. "You cheater! That's a truth!"

"No, I *dared* you to tell me." He gave me a playful wink.

"Well, I'm not answering it."

"Come on, Ally, it's just a game."

I huffed out a frustrated breath and tried to think of the least important thing about myself that I could tell him.

"Fine. Something that nobody else knows about me is that I brush my teeth in the shower. It's a time-saver and it gives me something to do while the conditioner is in my hair."

Scott's smile was radiant. "There, that wasn't so hard was it? Truth."

"Tell me about when you lost your virginity."

"I was seventeen. It was after the junior prom in the back of my parents' car."

"Dare," I said.

"I dare you to tell me if you've ever been in love," he taunted.

"Oh, come on! This isn't a game of Truth or Truth."

Scott laughed. "If you don't want to fulfill the dare, you can take off a piece of clothing."

"Fine." I removed one of my shoes and tossed it to the other side of the room. Getting naked was much easier than answering the questions.

"Truth," he said before I could ask his preference.

"What's your favorite sex position?"

"Reverse cowgirl. Let me guess, you want a dare?"

I nodded.

"I dare you to go out with me tomorrow. No sex. No payment. A date."

"What? No way!" I took off my other shoe and squeezed it tightly.

Scott's face fell just a little, and I actually *cared* that I'd hurt his feelings. I tried to think about what it must feel like to know that a person was only spending time with you because you were paying them. I was sure it wouldn't feel nice.

Against everything I believed in and my own better judgment, I sighed. "Oh all right. But don't take sex off the table. I'll spend the day with you, but it's not a date. It's just two people hanging out, and if they happen to have sex too, then so be it." I put the shoe back on.

I needed to put the sex clause in. It was the only way I'd feel like I was myself and not someone pretending to be on a date.

His eyes crinkled at the sides with the size of his smile. "I accept your terms. Truth."

"Why are you doing this?"

He shrugged his shoulders. "I really wish I knew. I never planned to feel drawn to you. All I know is that when I'm with you, I feel good. I feel happy. I just haven't had that in a while."

"Is your life lonely?"

"You already asked your question," he said in a mock warning voice.

"Hey, I'm talking. Do you want me to go back to not wanting to talk at all?"

He chewed his lip. "It is and it isn't," he said, answering my earlier question. "I have people around me all the time, needing things from me. But I don't have many people who actually *care* about me."

I didn't want to point out that I was just another person who was around without caring. He didn't need to hear that. If he took comfort from our time together then I was doing my job. I supposed that emotional comfort and physical comfort were pretty similar.

The energy in the room had dropped. Suddenly, this game wasn't fun anymore.

"Do you want to keep playing?" I asked.

He shrugged his shoulders.

"Well, I'm the most undressed so that means that I have to give you oral sex," I said, trying to give him an encouraging smile, but he didn't return it.

"You don't have to, Ally."

"I want to. Come on, let's have some fun. You said earlier that you hoped tonight would end in the bedroom. Well, here we are, in the bedroom. Let's end the night on a high."

I stood up, kicked off my other shoe, and slowly unzipped the back of the dress, letting it slip over my body into a puddle on the floor around my feet. I stood before in him in just my panties. I hadn't been able to wear a bra under that dress, and my nipples hardened at the contact with the cool air.

His eyes grew dark as he looked up at me, and when I reached my hand down to help him up, he took it.

# CHAPTER SIX

"These eggs are delicious," I said, shoveling another forkful into my greedy mouth.

I'd broken another of my rules—no sleeping over. Scott had paid for the whole night, but that usually entailed a sweaty marathon. Scott and I had indulged in each other twice before we'd fallen asleep and again when we'd woken up.

Scott smiled. "Noted. You like scrambled eggs."

"What's that supposed to mean?"

"Just that I learned something about you." He took a sip of his coffee and then gave me a toothy grin. "You're a difficult nut to crack."

I tried not to let my irritation show. Instead, I took another bite of eggs.

"Are you backing out of the dare?" he asked, his voice casual as he took another sip of his coffee, but I could see the sparkle of interest in his eyes.

"I thought you always flew home on Monday mornings."

"Normally I do, but I decided to extend my stay. I'll fly home tomorrow."

"You postponed your flight because of the dare?"

I really hoped he was going to say no. Under the table, I crossed the fingers on my right hand and as many toes as I could manage.

"In part. There is some business that needs my attention this morning. I *could* have handled it from my home office, but since I had the incentive of a date with a lovely lady, I decided to stay."

"When did you even have time to call the airline?" I asked.

"I sent a text to my assistant and she made the arrangements for me." He poured another cup of coffee.

"Will you be working all day?"

"Just for a few hours. When we finish breakfast I'll go into the office, but then I'll meet you for lunch and we'll spend the rest of the day together."

I nodded. That would give me time to go home and have a shower.

"Unless you're backing out," he added playfully.

"I don't back out of dares."

He smiled. "Start thinking of things for us to do. I'd like you to give me a local's view of the city."

My mouth gaped and I cleared my throat. "This is *your* day. I'm happy to do whatever you want to do."

"Great! What I want is for you to show me what a local does."

I groaned. He was the master of turning things around onto me. Just like with the dares.

An hour later I was chewing my lip as I rinsed the conditioner out of my hair. I had *no* idea what activities to do with Scott. I wasn't really a local myself, having only moved to the city for college. And to be honest, when I had a day to sight-see, the *last* thing I wanted to do was any of the cliché touristy things. In fact, getting *out* of the city was what locals loved to do in their time off.

I applied a coat of powder to my cheeks and stopped to wonder why I even cared what we did. I should just take him to the Empire State Building and Central Park and be done with it. Or I could just stay home. He didn't have my phone number or know where I lived. In a city of eight million people, he'd never find me.

I put the lipstick down on the sink and looked in the mirror. I had on a little makeup, not enough for a night out but enough of a mask so I didn't look like Alison. The woman staring back at me wasn't a liar or a quitter. She'd promised she'd be somewhere, and she would be. I couldn't strand him all alone, no matter how uncomfortable the day would be.

Once I'd decided to go through with the dare, an idea formed in my head of what we could do for the day, and I called my brother for some help. I'd never had the opportunity to use his job as the manager of a car rental agency to my advantage before, but there was a first time for everything.

"Do you have an extra car today? Maybe a convertible?" I asked when Zach answered the phone.

"Hello to you too, little sister."

"Can I get one?"

"I dunno. What's in it for me?"

"Please, Zach? I never ask for favors."

"You'll take extra special care of it?"

I sighed. "Of course I will. I'll have it back tonight in perfect condition."

"All right."

"You're the best. I'm on my way over now to grab it."

I hung up the phone and looked myself over in the mirror. So far Scott had only seen me dressed for work, and I wondered what he'd think of my jeans-and-tank-top ensemble. I dragged my fingers through my hair to pull it up into a messy ponytail, then rifled through my purse for my driver's license. I didn't carry it normally because I never drove.

It was just after eleven in the morning when I left my apartment. I wasn't meeting Scott for another hour, but that would give me time to pick up the car and get a few more things ready for our day.

I caught the subway and power-walked to the rental agency. Zach was out front, leaning on the hood of a silver convertible.

"Thanks, Zach!" I said when I grabbed the keys dangling from his outstretched fingers.

"You're the only one who drives it. I don't want *anyone* else behind the wheel."

"Scout's honor!" I gave him a little salute.

"You were never a Scout!"

I rolled my eyes. "I swear I'll deliver the car back to you in perfect condition."

"With a full tank of gas," he reminded me.

"Yes, Zachary."

I gave him a quick hug and climbed behind the wheel. The rumble of the engine sent a thrill through me as I drove uptown. I wasn't sure what it was, but the hum of the car made me feel calm. It was almost noon as I battled the traffic back to The Plaza to meet Scott. He was standing outside waiting for me when I pulled up and honked the horn.

He looked over the car with a raised eyebrow and reluctantly climbed into the passenger seat.

"What's this?" he asked.

"Our activity for the day."

"I thought true New Yorkers used the subway."

"To get around town, that's true. But we're leaving the city."

I pulled into traffic and drove north, past Central Park.

"Is this your car?" he asked.

"No. My brother manages a car rental agency and he has very kindly let me borrow it for the day."

"You have a brother. Noted."

"What's with that *noted* shit? Are you creating a dossier on me or something?" I glared at him, then turned my attention back to the road.

"Just trying to remember details. You give so little of yourself away that I have to take the small crumbs you drop by accident."

His smile was killer, and even though I wanted to be annoyed that he'd wheedled out some knowledge of my personal life, I couldn't help but soften to him. Stupid happy eyes and sexy grin!

"Where are we headed?" he asked, changing the subject.

"We're just driving until we find somewhere to stop. You said you wanted to do what New Yorkers do. Well, New Yorkers love to get out of the city when they have time off. So we're getting out of the city."

Scott settled back in his chair and started fiddling with the radio dials, changing the station to an easy listening station from the nineties and then turning the volume down. He watched me as I kept my gaze on the road, but after several minutes of that, I snapped.

"Why are you staring at me?"

"You're very focused when you drive."

"Yes, well, I'm trying not to kill us, and I promised my brother that I'd bring this back in one piece."

"That's true. This car is probably a little too powerful for you. A BMW would probably have been more appropriate than Porsche." His expression was so serious, and I suppressed a smirk.

"Trust me, I can drive just fine. And I didn't know you were into cars," I said instead of teasing him about being a car-nerd.

"There's a lot you don't know about me. In fact, are you up for a little driving game?"

"You sure do like games. First Truth or Dare and now this?"

"I think you'll like this one — it allows you to lie about who you are. Isn't that your comfort zone?"

"Lying and withholding are different."

"If you say so. Do you want to play?"

"Okay. What's the game?"

"Two truths and a lie. Do you know it?"

I nodded. Of course I did. It was a popular drinking game while I was in college. You told two true things about yourself and one lie, and the other person had to guess which fact wasn't true. If they guessed right, you had to take a shot.

"You go first," I told him.

"All right. My favorite color is orange, I spent a year in Australia as a teenager on exchange, and I had a sixth toe removed from my left foot when I was eight years old."

"Hmm." I tried to think about the options. I honestly had no idea what his favorite color was, and though he'd never mentioned living in Australia or having an extra toe, we hadn't spoken about his childhood. It would have to be a complete guess. "The sixth toe?"

"Damn, you're good!" He laughed and smacked his hand on his thigh. "I really thought I might have had you with that."

"Orange?" I asked.

"Yes, it's so happy."

I poked my tongue out. "Orange is my least favorite color."

He raised one eyebrow but didn't respond. Instead, he waited for me to take my turn.

"Okay. I'm terrified of birds, before this career took off I'd planned on being an architect, and I believe in aliens."

"That's easy. It's got to be the aliens." He smirked and twisted to face me.

"Wrong. I majored in journalism in college, not architecture."

"You believe in *aliens?*"

"You *don't?*"

"Of course not." He shook his head and then looked at me again. "Do you believe in ghosts, too?"

"Look, I just think it's arrogant to assume that out of all the billions of planets, in a universe so big that our minds can't even comprehend it, that there isn't one other planet out there capable of supporting life and that, just like on Earth, life has developed. I'm not saying that there are little green men in orbit abducting people — just that somewhere out there, life exists on other planets." My tone was a little more forceful than I'd intended, but I didn't like to feel that I was stupid for thinking scientifically.

Scott was silent as he pondered my words, and I drove toward the Connecticut border.

"I suppose when you put it like that, there's a possibility," he finally said. "It's nice to see you're passionate about something besides sex."

"What's that supposed to mean?" I glanced away from the road for a second to gauge his expression.

"Just that all you've seemed to care about since we met is sex. Conversation seems to be trivial to you, and you don't appear to have any need for companionship. It's reassuring to see that something matters to you, even if it is something as strange as aliens."

I let out a long breath and pulled the car over to the side of the highway. I left the engine idling but pulled the handbrake on so I could give Scott my full attention.

"Sex is important to me because it's my *job*. I'm sure you take the publishing of books seriously. I don't want to talk too much about myself or be friends with you because I'm working and you're a client. I assure you that I am capable of caring about people. I love my family, and I have some very close friends. Things matter to me just as much as they matter to you, I just don't talk to my clients about them. It wouldn't be professional."

I waited for him to respond, but when he didn't, I pulled the car back out onto the highway and continued east. We traveled about ten miles in complete silence, and I was just about to reach for the volume knob to turn the music up when Scott finally spoke.

"I spy with my little eye, something beginning with L."

"Another game?" I asked, shaking my head and laughing.

We played I Spy for nearly an hour, and surprisingly, we didn't break out in an argument. When we arrived at New Haven, it was almost two p.m. and we were both starving.

We found a cute café on the waterfront, and with the smell of the ocean to enhance the mood, we settled into a relaxed lunch.

"Is there anything exciting to see in New Haven?" Scott asked the waiter when he cleared our plates.

"Not really. The Yale campus is nice though. They run tours if you go to the visitor's center."

"Thanks." Scott left a very generous tip, and we drove off again, parking near the Yale campus. When we got out, he grasped my hand.

As we walked down the street, I took in the city and realized it had much more to offer than just the college campus. Sure, the school was a huge part of the town — you could see it everywhere, blue-and-white decorations and the school logo in window displays — but it looked like there was a lot more to it.

I breathed in deeply and enjoyed the fresh air. The only place in New York City where I could breathe this clearly was in the park.

"Wanna look around the campus?" Scott asked.

"Sure."

We decided not to join an official tour and just strolled the winding paths ourselves.

"Being here," Scott said, taking a deep breath, "reminds me so much of my own time at college. I feel like I should be headed to a class somewhere."

I smiled. The wind ruffled his hair and his eyes held a sparkle as he grinned at me.

"I suppose, despite being in the Ivy League, all college campuses have some similarities."

Just then, a flood of students left one of the buildings and we were caught in their wake, being herded toward another building.

Scott grabbed my hand and tugged me in the opposite direction. Some of the students let out grunts of frustration as we pushed past them, but soon they had moved on and we were standing alone on the path.

"What was that?" I asked, laughing.

"Some very eager students on their way to class."

"I don't remember ever being that excited to get to my classes."

"Perhaps your classes weren't as interesting as theirs," Scott offered.

"Journalism was pretty interesting."

Scott's eyebrows shot up. "Did you graduate?"

"No. I attended for three years before I found my *other* career of choice." I laughed.

We started down the path again. The sun was warm on my face and arms, but I wasn't sure where we were headed, so I let Scott lead the way.

"Why didn't you finish? You were so close to the end."

"Halfway through my junior year I had some personal issues, and studying wasn't high on my list of priorities." I shook my head to push away the memories that threatened to well up. "This is better, though. I would have made a terrible journalist. I can't stick to deadlines."

"Oh, I don't know. I can picture it. '*Hard-hitting journalist, Ally Whatshername reporting.*'"

"Ally Whatshername?" I giggled.

"That's my best guess."

I punched his arm and snorted softly. "Good try."

"You mean I'm *wrong?*" He gave me his best mock-horror expression.

"No, you're right. I come from a long line of proud Whatshernames."

"Maybe *I* should be the hard-hitting journalist."

I punched him again and marveled at how easy it was to play with Scott. It was true that I wasn't being paid for this *date,* but he was technically still a client.

I took a few more steps before I realized that Scott had stopped walking.

"Is something wrong?" I asked.

He shook his head. "The sun is getting low in the sky."

Through the tree branches, I saw that the light had turned golden and the clouds were rimmed in pink.

"We should probably head out. I need to get the car back."

"All right."

The jovial mood from before was gone as we walked back to the car. Scott shuffled his feet and kept his eyes low despite my trying to initiate conversation several times. The drive back wasn't any better. He showed no interest in the games that he'd been so excited about earlier. It wasn't until we were again surrounded by the tall buildings of Manhattan that he looked at me and finally spoke.

"Will you stay with me tonight?"

I bit my bottom lip. It was my day off, so I knew that Todd wouldn't have any other clients for me, but I cherished those nights when I could curl up alone in bed and read.

"My brother will kill me if I don't get the car back to him." It was the best excuse I could think of.

Scott frowned. I hated to see the light go out of his eyes—and I hated that I hated it.

"Return it and then join me for a late dinner."

"The rental place isn't close. By the time I got back up to you, it would be late."

"I don't mind waiting."

"Scott." I tried to keep a stern tone in my voice.

"Ally," he said gently, "I've enjoyed getting to know you today."

I took a deep breath and pulled the car up to the curb of the hotel. The doorman rushed over to open the door, but Scott waved him away. He reached over and took my hand off the steering wheel, clasping it tightly in his own.

I stared down at where our fingers were joined, and my heart thudded in my chest. I shouldn't have liked his touch as much as I did. I tried to pull away, but he held on.

The mood in the car was far too serious, so I tried to break the tension. "You got today as a freebie because I lost a bet, mister. Don't forget that."

Scott let out a slow breath. "If I have to pay for your time, I will."

"Look, I had a great time but—"

"Please."

I don't know why I agreed. It was stupid and the last thing I should have done. All I knew was that I hated to see him sad and that I genuinely *did* enjoy spending time with him.

I sighed. "All right. Let me return the car and I'll come back."

"Don't stand me up." His smile was radiant. The change in his mood was ridiculous. It was as if I'd just told him that he'd won the lottery.

My phone beeped with a text message from Zach asking where I was and why the car wasn't back yet. Perfect timing, as always.

"Hurry back," Scott said as he climbed out of the car.

I nodded a goodbye and pulled out into the early evening traffic.

I returned the car, full of gas, to Zach as quickly as the traffic would allow, and then I made a quick trip home to shower and change. As I applied a new layer of makeup, I tried to talk myself out of going back to The Plaza. I was home. It would be so easy to curl up on the couch and watch some bad reality television. All that was waiting for me uptown was trouble. Trouble, and the sweetest blue eyes I'd ever seen. With a defeated sigh I touched up my mascara and put on some gold hoop earrings. Scott was waiting for me, and it would be rude to cancel. I might be a hooker, but manners were still important to me.

Jamie wasn't home, and I was grateful for that. I didn't want to explain to her why I was going out on a night off. Unfortunately, that also meant she wasn't around to talk sense into me either.

Half an hour later I was standing on the street, staring up at the hotel. *What am I doing?* I had never spent any of my down time with a client. Scott had offered to pay me, but after spending the day together, it just didn't feel right. Scott had brought down all my defenses. A few lines from Beyoncé's song "Halo" ran through my head. Just like in the lyrics, my walls were tumbling down.

My instinct told me to run. *Quick! Get out of there and back to the safety of your empty apartment!* But I stayed. There was also a calmness inside me at the thought of seeing Scott again. It would have to be a professional meeting, though. I would be firm on that. I couldn't have him think that we were starting to date or that I was going to be his girlfriend. Tonight would be back to basics. Sex for money. End of story.

I strutted through the lobby with determination and tapped my high-heeled shoe for the entire elevator ride. Three firm raps on his door and his smiling face appeared.

"You came!"

"You're surprised?"

He smirked. "I hoped, but I wasn't sure."

"Well, I'm a girl of my word." I pushed past him into the room and saw the thick cream envelope sitting on the coffee table.

Scott followed my line of sight and cleared his throat.

"That's for you."

"Thanks."

I didn't move to pick up the envelope. Instead, I removed my coat and hung it over the back of the couch.

"I was just going to have a shower," Scott said.

"All right. I can entertain myself."

"Actually, I thought you might join me," he called over his shoulder as he disappeared into the bedroom.

# CHAPTER SEVEN

I got to the bathroom just as he turned on the faucet and a waterfall of hot water sprayed onto the tiled floor. The shower was plenty big enough for two people, with a rainwater showerhead hanging in the center. Steam quickly filled the room as we undressed and stepped inside.

The water stung my skin in a delightful way and I turned, allowing it to cascade over my back.

"Let's get all this junk off your face, shall we?" Scott said.

"What?"

"Your makeup. I'd like to see your actual face."

I pulled away and shivered once I was out of the warm water. I needed my makeup. It was the only thing that separated Alison from Ally. I couldn't be *Alison* with a client. No way. That was absolutely out of the question, no matter how much I liked him.

"I'd much rather suck your cock," I offered, hoping to dissuade him.

He gave a half-smile but shook his head. "All in good time."

He lathered up a washcloth and came toward me, holding it up to my face.

I twirled out of his reach and stepped out of the shower, quickly pulling a towel around my dripping body.

"I'm sorry. I know you've paid for tonight, but I have some boundaries that I don't cross. Not for any amount of money."

He left the shower as well, crestfallen.

"Like the kissing."

"Exactly." And before I could stop myself, I burst into tears.

*Why the hell am I crying?* The salt water burned my eyes and caused me to sob harder. I hadn't cried in years and *never* in front of a client. I hated each tear as it fell.

"It's all right," Scott whispered gently, pulling me into a hug.

His body was warm, and I sank into him. The water still rained down behind us, billowing steam throughout the room.

The tears eventually stopped, but the deflated feeling didn't go away. I was a balloon without air, clinging to Scott's embrace.

"Come on."

He led me into the bedroom and sat me down. He wrapped a robe around me, but I didn't raise my head to thank him. I didn't have any words that could express how his comfort and kindness made me feel even worse.

Why couldn't he have just been like all the others? My job was to give him pleasure, suck his cock, and fuck him silly. I didn't want him to be *nice*. It made me feel cheap. At least if they treated me like I was worthless, I didn't have to live up to anything.

Scott made me *want* to be Alison. And that was absolutely unacceptable.

He was kneeling in front of me, looking up with concerned eyes.

"Are you all right? Can I get you something? A drink?"

I shook my head. "You can keep the money for tonight," I whispered.

I'd never screwed up a job before. And with Todd's cousin of all people! I hoped I wouldn't get fired.

"Keep it. I wasn't paying for the sex. We don't even have to do anything tonight. I just wanted to spend the evening with you. And we had a lovely day together, didn't we?"

I lifted my head and looked into his warm, blue eyes. I nodded and gave him a shy smile.

"That's my girl. How can I keep that smile on your face for the rest of the night?"

I gave a little shrug, and he chuckled. I knew I must look like a sulking child, but I couldn't lift my mood. It probably would have helped if he'd turned me around and fucked me from behind. At least that would have been in my comfort zone.

"How about I order some ice cream from room service and we watch a movie?"

"I could just go home," I said.

He frowned. "I'd like you to stay…if you want to."

I thought through my options. I could leave, which would probably offend him, and he'd tell Todd about what a wrecked mess I was. I could switch my emotions off and tell him I was fine, fuck him senseless, and cry when I got home. Or, I could cuddle up with him in bed and eat ice cream as I sank into the softest pillows I'd ever slept on.

My instincts told me to go with option number two, but I really wanted that ice cream.

"That sounds nice."

His face lit up, and he kissed me softly on the forehead. He called down to the kitchen and ordered one scoop of every flavor they had, and then went and turned off the shower. The steam had started floating out into the bedroom, and the ground had a dry-ice look to it.

Before I knew it, we were snuggled up under the blankets with a large bowl of ice cream. They had only brought one spoon.

"Do you mind sharing?" Scott asked.

"Not at all."

He let me take the first bite while he fiddled with the remote control. Soon we were watching some sappy romantic comedy.

"How is the chocolate?" he asked.

"It's good. Not too sweet. The mango is really nice."

He took a spoonful of the mango and hummed in appreciation. I was about to tease him about being greedy, when he took another scoop and held it up to my lips so I could lick it off.

I let him keep the spoon for the rest of the night. He ate more of the ice cream than I did, but that was because I kept turning down his offered spoonfuls. I couldn't eat too much dairy or I'd get bloated. No one wanted a puffy prostitute.

After we were finished, we lay back on the stacked pillows, and he pulled me to rest against his chest. He really was getting the whole girlfriend experience tonight.

When the movie finished and the credits started to roll, an uncomfortable sensation crept over me. I'd been lulled into a safe movie-bubble, and now that was gone.

"Did you like it?" he asked, grabbing for the remote and turning off the television.

"I thought it was a bit mushy," I admitted.

"I get the feeling that romance isn't high on your list."

"It's not that. I'd love to fall in love one day. I just think that it's not as wonderful as everyone pretends it is. Love is hard, and it hurts you. You have to make yourself very vulnerable."

"And you're too strong for that?" he asked.

The tears started to well behind my eyes again. "No. I'm not strong enough," I whispered.

I wasn't sure why I was telling him any of this. I didn't even know him. In my mind, I did the mental switch of going back to formalities. I'd gotten too comfortable with Scott. Mr. Walker. No, even better — *Client Number Five.*

I had to remember that he was *only* a client. A client that had paid to fuck me, just like all the rest.

"Let's take a bath," he said, standing and holding out his hand for me.

We walked slowly to the bathroom, and he turned on the water and jets in the giant spa bath. The water bubbled temptingly, but without the steamy side effect of the shower.

Scott dropped his robe and stepped into the water, sitting down in the far corner. I let my robe fall to the floor as well and followed him into the tub.

"Come sit by me," he said.

The tub was triangular and I could have easily sat out of his reach, but at his request, I sat next to him so our knees were touching.

From my seat I could see into the mirror. My skin was pale and my breasts were sitting just at the surface of the water, nipples pointed and being lapped by the small waves from the jets. My face was a mess. Mascara lines and smudged eyeliner smeared my cheeks, and I rubbed at them, trying to clean myself up.

"Let me," Scott said, pulling a wash cloth from the bench. This time I didn't pull away.

He dipped it into the water and gently rubbed it over my cheeks. The white material came away streaked with black and orange. He continued to wipe my face, and I closed my eyes, allowing him to remove what liner had remained in place.

I was exposed—and afraid. I wanted to hide in the darkness and never look at myself again.

"Open your eyes. I want to see you," he whispered.

I took a deep breath and slowly peeked out from between my lashes. In the mirror, Alison stared back at me. Naked. Washed clean. My lip quivered.

"You're beautiful," he said. His eyes shone, and his smile was sincere.

And he was looking at Alison. He was looking at the *real* me. I'd never felt so raw and open.

"Please don't run." His voice was laced with worry.

I looked up at his words and saw that I had instinctively slid away from him along the bench seat in the tub.

"I like you better like this," he admitted.

"I don't."

He moved through the water toward me, and the tip of his hard cock poked out of the water. He was turned on, and I wasn't even wearing any makeup. If he was hard, then it was time for me to go to work. Finally! Something to make me feel in control again.

I slid back across the bench, as close to him as I could get. His hand touched my cheek, and he swiped his thumb along my jaw.

"Is Ally short for anything?" he whispered, looking into my eyes.

"No," I lied.

My full name wasn't for clients. It was only for my family. Mister Five was attractive and kind, but he wasn't family.

He wanted to kiss me. His eyes kept darting down to my lips, but he didn't do it.

I slid my hand along Scott's thigh and grasped his cock. He was rock hard. I pumped a few times, and his pupils dilated. I held his stare because it was what he wanted. The connection. I could fake that.

"I want you," he breathed.

Those were the magic words. I was on the clock again. Time to pay my rent.

A box of condoms was sitting on the bathroom counter. He must have planned for us to use one in the shower earlier. I reached across for the box, but I missed and it fell onto its side, spilling foil packets across the counter and onto the floor.

I grabbed one and ripped it open. He grinned. Happy dick. Happy man.

He thrust his hips up out of the water so I could place the rubber over his shaft. I did it with my hand this time instead of my lips. I had to show him some variety.

I realized it didn't matter if I was wearing makeup or not. Ally wasn't created using paint and brushes. She was inside me. I just had to turn her on and switch off my heart.

Mister Five settled back on the bench, and his cock disappeared beneath the water. A blow job would be difficult but not impossible. I'd just have to come up for air.

I leaned down to submerge my face, but he put his hand on my shoulder and shook his head.

"I thought you wanted—"

"I do. But let me do you first."

*Me?* Guys never cared about my pleasure. Sure, they all wanted to think they had given me an orgasm; it made them feel like sex gods. But none of them actually cared enough to give up their own pleasure.

He pulled me into his lap and fiddled with something under the surface. I wondered if he was just going to stick his cock straight in me and get going. But then a rush of water hit my labia, and I cried out.

He smiled. "These jets can be moved."

He moved it again, just slightly, and it shot a stream of bubbly water right onto my clit. The pleasure was intense and unrelenting, unlike any other sensation. Getting fingered or licked was a single motion over and over again with a small break between movements; this was constant pressure. My nails clutched at his arms for balance as he played with my left nipple, and I came quickly.

"Fuck. Oh God. Yes!" Words I'd said a lot but very rarely meant. *Except* with this man. When the orgasm faded and the pressure got too much, I pulled away.

"You're so beautiful when you come," he said. "Your skin flushes, and you smile the prettiest smile I've ever seen."

"My normal smile isn't pretty?" I teased.

"It is. Of course it is. But you always have this hardness about you. Like you're bracing for a fight. When you come, you lose that and just let the feelings overwhelm you. It's breathtaking to watch."

I didn't know what to say. The hardness he was talking about—that was Ally. She kept me safe. Maybe Alison was the only one who could truly let her guard down enough to feel the amazing sensation of orgasm. Interesting.

Instead of speaking, I ran my hand up his leg and grabbed his still-hard cock. He thrust his hips slightly in my hand. I slid through the water and straddled him, pressing my breasts against his chest and bracing my legs on the bench.

"Do you want me?" I whispered in his ear, licking down the outer shell and sucking the lobe into my mouth.

"God yes," he breathed out.

I lowered myself onto him and gasped as he filled me. I was still tender from my orgasm and didn't need much stimulation to get my blood flowing again.

His eyes closed, but then they opened and stared directly into mine. Craving that damned connection again.

I moved up and down slowly, sliding my breasts along his body. My nipples loved the sensation of his warm skin.

"I want to kiss you," he whispered.

His eyes burned into mine, and I really wanted to kiss him, as well. That was exactly why I shouldn't. I shook my head and turned my face to the side. His arms held me close and helped to lift me out of the water with each thrust.

Fucking in water was different than any other kind of sex. The water lapping at your body was like another set of hands stroking your skin.

We moved slowly together, the closest to making love that I'd ever experienced.

Pleasure flowed through me in soft waves, building to what I knew would be a tsunami at the end.

He started to meet my thrusts with his own, and soon we were crashing against each other in a desperate collision of flesh. The water splashed around us and splattered as it spilled over the edges of the tub to the tiled floor. Neither of us cared. All that mattered was the feeling. And it felt fucking amazing!

"You're so tight," he whispered as he nuzzled into my neck.

His stubble grazed my skin, adding to the sensations overwhelming my body.

"Fuck! Your cock is so big," I whispered.

We moved hard against each other, our desperation for one another increasing as the intensity grew.

"I want to fuck you," he groaned.

The smart-ass bitch inside my head wanted to tell him that he was already fucking me, but I knew he meant that he wanted to be in control. I didn't want to break the mood with a stupid comment.

"Then fuck me," I breathed out.

I climbed off him and knelt on the bench facing away from him, my arms braced on the edge of the tub. His hands grasped my hips tightly, and he pushed inside. He wasn't gentle, and we both grunted at the contact.

His fingers dug into my skin as he thrust into me over and over with all the leverage he could get. I knew I would have finger-shaped bruises on my hips tomorrow. I'd had them before.

My breasts swayed with our movement, dragging across the surface of the water. Another sensation to add to the mix.

He leaned over my back, and through the bubbly water I could see that he was adjusting the jet again. Hell yes!

The strong stream of bubbles hit my clit straight on, and I moaned. The sound echoed off the tiled walls.

"You like that?" he asked in a strained voice.

"God yes!"

"Your pussy feels so good."

I groaned and lowered myself over the ledge, pushing my ass up higher to give him better access. His speed increased, and he grunted with each inward movement. He was close. Each time he plunged into me, I let out a breathy "Fuck!"

His cock pounding me and the bubbles assaulting my clit were all too much, and I came again. Hard.

"*Ah, God!*" I screamed.

"Shit…Fuck…Yes!" he swore as my muscles convulsed around him and pushed him over the edge to his own release.

I moved away from the bubbles before I lost all sensation in my clit, and he fell onto my back, breathing hard.

I braced both of our weights on the tiled ledge and moved back into the bubbles again. This time I didn't let them hit my clit directly but rather the inner lips where he was still sheathed. The sensation was wonderful without being overwhelming.

"That's nice." He chuckled.

"Mm hmm."

We both let the bubbles drag the pleasure out a little longer, and then he pulled out and sat down on the bench.

"You're amazing," he said, pulling me into his lap.

"I've had a lot of practice." I smiled at my little joke.

He frowned.

"I'm sorry. I was just trying to be funny," I said.

"But that's the thing. It's not a joke."

"You can't seriously be mad about that."

"Who said I was mad?"

I scoffed. His arms were folded tightly across his chest, and the lines in his forehead were so deep I could practically see his brain. I slid away from him and gave him a curious look.

"You know who I am. *What* I am. I've never hidden that from you. You've *paid* me!"

Suddenly I was angry. And so was he.

"You hide *everything* from me!" he said.

I cupped my breasts and squeezed them tightly. "Does it look like I'm hiding? I'm fucking naked."

Scott rolled his eyes. "You hide *you*. I don't care about your tits or your ability to suck my cock. I care about what's inside."

"And you've been inside me a lot," I spat out.

His face hardened. "Maybe I'm wrong. Maybe you're just *this*. A New York whore who's too broken to let someone care about her."

We stared each other down. Tears prickled my eyes again, but this time they were tears of anger. I wanted to slap him.

"I think you should go. Your money's on the table."

"Keep it."

I stood up and quickly dried myself. I turned away so I wouldn't be tempted to look at him, but I caught his eyes in the mirror and his expression was sad, not furious, as his words and tone suggested.

I wanted to hurt him the way he'd hurt me. I'd never let anyone call me a whore before.

"You know what?" I said once I had my dress back on, "I *will* take the money. This wasn't a date. You booked me, and I fucked you. I deserve my payment."

I strode out of the room without waiting for his response and, as I walked through the suite, I wrapped my half-wet hair up into a tight bun. The envelope was sitting on the table where we'd left it, and I grabbed it quickly before slamming the door behind me and leaving the hotel.

That was the end of Client Number Five.

# CHAPTER EIGHT

I didn't sleep well that night. Monday morning dawned, and I had to get ready to meet Amy, the receptionist from the hotel, for lunch but it felt like my eyelids were made of sandpaper. I made myself a triple-shot coffee and sent Todd a quick text.

Having lunch with a possible new girl for the team.
I'll let you know how it goes. -A

When I walked into the diner, Amy was already waiting for me and gave an excited wave. Her hair wasn't black and red anymore; it had been dyed platinum blond. I barely recognized her.

The diner was styled like it was from the fifties, with checkered tabletops and round booths. The smell of coffee and waffles made my mouth water.

We greeted each other and ordered our food. I wasn't really hungry but got another coffee and a slice of chocolate pie with whipped cream. Comfort food.

"So, did you give some thought to what I said? Do you have questions?" I asked.

"Lots! Like, how much do you get paid? Is it dangerous? Do you ever feel scared? Do you have a pimp?"

I got the impression from her rapid-fire questions that she could have carried on like that all afternoon, so I held up my hand to silence her, smiling.

"One at a time. Let me catch my breath. I charge seven hundred dollars per hour, and half of that money goes in my pocket. The other half goes to my manager, Todd. I guess you could call him a pimp, because he books all my appointments and pays for all the advertising. Just don't call him that to his face!"

"Are you ever scared?"

I took a bite of my pie as I thought about the question.

"I was a little bit at the beginning, but not so much anymore. Most guys are a bit embarrassed about calling a hooker or so horny that they wouldn't dream of risking their potential orgasm by messing with me. Plus, Todd keeps extensive personal details on file so if anything did happen, we could notify the police right away."

"It must be so great to have sex all day long!" Her eyes lit up, and I laughed.

"You'd be surprised. I hardly ever come with clients. My job is to please them, not the other way around."

"But you still enjoy it, right? I mean, you're having sex, so it has to be good."

I shrugged my shoulders. "Some guys are into fetish stuff or just aren't very good in bed. As long as I make them squirt, I've done my job."

"So you've never orgasmed with a client?" Her eyes were huge as she stared at me in shock.

Mister Five flashed into my head. Water splashing. Jets of bubbles cascading over my clit. Him pounding into me from behind. I shivered and shifted in my seat.

"Maybe once or twice, but it's rare."

Amy pouted.

"Are you interested in this work because you like sex?" I asked.

She blushed and took a bite of her sandwich. Then she leaned forward and whispered, "I love sex so much. I lost my virginity last year, and now I can't get enough. It just feels so good."

I tried not to laugh, but she was so cute. Innocence. The guys would lap her up.

"This work isn't just normal sex, though. Sure, you get the guys who like vanilla, but there's a lot of fetish work involved, too. I recently had a client who was into pony play. Then there are threesomes, or girl-on-girl." I had to be honest with her. The last thing I wanted was for her to end up traumatized.

She nodded vigorously. "I've kissed a girl before."

"Have you gone down on one?"

She looked at the table and shook her head.

"It's a part of the job. You'll probably enjoy it. I look forward to the clients that like to have another girl there. It breaks up the monotony a bit."

"I'd like to try it."

It was always difficult to tell if someone was cut out for this business. A love of sex was a good start, but there was a lot of strength and self-esteem needed. I'd known some lovely girls over the years who had either fallen into drugs or who cried every night when they got home. I didn't want either of those things for Amy.

I looked her over again, really trying to picture her in the role. She was eager, that was for certain, and maybe if I took the time to mentor her, to make sure she was okay, then she might make it through.

"If you think you can handle it, then I'll get Todd to give you a call. He'll want to meet with you, and there'll be a test."

"A test?"

"More like an audition. He'll want to have sex with you to make sure he's selling a quality product. Basically, he wants to make sure you're a good fuck."

She swallowed thickly. "All right."

I laughed and patted her hand across the table. "Don't worry, he doesn't bite."

I pulled out my phone and dialed Todd.

"If it isn't the Queen of Muff-town," he answered.

"Shut the fuck up. I'm calling for work."

Amy's eyebrows rose. I supposed that not many people said "fuck" to their boss. Ha! Todd loved it.

"How's Bambi?"

"I think you'd like to meet her. She's keen."

"Awesome! Get her blood screened, and bring her by tonight. We'll test her out."

"Both of us?"

"Sure. I'm getting a lot more girl-on-girl requests. Need to make sure she's up for it."

"I gave you Adam for free because you'd given up a commission for me. I'm charging you for tonight." I had to be strict with Todd. I didn't want him to think I was going to fuck for free whenever he wanted.

"Yeah, yeah. Two hundred for a test run."

"Deal."

We hung up, and I smiled at Amy.

"You're in."

"As easy as that?"

"You have to prove yourself in the test tonight and get a blood screening. But, if Todd likes you and you're bug-free, then you'll be getting paid by the end of the week."

She reached into her bag and pulled out a piece of paper. She unfolded it and slid it across to me.

Blood tests. This girl was prepared. She was also clean. Perfect.

An hour later, Amy and I were browsing a sex shop. She'd wanted me to show her some of the tools I used, and I was happy to do something that would distract me from thinking about Mister Five.

"What about this?" Amy called across the shop, holding up a long string of golf ball sized anal beads.

I wandered through the aisles to her.

"Those are for experts. You need to work your way up to them." I laughed, taking them from her and hanging them back on their hook. "Try these." I handed her a string of marble-sized balls.

"What were you looking at over there?" she asked, winding the string of beads around her hand.

"Dildos. I've been thinking of updating what I have."

"Show me?"

I led her back to the display I'd been checking out, and she looked at them in awe.

"What do you use now?" she asked.

"I have this and this and that one," I said, pointing.

She picked up a double-ended vibrator and weighed it in her hand before placing it back gently.

"What are you looking at getting now?"

"Well, I thought this glow-in-the-dark one might be fun," I said, taking it off the shelf. "And I've had a few guys over the past month who wanted me to finger their ass, so I thought an anal dildo would be a good investment."

"An *anal* dildo?"

"Here," I said, handing one to her. "See how the shaft is narrower? More like a finger?"

She nodded and grabbed one as well.

"Okay, let's get you a starter kit so when Todd interviews you, you can be prepared."

"Yay!" She clapped her hands. Her enthusiasm was adorable.

When we left the store two hours later, I had the two dildos, three pairs of crotch-less panties, and a bulk pack of one hundred condoms—about a month's supply. Amy had three dildos, four pairs of crotch-less panties, the same pack of condoms, the anal beads, three flavors of lubricant, a corset, and three sexy costumes. She would build up more as she worked, but it was a good amount to start with.

"Will you show me how to use some of these things?" she asked as we walked down the street.

"Absolutely. And let me ask you something—what's your personal grooming ritual?"

"I shower twice a day."

I chuckled and placed my hand on her arm. "Are you smooth or rocking it seventies style in the fur department?"

She giggled, and that adorable blush covered her cheeks again.

"I'm not completely bare, but I keep it neat. Is that okay?"

"It's up to you, really. Most guys seem to prefer bare, but you do what you're comfortable with."

"What do you do?"

"Full Brazilian. It's easier to keep clean and maintain. But that's just my preference."

She sighed. "I think I want to go get a wax."

I took her to my beautician who squeezed her in as a favor to me. When she was hair-free, we headed for a coffee shop to refuel. We talked a lot — not about work, just about us. It turned out that Amy was twenty years old, a student at NYU, and she worked at the hotel part-time to help pay her tuition. She was very sweet, and I thought if things worked out with Todd, we could become good friends.

"Don't be nervous. You love sex, so just enjoy it," I told her when we got to Todd's apartment.

I knocked on the door, and Zach answered it. Shit. Todd usually only invited people over for sex in the apartment when he knew Zach was going to be out. Zach knew what Todd did for a living, but he didn't exactly approve.

"Hey, sis." He pulled me into a hug. "Whatcha doing here?"

"Just thought I'd bring my friend Amy over to meet Todd."

"Hey, Ally!" Todd said, shooting me an apologetic look. "Wanna go out and get a drink or something?"

"Sure, sounds good."

"You just got here!" Zach objected.

"Why don't we go see a movie this week? Sibling bonding time."

"Yeah, all right. Can we go see that new super hero movie?"

"Which one?" I asked.

"I don't know. Isn't there always a new movie about a super hero?"

We both laughed and hugged.

"Okay, I'll let you know when I'm free. The movie is on me," I said.

I turned back to Todd and Amy, who were talking quietly. It looked like I wouldn't have to introduce them. Todd was running his fingers up and down her arm.

Finally, the three of us left and stood aimlessly on the street outside the building.

"What happened, Todd?" I asked.

"He was supposed to have a date tonight, but the girl got called in to work so they rescheduled. Shit! What are we going to do?" Todd ran his hands through his hair. He was one of those people who always liked to plan ahead, and having something go wrong at the last minute stressed him out.

"Should we get a hotel room?" I tried to keep my voice even, hoping to calm him down.

"Your place?" he asked.

I agreed that we could use my apartment, but not my bedroom. That was my sex-free zone, which was a bit ironic seeing as the bedroom was the one place that everyone else had sex.

Amy told Todd about herself as we walked around the corner, and I let us into the empty apartment. Jamie had four clients that evening and wouldn't be home until well after midnight.

"How do you want to do this? A threesome?" I asked.

Todd considered it for a moment and then shook his head. "Why don't you test her out first and then I'll join in."

Amy looked at me nervously, and I gave her an encouraging smile.

"Come here, honey," I said, holding my arms open.

Sex with girls was completely different than sex with guys. First off, I had no problem kissing girls because I would never date one in my personal life, so it wasn't a breach of my boundary. Their lips were always soft, and they never tried to push their tongues down your throat.

Second, it was always more sensual. Girls had soft skin and curves. Boys were all sharp edges and hard muscles.

Todd settled himself on the recliner but didn't pull the footrest out. Instead he sat forward, watching us intently. It was his lucky night.

Amy sat next to me on the couch. I leaned in to kiss her cheek.

"Pretend that you're in love with me and can't get enough of touching and kissing every part of my body," I whispered in her ear.

She gave a small nod and turned her head, catching my lips with her own.

Her mouth was soft at first. Just small pecks to test the water. She tasted like cinnamon, and I wondered if she'd popped a breath mint when I wasn't looking.

I ran my hand around her waist and pulled her flush against my body. She mirrored me, and soon we were pressed against each other. She opened her mouth and deepened the kiss.

"Undress me," I mumbled into her mouth.

Her hands glided up my stomach, taking the bottom of my shirt with it, and we stopped kissing only long enough to pull it over my head before crashing back together. Her shirt was a button-up, so we didn't have to break apart. It fell easily from her shoulders.

She wasn't wearing a bra, and I'd been right about her having a nice rack. Her breasts were small but firm. Her nipples stood out straight, begging to be sucked. I wanted to lick them, but this test wasn't about pleasing her—she had to please me.

Still, I couldn't resist sliding my fingers lightly across her ribcage and palming a breast. She had a perfect handful. Guys would have trouble titty-fucking her, but hopefully her cock sucking skills would make up for that.

Amy moaned softly into my mouth and reached around to remove my bra. It dropped from my arms and she broke the kiss to take me in.

"Touch me how you like to me touched," I told her.

She gave me a devilish grin and pushed me hard so that I fell back on the sofa. She crawled up my body and then licked her way down my throat.

I glanced to the side, and I wasn't surprised to see Todd stroking his cock. I couldn't really blame the guy. He had two hot-as-fuck chicks going at it just a foot away from him. What guy *wouldn't* be palming himself?

She sealed her lips over my nipple and flicked it with her tongue. I moaned. She was doing so well.

Her left hand had snaked its way down my body, through the fly of my jeans, and was in my panties rubbing circles on my clit. But I wanted more.

"Are you ready to try eating me out?" I asked.

She released my nipple and looked up at me with hooded eyes. "I can't wait."

Evidently she was enjoying herself. A good start.

My jeans and panties were quickly disposed of and she spread my legs wide.

"Your pussy is so pretty." She giggled.

"I remember it tastes amazing too," Todd added, still stroking his cock.

She smiled at him and leaned down. Her tongue was tentative, softly lapping at my clit. I could barely feel it.

"Are you all right?" I asked.

She looked up at me with a slight frown. "I don't know what to do!"

"Yes you do. Think about what you enjoy. What do guys do that drives you wild? Do that."

She dove back in and sucked the nub into her mouth.

"Fuck," I cried out.

She giggled.

"Just like that," I said as she sucked and licked.

Todd was practically panting. He had stopped stroking his dick, obviously not wanting to use up all his stamina before he got to fuck her. It must have been torture for him though. His cock was oozing pre-cum like a leaky tap.

"You like what you see?" I teased.

"You have no fucking idea!" He looked like he was physically holding himself in the chair so he didn't stand up and join us.

"Tell me how good it feels," Amy said, looking up at me. She shoved her tongue inside me and swirled it around.

"Fuck. It's so good, Amy. I'm going to come on your tongue."

I grabbed my breasts and squeezed, flicking the nipples. I'd been eaten out last week by Adam and he'd been good, but he didn't compare to Amy. She knew right where I needed to be touched and how much pressure to apply. She knew when to suck and when to lick.

I rolled my head to the side and glanced at Todd. I licked my lips and his hand shot to his cock, giving it a few brisk pumps before letting out a soft grunt.

"I want to make you come!" Amy mewled.

"I want to come! Make me come!"

Her mouth found my clit again and she sucked lovingly, as if it were the sweetest treat. Two, and then three, fingers pushed inside me and I thrust my hips up to meet them. She pumped them into me over and over.

I was about to combust and burst into flames. Finally, I couldn't handle the amazing sensation anymore and I let myself go.

"Oh, God! Yes! I'm coming!"

Amy didn't stop. Wave after burning wave of bliss crashed over me and just when I thought the orgasm was dying down…it didn't.

Amy crooked her middle finger up inside me and rubbed my G-spot. A second orgasm hit me like an earthquake.

My legs spasmed and my back arched off the cushion.

"Fuck! Fuck!" I cried. "Oh, shit!"

My breathing was ragged when she finally removed her fingers and gave my clit one last lick. My heart pounded in my throat.

She lay on top of me and kissed my breasts, nuzzling them and running the tips of her fingers lightly over my erect nipples. I grazed my hands lazily through her hair.

"My turn!" Todd said. I guessed that he'd almost come undone watching us and was desperate for his own release.

"All right, I'll give you guys some privacy," I said. I stood to go to my bedroom.

"Or," Amy said softly. "You could stay?"

I looked at Todd to see his reaction, and he nodded.

"All right," I said.

I sat, still completely naked, on the chair Todd had just vacated.

His erect cock was already sheathed in a condom. He wasn't wasting any time.

Amy knelt on the arm of the couch, hands splayed in front of her. Todd approached her from behind and they both cried out when he pushed in.

"Holy shit! You're so wet!" he exclaimed.

"Ally got me really excited," she panted as he slid out and rammed back into her.

She was rocking back and forth, increasing their momentum.

"God, I love your hard cock so much!" she cried.

My body reacted to the display in front of me. I had always been a bit of a voyeur but very rarely got the opportunity to watch others having sex. I was always participating or the one being watched.

"I wanna ride the fuck out of you," she barked.

I knew from previous experience that Todd loved dirty talk, so he must have been in heaven with Amy. The shy, petite girl turned into an animal as soon as she was stuffed with cock. What a transformation!

Todd got down on the floor right in front of me and gave me a cheesy grin. Amy swaggered over, sat down on his cock, and started bucking her hips. She wasn't going to take this slow. They were both breathing heavily, and with them so much closer, I could hear every exhalation. It was fucking hot.

Amy pressed her hands into his chest and lifted her body up and down, penetrating herself on him. She was beautiful to watch in action.

I let out an involuntary gasp when she straightened her body, lifted her arms above her head and started rocking her hips back and forth. The new position showed off her breasts and tight body to perfection.

I'd never been attracted to women. I fucked them for money if a client wanted it, but it was always for the client. I had never looked at a woman in my daily life and craved her touch. Despite that fact, I couldn't deny that Amy was exquisite.

As I watched her move, my hand found its way between my legs and rubbed gently. I didn't need much stimulation, as I'd barely recovered from the two orgasms I'd just enjoyed.

Todd smiled at me and winked when he saw me touching myself, then his eyes went straight back to Amy. I couldn't blame him. I couldn't tear my eyes away from her either.

She was breathing out a steady stream of, "Yes! Yes! Yes!" with each movement.

Todd's eyes were scrunched up, and his jaw was clenched. He was going to shoot any second.

"Let me fuck your mouth!" he begged.

She jumped off him and kneeled as he stood above her. My fingers pushed inside my pussy, and I pumped furiously.

I closed my eyes for a second to allow a particularly strong wave of bliss to wash over me. When I opened them again, Amy's nose was buried against Todd's groin.

"Fuck!" he moaned as she sucked him in.

He pumped his hips back and forth, and she took it all without gagging. She was born to be a pro.

Todd roared his release and then fell backward onto the couch. Amy crawled up beside him and stroked his cock softly, milking the last of the cum from him.

She had an expectant look on her face, and I knew that she hadn't come yet.

"Do you feel frustrated?" I asked.

"I need to come so bad!" she begged.

"Get used to that feeling because with most of your clients, you won't be satisfied."

She pouted.

"But you did a great job tonight. Don't you think she deserves to be finished off, Todd?"

She turned her head hopefully, and he cracked a grin.

"Let me taste you," he said.

She eagerly lay back and spread her legs.

I'd stopped rubbing as I watched Todd climax, but my fingers quickly went back to work.

Todd buried his face between Amy's legs, and she started gasping. I couldn't see exactly what he was doing, but I knew he had good oral skills. I'd experienced them a few times myself.

Her eyes locked with mine, and they'd occasionally flick down to where my fingers disappeared inside my body.

Todd popped his head up. "God, you're so wet."

She lifted her hips to his face, and he dove back in. The only sounds in the room were the whimpers and moans of pleasure that Amy and I were creating. She was tugging on her nipples and bucking against Todd's face.

I went over the edge first, falling gracefully into release. It was bliss. Not the earth-shattering orgasm I'd had from Amy's touch, but beautiful waves of pleasure coursed through my whole body.

"Ugh! Fuck me!" Amy cried.

I was still shocked at what a tiny little firecracker she was. A pocket rocket.

Todd started pumping his fingers in and out, completely lost in her. I knew already that she had the job.

She bucked off the sofa and cried out one last time before gasping against the cushion.

All three of us sat in silence for a moment, catching our breath.

"That was amazing!" Todd declared. "You're hired!"

Amy curled into the back of the sofa and started giggling with her hands over her face. I walked over and sat beside her, placing a hand on her shoulder. "Are you okay?"

She rolled over, laid her head in my lap, and pressed a kiss to the underside of my bare breast.

"This is going to be the best job ever!" she said.

# CHAPTER NINE

"What would you like to watch?" I asked Zach as we stood outside the theater, staring at the "Now Showing" posters.

"I can't believe there are no super hero movies!"

"Well, I think this one has a guy who can see through walls. Is that a super hero thing?"

"If it was, then the movie would be called *X-Ray Man* and he'd be wearing a cape. That looks like a suspense thriller," Zach said. His expression reminding me of the little boy he used to be.

I rolled my eyes. "Look, we don't even have to see a movie!" I was losing my patience. We'd been standing there for a while. "We can watch *X-Ray Man* or we can go get something to eat."

He grinned, and I knew that he loved getting under my skin. Stupid big brother!

"You know, it's actually called *Lying in Wait*." He pointed toward the poster.

"Oh, shut up!" I tried to sound mad, but I was laughing. "Buy me some Sour Patch Kids."

I went to the box office to buy our tickets, and Zach went to the concessions stand to get our food. Twenty minutes later, we were seated and chewing happily on popcorn as the trailers ran.

About twenty minutes into the movie, I lost track of the plot. The main actor had eyes that were so similar to Scott's that a few times I had to look away from the screen. It really annoyed me that I couldn't escape that man.

When the credits started to roll and the lights came back on, Zach turned to me with a smile. "That may have been the worst movie I've ever seen in my life."

"Oh, come on, it wasn't that bad," I countered.

"Were we watching the same movie?" Zach raised his eyebrows in mock-horror. "The plot was full of holes, the dialogue was corny, and the ending didn't make any sense."

"Only because you weren't paying attention at the beginning."

"I was!"

"Oh really? How many dogs was the lady walking in the first scene?"

"What dogs?"

"My point exactly."

"I remember the lady. She was wearing short-shorts, right?"

"Yes, and she was walking four dogs. They kept getting tangled around her legs." I shook my head when the blank look on his face didn't change.

He shrugged his shoulders. "It wasn't a total waste, though. At least I got to have popcorn."

"You know you can cook it home, right?" I teased.

"It's just not the same out of a microwave."

"What are you up to for the rest of the day?" I asked.

"Shopping. Todd wants to buy one of those new 3D TVs. What about you? Big Saturday night plans?"

"I'm just going to head to the gym before work tonight."

"Who opens mail on a Saturday night?" Zach asked.

"The paper gets a lot of mail. It's never ending."

I'd managed to keep up the façade that I did the night shift in the mail room at *The New York Times*. It was semi-related to the career I'd wanted in my youth, but entry level, so I didn't have to have much knowledge on the running of the paper if anyone asked questions.

Lying to my brother was hard. Every time I did it a lump would settle in my stomach, but I knew he would flip out over the truth. I'd long ago come to the conclusion that the lie was for his own benefit.

Zach and I hugged goodbye. As I walked away from him to the subway, I wondered how much longer I'd be living a double life. The thought that it might be forever unsettled me, and I rushed to the gym, eager to work off the stress.

The party was in full swing. Music blared from the speakers, causing the ground to vibrate slightly under my feet. Todd thought it would be a nice idea to throw a party to welcome Adam and Amy to the family. He'd chosen a tropical theme, which I thought was just an excuse for him to see his girls in skimpy bikinis or coconut bras. But I wasn't complaining. I loved piña coladas and looked great in a bikini.

Kimberly, Nicole, and I were sitting at the dining table, watching the others dance.

"This is fun! We should all catch up more often," Nicole shouted over the music.

I nodded. "What have you been up to lately?" I asked them both.

"Mostly just work. I'm so busy right now. How about you?" Kimberly asked.

"Same. Todd's pressing me to take more guys on, but I don't have the time. Speaking of which, I have two wanna-be regulars up for grabs if you each want one?"

"Who are they?" Nicole twirled a piece of her auburn hair tightly around her finger and then let it spring free.

"I have a young guy, Pony Boy, who I thought might be perfect for you. He's sweet and shy, but a bit clingy. He likes to be ridden like a horse."

"I can do that!" Nicole said. "Ride 'em, cowboy!"

"What about the other one?" Kimberly leaned forward to hear me better over the music.

I thought instantly of Toothpick Guy.

"I have an older man who comes into town once a month for business. He'll probably turn into a regular. He's all yours."

The other girls didn't have the same boundaries that I did about regular clients. That was just my thing.

"What are his kinks?"

"He's pretty vanilla," I told her. "Nothing out of the ordinary. As long as you make him spray, he's happy."

She frowned but accepted him anyway; Kimberly loved the kinky ones best.

A phone was ringing somewhere, but no one moved to claim it. I could see the screen flashing on the coffee table and recognized it as Todd's phone.

"Todd!" I yelled.

He either was so absorbed in dancing with Amy that he was ignoring me, or he hadn't heard me over the music.

"*Todd!*"

He turned his head curiously, as if he had only just heard his name, but wasn't sure if he was imagining it.

I waved to get his attention and pointed to his phone. He nodded and leaned down to say something in Amy's ear before picking it up.

Zach was sitting on the couch, looking very uncomfortable next to Adam and Jamie who were making out like teenagers. My poor brother.

Todd yelled at Adam and Jamie to get a room as he passed them and headed for the kitchen to talk in private. When he went by me, I heard only a bit of what he was saying.

"Sorry, but I don't give my girls' phone numbers out to anyone. Not even family. It's company policy."

My ears pricked up. *Family?*

Was that Mister Five on the phone?

I excused myself from Kimberly and Nicole and followed him into the kitchen.

He had just hung up the call when I walked in.

"Just the girl I was looking for," he said, smiling.

"Who was that?" I demanded.

Todd opened and closed his mouth nervously. "Scott said you guys had a misunderstanding."

"A misunderstanding? How can you *accidently* call someone a whore?" I spat out.

Todd's brow creased. "That doesn't sound like something Scott would say."

"Your cousin can go fuck himself!" I said, crossing my arms over my chest.

"Okay, cherry pie, calm down. He said he wants to apologize. He's booked you for Sunday night. Why don't you just hear what he has to say?"

"Go. Fuck. Himself."

Todd sighed and punched some buttons on his phone. My cell, which was in my pocket, vibrated.

"There. I've just texted you his number. You tell him that you're not coming. I'm *not* getting involved."

He stormed out of the room and back to the party. It was very rare that Todd showed any kind of annoyance or anger, so the fact that he was upset now surprised me. He must have been offended that I didn't want to talk to his cousin.

I stared at the numbers on my screen that would instantly connect me to Mister Five. My thumb hovered over the call button for several seconds and then I locked the screen, put it back in my pocket, and rejoined the others.

Kimberly and Nicole were now dancing together, and Jamie and Adam had disappeared, probably to one of the bedrooms for some privacy. I sat down on the couch next to Zach.

"Why are you sitting over here all by yourself?" I asked.

He smiled. "Just trying to work out which of these girls work for Todd and which are just friends."

I held back my laughter. I wondered what he would think if he found out that *everyone* at the party worked for Todd.

"Don't strain your brain over it. Do what I do and try to ignore what Todd does."

"Speaking of Todd, don't you have a problem with *that?*" he asked, pointing to Todd and Amy dancing together.

"No, why would I?"

"Um, because your boyfriend has his hands all over that girl."

"Oh! Right. It's okay. I mean, I trust him."

"Well, just don't come crying to me when he breaks your heart. He might be my best friend, but I'll bash his scull in." He took a swig from his beer bottle. "Does Kimberly have a boyfriend?" he asked, turning his view away from Todd.

"It's complicated. I don't think she's your type." It seemed like the easiest answer. He watched her sway to the music and drank more of his beer.

"She looks like my type."

"I thought you were dating someone," I said, trying to get his attention off Kimberly. I grabbed his beer and took a sip.

He sighed. "That didn't work out. Sparkle had a bad temper and I just wasn't feeling it."

I spat beer all down my shirt. "Sparkle?" I sputtered.

"Hey, it's a ridiculous name, but she didn't choose it," he said defensively.

"I'm sorry. It just sounds like the name of one of those tiny yappy dogs."

I ruffled his hair playfully. He shrugged, grabbing his beer back from me, and emptied the bottle. He stood and disappeared into the kitchen, presumably to get another one from the fridge. Instead of rejoining me on the couch, he walked up to Kimberly and started to dance with her. I just hoped that didn't end badly, or wind up exposing my secret career.

Todd and Amy were slow dancing in the corner, despite the pumping beat of the dance music. They were lost in their own world, swaying together.

I tried to enjoy the party, but all I could think about was the call I had to make to Mister Five. Deciding that the sooner I did it, the sooner it would be over, I stood up and walked down the hall.

Groaning was coming from Todd's bedroom, so I bypassed that and went into my brother's. A photo of our parents hung on the wall. I wondered how he could bring a girl here with them staring at him through the whole thing. It was kind of creepy.

I sat on the bed and stared at the digits on the screen again. I told myself to just get it over with and searched through the menu to find the function that would allow me to block my number. The last thing I wanted was for him to be able to call me whenever he felt like it. I hit the call button and waited. It only rang a few times before the voice that shouldn't be so familiar answered.

"Scott Walker."

That voice had whispered delicious, naughty words in my ear, but it had also called me a whore. Conflicting emotions washed over me.

"Hello?" he asked.

"Hi," I said softly.

He was silent for a moment. "Ally?" he asked, hopefully.

I regained my backbone and let the anger I still felt sit in my voice. "I'm just calling to cancel your booking for Sunday night."

"Why?"

"Todd said you wanted to talk to me, but there's nothing to say."

"There's a lot to say!"

"Please enlighten me."

"I owe you an apology."

I waited.

"It's not something I want to say over the phone though. Will you please meet me on Sunday night?"

I wanted to reiterate the "go fuck yourself" comment I'd made to Todd, but I couldn't bring myself to say it to him.

"Please," he added.

I let out a frustrated sigh. "Okay, but I'm not meeting at your hotel."

"Thank you, Ally. Can I call you tomorrow with the details of when and where?"

"You can tell Todd. He'll send me the job details." I tried to keep my voice neutral.

"All right." He sounded disappointed, but I'd already broken enough of my rules for this man. I was breaking the no repeat clients rule — again! — just by agreeing to see him. I wasn't giving out my personal number. No way!

"Ally," he said softly, just as I was about to hung up.

"Yes?"

"I don't think you're a whore."

The word hung in the air, and I didn't know how to respond. I ended the call without saying another word.

I joined the others in the living room, but the music was giving me a headache and the conversations were dull. The party had completely lost its spark for me.

"I'm going home," I said to Zach, who had returned to his spot on the couch.

"You okay?" he called over the music.

I gave him a thumbs-up and the best smile I could and then waved goodbye. The temperature outside had dropped, so I hugged my arms around my flimsy tropical outfit as I walked around the corner.

A guy with windswept black hair and a khaki jacket crossed the road and walked ahead of me. I froze and stared at the back of his head. From behind he was a dead ringer for my ex-boyfriend, Nick. The last boyfriend I'd had.

I silently prayed that he didn't turn around. I didn't think I would have been able to cope with seeing his face if it was him. I slowed my pace to allow him to move ahead, and soon he was out of sight.

The damage was done though. All the thoughts of negativity and feelings of inadequacy that he'd brought out in me came surging back. I ran the rest of the way home, holding back my tears, and collapsed on the couch.

*Fucking Nick!*

It had been months since I'd last thought about him, the longest span of time in a while. I'd hoped that I was finally moving past that relationship.

I wished Jamie would hurry up and get home from the party. She was always able to snap me back to myself and distract me.

But Jamie might not be home for hours. I was on my own. I tried not to listen to the voice in my head that told me the reason I was alone was because I was unlovable. But it was impossible to ignore, and it wasn't saying anything that I didn't already know.

# CHAPTER TEN

knocked on the door and waited. Very rarely did I go to a client's home, but this was a special occasion. Robert was the closest thing I had to a regular client, but I didn't really think of him like that. He only booked me once a year and always on the same date. This would be our third meeting, and he never wanted sex.

The door opened and Robert smiled at me. He was in his mid-forties, had soulful brown eyes, and brown hair streaked with silver. He was one of those men that got better looking as he aged.

"It's good to see you again, Ally," he said, holding the door open for me.

"You're looking well."

He gave me a sad smile. It was his wedding anniversary, and he hated to spend it alone. His wife, Carol, had died of cancer six years before, and he was still madly in love with her. The first time he booked me, I'd arrived expecting sex. Instead, we'd spent the night sitting by a roaring fire with him crying as I held him. Last year, he'd had me read aloud entries from her journal about when they'd first met.

The journal entries spoke volumes about how much she'd loved him. It would have been magical to see them together. Robert had both restored my belief in true love and frightened me away from it. I couldn't bear to love someone as much as he loved his Carol and then lose them. It would be like living in hell.

"Would you like a drink?" he asked.

"Champagne?"

"Of course."

We walked into the living room and he poured us both a glass. It was nice, but it didn't go down as smoothly as the champagne Mister Five had served.

"How are you?" I asked.

"Same old. Working hard and trying to keep busy."

"Have you made any new friends?"

We both knew I was asking if he'd met any women, but it seemed a bit harsh to ask it straight out.

"Oh no. Carol is the only one for me. The only one there will ever be."

It made me so sad to think that this handsome, sweet man planned to spend the next forty-plus years of his life alone. It was tragic and romantic. I struggled not to cry.

"I thought we could do something a bit different tonight," he said.

"Whatever you'd like." I gave him what I hoped was a comforting smile.

"It's been so long since I've known the touch of a woman…I don't want intercourse, but it would be so nice just to hold someone."

"I happen to be fantastic at holding people."

"Naked," he added shyly.

I nodded and held out my hand to him. I knew him well enough to realize this was going to be difficult for him. Maybe impossible. But I wanted to try to make it a good experience.

I led him up the stairs to the spare room. I didn't think he'd want a naked woman in his bed. Carol's bed. I closed the door behind us and sat him down. The room was dusty, and it was obvious that it hadn't been used in a long time. There was a crocheted blanket covering the bed and I wondered if Carol had made it. Robert kept looking down at the carpet and wringing his hands. His body needed the sensation, but his heart was resisting.

I undressed slowly, and his eyes followed every movement I made. When I was naked, I walked to his side and took his hands. I ran them down my body, over my breasts, and rested them on my hips.

"Your skin is soft," he whispered.

"Is this what you want?" I asked.

He nodded and started to remove his own clothes. A moment later he was naked and looking at me nervously.

"Let's lay down," I suggested.

I lay flat on my back with my hands by my sides, allowing him to get comfortable. Robert mirrored my position, hesitant to touch me.

"Come here," I said softly, pulling him to cradle against my chest.

His cheek was warm against my breasts; his breath cascaded over my nipple. I swept my fingers through his hair, and he ran his in small patterns on my belly.

"Is this what you were hoping for?" I asked, making sure that he was satisfied.

"Yes." He let out a content sigh and hugged me tightly.

His eyes were closed, and he was murmuring quietly to himself. I heard him say his wife's name. It was a private moment, so I didn't interrupt.

His hand moved up my stomach, and he cupped my breast lightly. My instincts took over at his hint that he wanted a more sexual experience.

He'd clearly said he didn't want sex, but that didn't mean that he didn't want pleasure. I knew he would be too shy to ask directly, so I decided to test the waters and allow his response to guide me.

My hand stroked down his body and rested on his hip. He didn't protest.

I ran the tips of my fingers around in circles, sometimes dipping down close to his pubic hair but then returning to his hip. Again, he allowed the movement with no response. Well, there was a response, but not a verbal one. His cock was growing hard against my thigh.

"Is this all right?" I whispered as I moved my hand down and tentatively ran my fingers up the length of his shaft.

"Yes." The word was barely audible, but now that I knew what he wanted, I wouldn't push him to talk.

I stroked him slowly. There was no rush, and it wasn't about just making him come. He needed to feel close to someone, and I could give that to him.

"Close your eyes," I said.

I thought he might like to imagine that it was Carol touching him, and that would be a lot easier if he wasn't looking at me. My hand kept a slow but steady rhythm as his wandered over my body. He pressed kisses into my chest and neck while his hand kneaded my breast gently. It was a very different experience than I was used to giving, but I was always there to give what the client wanted.

His breathing sped up, so I moved my hand a little faster. It was still slow by my usual standards but enough to give him a little more friction. This beautiful man hadn't been touched by a woman in over half a decade. He deserved some pleasure.

Soon, his hips were moving in time with my hand and he was clutching me, gasping in my ear.

He came with a groan, and I felt a warm puddle pool on my leg.

"Thank you," he gasped and held me tightly.

He began to pepper light kisses along my jaw, and I did something that I'd never done with a client before. I turned my face down and caught his lips with my own. He kissed me back hungrily, capturing my face in his hands. It wasn't a tongue bath like I might have gotten from some of my other clients; it was a thank you kiss. An intimate moment of gratitude and sorrow.

When we pulled apart, he had tears staining his cheeks. I held him awhile longer as he cried, and my heart broke. I'd once heard that the worst day of loving someone was the day you lost them. But what about all the days after that? It seemed easier not to risk it. Love always ended in pain. Break-up or death were the only options.

When he walked me to the door, he gave me a tight hug.

"Thank you, Ally. You always know exactly what I need."

I smiled, but I didn't feel happy. His situation broke something inside me. It was too close to my own pain.

"Maybe next year, if you're happy to come back, I'll be ready for more."

"Whatever you want," I said.

I meant it. I felt like Robert was someone I would be willing to allow my defenses down for. He understood the hurt of love. We could share a slow, sorrowful fuck. Maybe next time.

We wished each other a good night, and I caught the subway home.

Once in bed, I couldn't get to sleep. For some reason, thinking about Robert and his love for a woman that he would never see again made me think of Scott. I would be seeing him tomorrow. Strangely, the sorrow in my chest lifted. Just a little bit, but it definitely lifted.

# CHAPTER ELEVEN

I tossed and turned for a bit, but sleep didn't find me. Thoughts of Robert and Mister Five were racing around in my head, tearing at my heart and making me think about canceling the booking for the following night. It was almost midnight when I got up with a heavy sigh.

I was in the kitchen making some warm milk when Jamie walked out of her bedroom, fully dressed for a night out.

"Did you get a client?" I asked.

"No, I'm meeting Todd and Adam. You should come."

"I'm not in the mood."

I took a sip of milk and sighed. Jamie's arms slipped around my waist as she hugged me.

"What's wrong, Ally Cat?" she asked.

"I just saw Robert."

It was all the explanation she needed. I'd been just as depressed after seeing him last year. I had a soft spot for that guy.

"Love hurts. We all know it. You especially know it!"

"I don't know why seeing Robert always makes me think about Nick."

"It's simple," Jamie said, taking the mug of warm milk and placing it down on the counter. "You thought you had forever with Nick, and he hurt you. You see Robert, needing his forever with someone he can't have, and it makes you feel rejected. You wish Nick was like Robert."

I shrugged my shoulders. I could see what she was trying to say but it wasn't exactly right. I didn't necessarily want Nick to be my Robert; I just wanted *someone* to love me like that. I hated admitting that to myself. I was so weak.

*Maybe I should have had booze instead of milk.*

"Come on!" Jamie grabbed my hand and pulled me out of the kitchen. "Amy will be there, and I know she'd love to see you. Plus, Adam's been dying to fuck you again."

"Is this a sex party? Todd and Amy, you and Adam, and then just me on my own? No way!"

"It'll be a *ménage á cinq!*" She giggled.

I rolled my eyes. "I'm not a fifth wheel."

"You'll be the main attraction. Come on, I know how you like to deal with emotional pain. Get your nasty on!"

I gave in. Jamie was right. She always was when it came to my moods. I needed a good hard fucking.

"Fine. But I'll need to be a lot more drunk."

"How drunk are you now?"

"Not at all."

"You square!" She giggled again and handed me a flask from her pocket. I took two long swigs before giving it back to her. The liquid was warm as it slid down my throat, and it helped calm me right away.

"Do I have time for a shower?" I asked.

"A quick one. They can start without us, and we'll join in when we get there."

I raced to the bathroom and stripped out of my pajamas. The hot water soothed my muscles and washed away the sadness. I promised myself that I wasn't going to think of Robert for the rest of the night. Tonight, I would concentrate on being strong again.

I pulled on some old jeans and a sweater, not bothering with underwear, and met Jamie in the living room. She was topping up the flask from one of the bottles in the liquor cabinet. We both took another shot and headed out the door.

We caught a taxi to Adam's apartment, and Jamie led me up several sets of stairs. Before we entered, she grabbed my shoulders and looked me straight in the eye.

"You are *Ally*. You are a wild sex goddess who doesn't want or need love. All you care about is that men bow down to your puss. You got me?"

I laughed. "Got it."

"Okay then, let's have some fun!" She grinned and squeezed my ass. "I can't wait to have my turn with you."

She opened the door without knocking and pulled me inside. She was right; they had started without us. Amy was kneeling on the couch with Todd ramming her from behind and Adam sheathed in her mouth.

I'd never been to Adam's apartment, and I automatically checked out the room. Everything was in neutral shades of gray and brown. There were two couches on opposite walls and a set of weights in the corner that I assumed had helped to sculpt Adam's firm body.

"Hello, lovely ladies!" Adam said with a grin as Jamie walked over.

"Ally! What a lovely surprise. Will you be fucking me tonight?" Todd asked, still plowing into Amy.

"Ha! You wish." I laughed, but who knew where the night was headed.

Jamie passed me the flask again, and I practically drained it before handing it back to her. My limbs were starting to feel heavy, and the edges of my vision were just starting to blur. Perfect!

Amy's eyes tracked me as she sucked Adam's cock.

"Hey, Amy," I said, smiling.

On the coffee table was a large glass bowl filled to the brim with shiny condom wrappers. There were already a few ripped packets on the floor, and I wondered how long they had been going before we'd arrived.

"Ally and I are just going to enjoy the show, and we'll join in once you've finished," Jamie said, pulling me to the other sofa and sitting me in her lap.

Her arms were around me, and I realized that it was exactly what I needed. A hard fuck would be good, but first I just wanted to be held by someone who cared about me, and I was pretty sure that no one loved me more than my best friend.

I swiveled so I faced her and pulled her close, ignoring the three-some on the other couch. I wanted a soft, tender kiss. I'd let Adam fuck my brains out later, but right now I wanted Jamie. I'd never initiated anything with a girl that wasn't for a job, but it felt right.

She saw the desire in my eyes.

"Or maybe we *won't* watch," she whispered, her warm breath flowing over my throat as she leaned in.

We kissed softly, our lips moving together. She tasted like whis-key. I slid my body closer, trusting her with my touch. Our breasts mashed together as we embraced. Her hands ran down my sides and pulled the sweater up over my head, leaving me topless. A chill ran down my back from the cool air, and my hardening nipples didn't go unnoticed.

Her kisses moved down my throat and over my chest, burning my skin as she went.

In the background, I could hear the labored breathing of Adam and Todd as they both worked on Amy. She was making muffled moaning sounds that were stifled by Adam's dick. Those sounds and Jamie's touch had me wet.

"Aren't you a naughty girl," Jamie teased quietly. "All ready for me."

She lapped at my nipple, and an electric shock ran straight to my clit.

"Take off your dress," I said. "I want to touch you."

We both stood up and as she removed her tight mini dress, I pulled my jeans off. Jamie hadn't worn underwear either. We settled back onto the couch, and I straddled Jamie's lap again. Her mouth started on my neck, moving down as her fingers moved up my stom-ach. My pulse beat between my legs, and I squirmed in Jamie's lap, desperate for friction.

One of the boys groaned loudly and then Amy's moans were no longer muffled. Adam must have come and pulled out of her mouth.

Todd was grunting, "Fuck. Fuck. Fuck."

Large warm hands stroked over my shoulders and past Jamie's mouth on my nipple. Adam's lips caressed the back of my neck and down between my shoulder blades as he knelt behind me. His fingers kept moving lower. In my mind, I begged him to keep going, just a little farther, to where I needed stimulation. He didn't disappoint.

His fingers found my clit and I cried out, not caring if Todd or Amy heard. I hoped they did.

"Yes." I breathed out loudly and grabbed Jamie's head. I pulled her face up to mine and hungrily captured her lips. She moaned into my mouth and sucked lightly on the tip of my tongue as Adam's fingers worked their magic.

The sensations were fantastic—Jamie's mouth and Adam's hands—but it was an uncomfortable position and my back was starting to ache.

"Let's move to the floor," I suggested.

Adam removed his hand from between my legs and lifted me up into his arms.

"Ally's had a bad night and needs to be cheered up. Are you up to it?" Jamie asked.

"Ugh! Fuck me harder with your big cock!" Amy grunted from the couch. I still didn't expect such a tiny girl to be so uninhibited.

As Adam carried me across the room, I felt secure in his huge arms. He didn't seem to have any trouble lifting me, like I was weightless. He laid me down on the coffee table, shoving the bowl of condoms to the side. It fell to the floor, and the gray carpet was suddenly covered in a rainbow of squares.

"Pass me one, Jamie?" he asked, holding out his hand.

He'd positioned me on my back with my legs hanging over the edge, my feet planted on the floor. Amy reached out a hand to me, and we were close enough that we could just grasp each other's fingers. There was something intimate about it.

"You having fun, Amy?" I asked with a grin, already knowing the answer because her eyes were rolling back in her head.

"Oh God, Todd fucks so good!" she groaned.

"Wait till you get me in you." Adam chuckled.

Amy's eyes flashed, and I knew that after he was done with me, Adam would have another customer.

As we'd talked, Adam had sheathed himself, and without warning, he pushed into me.

"Unf!" My unintentional grunt at his size had Adam smirking down at me as he started to move.

I bit my lip and closed my eyes, enjoying the feeling as he filled me completely.

Amy's fingers were still grasped tightly in mine, and her hand was moving back and forth as Todd thrust, tugging on my arm.

"I wonder if this is the best orgy there has ever been," Jamie posed as she walked over to the couch and sat next to Amy. "I mean, we're all *trained* in how to give the most pleasure."

Adam laughed and sped up his thrusting. "I'll show you pleasure."

I glanced up at Todd and saw that his eyes were closed tightly; his whole face was scrunched up. "Watch out, Amy, he's going to blow," I warned with a giggle.

She didn't acknowledge me, and I looked down to see that Jamie was now leaning against the arm of the couch with her legs spread open and Amy's face was buried in her.

"Oh shit." Todd came and fell onto Amy's back, pushing her farther into Jamie's crotch.

Adam was holding a steady rhythm inside me, no variation in speed or pressure. It felt good, of course, but nothing earth-shattering. He was relying on his size and letting his technique be lax. The professional inside me didn't like that. So much for the amazing pleasure he'd just bragged about. I was about to get up and push him onto the floor so I could ride him when his movements changed. His speed increased, and his hands stroked over my belly. His thumb teased my clit as he continued to thrust, and then he pressed down hard with his thumb and twisted his hand.

Just as they had when I'd first fucked Adam at his audition, stars exploded behind my eyes and I cried out, gasping for breath, desperate for the oxygen that I couldn't get enough of. Both times we'd fucked, he had lulled me into thinking his technique was lacking and then blown me away by the intensity of the orgasm. It must have been *his move.*

"Keep the fireworks going; she needs it tonight," Jamie said, but she sounded so far away.

Everything was far away. I was only partially aware of being lifted and turned so that I was kneeling. At least, I thought I was kneeling. Then there was more pleasure.

My nipples were tingling from an unknown touch, and I was rocking back and forth. Was he fucking me again already? I couldn't tell. All I knew was that I was in heaven. Every single cell in my body was electrified. Wave after intense wave of pleasure crashed over me. Wet lips traced their way up my back, and I let my head fall forward to give him complete access to the back of my neck. My hair was hanging down around my face, tickling me.

The pounding was intense. I was definitely being fucked. My head swam with the alcohol that had taken full control of my faculties and made everything a bit hazy. Or maybe it was the intense pleasure that had dulled everything else.

There were lips on my mouth; they couldn't possibly be Adam's because he was behind me. Wasn't he? My eyes fluttered open but the sensations were better in the dark, so I kept them closed instead.

My whole body was being pushed forward with each of Adam's thrusts, and my face was mashed against someone else's. Someone with stubble. Todd. I was kissing Todd. I wanted to tell him that I didn't kiss on the lips, but his mouth felt so good against mine. His tongue was necessary to the pleasure I was experiencing.

"I miss fucking you, cherry pie," he mumbled against my mouth.

"We can't."

The words came automatically, and a part of my brain that wasn't letting go of everything else in favor of the pleasure was glad that I still held the boundary of no sex with my boss.

"Remember how good we used to be?" he asked. "You wore me out that first night we were together."

I cringed away from him. That might have been a good memory for him, hours of crazed fucking, but it was one of the worst memories I had. That was the night I'd been broken. The night I'd said goodbye to Alison.

"Stop."

I tried to push Adam off, but he was lost in his own world.

The pain of that night, all those years ago, had burned through everything else and was crushing me. Instantly, the pleasure was gone. I was worthless, unlovable. Adam didn't love me; he just loved the way I felt wrapped around his cock. And it wasn't even specifically *me* that he needed—any girl would do.

"Stop," I said again. Tears burned behind my eyes, and I needed to get away.

"What? Are you okay? Am I hurting you?" Adam asked. He stopped thrusting but was still inside me.

"I just need to use the bathroom," I said, trying to hold myself together.

"Right now?" he asked, incredulous.

"Let her up, Adam." It was Jamie's voice that finally made him let me go.

"I'm not finished," I heard Adam say, sounding like a sulking child.

"Here, fuck me until she comes back," Jamie offered.

I scrambled from the room on my hands and knees and locked the bathroom door behind me. I looked at myself in the mirror and cringed. My eyes were red from the alcohol, and my hair was a bird's nest.

"Fuck." I slammed my hand into the basin. My palm stung. The vanity sprung open from the impact, and I could make out several razors, some ibuprofen, and more condoms.

"Ally." Todd's voice was soft on the other side of the door. "I'm sorry. Can I talk to you for a minute?"

"What do you want, Todd?" I snapped.

"I didn't mean to upset you. I just wanted to remind you how good we were. I helped you that night."

I laughed darkly. He hadn't helped me at all that night. Or had he? I remembered the emotional pain and how fucking him had made me feel strong. He'd *needed* me that night. I wanted to feel that strength again. I opened the door and dragged him inside. He was still naked.

"You want to help me again?" I asked.

His eyes were wide with shock. I didn't wait for an answer. I dug around in the vanity and removed one of the condoms, slipping it onto him. I pushed him down to the floor, straddled his hips, and sank down on his cock. He wasn't fully hard but with a few quick movements he was hard enough.

"Ally," he said hesitantly.

"Help me again, Todd. Tell me you want this. Want *me*."

"I want you," he said, finally catching on.

His hands cupped my ass and helped me rise up and down on his dick. He was fully hard now, and my movements were easier.

"Tell me you need me."

"Ally, I need you." The words were exactly what I wanted to hear. "I always picture you when I jerk off. I've wanted you every single night since our first fuck."

"Yes," I breathed. "Fuck me, Todd. Show me how much you've wanted to fuck me all this time."

We rolled over and he pounded into me, his head resting on my shoulder as he pistoned his hips. Just as the first time we'd fucked, the physical pleasure was there, but I was getting so much more than that. My self-worth was inflating like a balloon.

A loud roar came from the other side of the door, and I guessed that Adam had just come. Good, he didn't deserve me running out on him like that. His release encouraged me to do the same for Todd. Wasn't that what this was all about anyway? Being needed. Giving a man something that he wanted from me. He wanted me to make him come.

"God, you're so fucking good, Ally," Todd grunted.

I wrapped my legs around his hips and scratched at his back. He hissed, and I wasn't sure if it was from pleasure or pain. Was there a difference? Not anymore. Not for me.

I needed more control. I was getting some power from giving him pleasure, but I wasn't *owning* it. I rolled us over again so we were pressed against the side of the bathtub. Todd sat up, leaning against the bath, and I straddled his lap. I stared into his eyes and moved over him, taking from him what I needed.

"Holy fuck," Todd gasped.

He was close, but I wasn't ready for him to be done yet. I needed more from him. And for once, I didn't care about the guy's pleasure. This was about what *I* needed.

I rode him hard and fast, and I could see when his orgasm hit, but I didn't stop. I wasn't ready. He didn't try to stop me. He just sat on the bathroom floor and let me ride him and take what I wanted, without complaint.

"You're beautiful, Ally. You're the best fuck I've ever had."

He kept up a constant stream of words that helped me put myself back together.

I was Ally Fucking Mitchell. I was the best fuck in New York City, and guys paid a fortune to have an hour of my time. My pleasure-giving skills were notorious.

With each stroke of Todd's softening cock, I could feel my wall going back up. Brick by brick.

"Sorry, Ally, I just need a minute." Todd winced and held my hips up so I couldn't slide back down. I let out a frustrated sigh, stood up, and started pacing the room.

"I'm sorry, this isn't fair to you," I said, truly meaning the words and yet knowing that I needed to use him to become myself again. It had worked before.

He chuckled. "I should have known to be careful what I wished for."

He was too good to me. He wanted the old me back, as well. I knelt next to him and removed the condom, dropping it on the floor and putting a new one on him.

"It's my lucky night," he said with a grin.

He was hard again now, and I mounted him right away, not wanting to waste another second. Yes! That was what I needed.

He watched me with half-lidded eyes as I fucked him hard. The face of my ex-boyfriend, Nick, flashed into my mind, and a burst of rage made me grind harder. Todd grunted in response. I pushed Nick away only to have him replaced by Robert with his sad eyes and big heart. I didn't mean to cry, but I could feel warm tears dripping down my cheeks.

"I'm sorry," I whispered. I wasn't sure if the words were to Robert, Todd, or myself. Probably for all three of us.

"Don't be sorry, cherry pie. I'm having the fucking time of my life here."

I ignored Todd's words and kept riding. Robert's brown eyes morphed into Scott's blue ones, and for a moment, they were the same person. Someone who believed in love.

My wall slammed down, and the faces in my head disappeared. No more!

I was close to orgasm, and I could see that Todd was struggling to hold off his second release. I leaned back and rested my hands on his shins, moving my hips faster.

"Yes," I breathed.

This was what was important. Sex. This was all that mattered. Pleasure. I didn't need love. I didn't want to have to answer to someone else, to worry about them, or have to consider their feelings.

I put all my own feelings away in a little box and locked it tightly. My orgasm hit, and I bucked violently in Todd's lap, grunting and gasping my release, and then I rolled onto the cool tiled floor.

Todd looked at me nervously, assessing if I was still broken. The fuck had been exactly what I needed to shed the emotions that Robert had brought to the surface. Alison was back in her box. I was Ally again, and all the pain was pushed down deep inside, exactly where it belonged.

"Thanks. You really helped," I mumbled, my chest rising and falling as I caught my breath.

He wore a cheeky grin. "I've wanted to do that again for a long time."

"I know, but it can't happen again. You're my boss. It shouldn't have even happened now."

"It was good though?"

"It was just what I needed."

He must have sensed that I didn't need him anymore, because he got up quickly and threw the condoms in the small trashcan under the sink. He looked back over his shoulder at me, but I smiled and waved him out of the room.

"Ally, if you ever need help again…"

"You're the first person I'll call. Thanks, Todd."

He nodded and left the room.

Once I was alone, I looked at myself in the mirror again. Ally stared at me with her hard smile and her cold eyes. I was strong again. I'd put myself back together. I was no longer the broken little girl who wanted to be loved. Or maybe I was more broken than before, just with a better Band-Aid. It was hard to tell the difference.

All that mattered was that I was strong enough to face Scott tomorrow night. I wasn't angry with him anymore. He'd called me a whore and I'd just proved him right. I'd owned it. I'd been the best fucking whore there ever was.

I didn't feel the need to stay and keep going on with everyone. I'd gotten what I'd needed, and I was exhausted.

"You okay?" Jamie called as I walked through the living room.

"Yeah, I'm just tired. I'm gonna get a cab."

By the time I got to the front door, they'd all forgotten about me completely. Both guys were sitting on the couch. Amy was riding Adam, and Jamie was riding Todd. The girls were leaning sideways and kissing each other. They were all lost in pleasure.

I smiled. My friends were certainly unconventional, but I loved them for it.

# CHAPTER TWELVE

I was getting out of the shower when I heard my phone ringing. I ran through the apartment, trying to clutch the damp towel to my body. I reached my bedroom, kicked the door closed, and picked up my cell just as it stopped. The missed call was from Todd.

I dropped the towel and dialed him back as I rummaged through my underwear drawer.

"Thanks for calling back, cherry pie."

"What's up, Todd? I'm just getting ready to go meet your cousin."

"Listen, about that. I need you to take a client before you go."

"What? I don't have time."

"Sure you do. You're not meeting Scott until seven and it's only five."

"Todd," I said, trying to be patient. "I'm not really jazzed about the idea of going to meet Scott smelling like another man's cum."

"You've done it before. The first time you met with him you'd seen four other guys."

"For fuck's sake!" I said. "I'm not taking another client, all right?"

"Yes, you are. He knows it's a last minute booking, and I've told him that he only gets you for thirty minutes. Just fuck him hard and get out of there. I know you have another appointment. I'm not *completely* unreasonable you know," he said as if he were the one doing me a favor.

I pinched my nose as I tried to calm myself down. As my rational mind caught up with my emotions, I thought that it might actually be good to fuck away my nerves and meet Scott with a firm resolve.

I'd planned on taking my time getting ready, making sure I looked as hot and sexy as I could, but now I had to rush. I sprayed product into my hair and scrunched it, hoping it would dry with some curl, and then quickly did my makeup.

The quickie client was staying near the Empire State building, so I caught the subway and was there in only a few minutes. He opened the door after my first knock and leered at me.

He was a middle-aged man with thinning hair and a gaunt face. His skin had the gray pallor of a heavy smoker, and I could tell just by his expression that this guy was horny as hell. He just wanted to get off hard and fast. I was happy to oblige.

As soon as I was in the room his hands were peeling off my clothes. I only stopped him long enough to ask for my payment and to shove a condom in his hand, and then I undressed and lay on the bed.

This hotel room looked just the same as every other hotel room in the city. I'd been in thousands, and they were all pretty much the same. White walls, white linen, low lighting, and uncomfortable, sparse furniture. This room did smell a bit mustier than most, but I didn't plan on being there long enough to breathe it for long.

I didn't want to look into his greedy eyes, so I rolled onto my stomach. He could do me from behind.

The bed dipped as he moved behind me, already breathing heavily.

His hands grasped my hips, but he didn't push in straight away. I'd thought this guy was just after some ass. He dipped his fingers into my wetness and swirled them around. He pumped them in and out a few times, and I moaned to give him a show.

Then, to my surprise, his fingers moved higher and he started spreading the moisture over my anus. It appeared he did want ass after all—literally.

I wasn't opposed to anal sex. I'd done it plenty of times before; I was just surprised because most guys would start with the girly parts and move to the ass after they were worked up.

"I'm going to fuck your ass."

*Thanks for stating the obvious!* I pushed my butt a bit higher to give him better access and moaned. "Mmm, put it in me."

Anal sex was probably a good option for Mr. Quickie. I'd found through experience that guys could go a long time in the pussy, but anal sex was usually over much faster. I guessed that the extra tightness and pressure was too stimulating for guys to hold out for long.

He pushed inside me slowly and I relaxed my body, letting him in. That initial thrust always felt strange. That hole wasn't made for things to go *in*. But once he was seated and thrusting, it felt great.

"Fuck. It's so tight," he gasped as he pulled out and then slammed back in.

I kept my eyes on the alarm clock on the bedside table, making sure I didn't go over my time.

As he moved behind me, I thought about what I was going to say to Scott when I saw him. Yes, he'd said some mean things to me, but he was only speaking the truth.

I heard a hocking sound, and then the client spat on my ass, working the saliva in for more lubrication. I cringed, but it wasn't the worst thing that had happened to me with a client. I didn't bother to stop him because I just wanted him to come as quickly as possible.

He was grunting and groaning but seemed completely disinterested in me. The majority of my clients loved touching my body. They stroked my soft skin, paid a lot of attention to my breasts and nipples, and played between my legs, at least for some of the time. This guy had gone straight for the ass and wasn't touching me at all.

I glanced back over my shoulder and saw that his eyes were scrunched shut as he thrust. He could have been picturing anything. It made me wonder if perhaps he was gay but not confident enough to order a male prostitute.

I made a mental note to talk to Todd about bringing a gay guy into our team. I hadn't spoken with Adam directly about it, but I was pretty confident that he was only interested in servicing women.

It was starting to feel really good, so I hummed, but he leaned forward and shushed me. Okay—I was just a vagina, or rather an anus, to him. That was fine. That was what I was to all of them in the end. The other clients just weren't so obvious about it.

I knelt there silently, letting him thrust as he wanted, and watched the clock. I couldn't help my deep breathing, but I did bite my lip to keep any moans silent.

He started grunting curse words under his breath, so I suspected he was close. I clenched my ass as tightly as I could and then released, sending him over the edge. He pulled out of me, the bed shifted again, and he was gone.

I was used to guys collapsing on me and rolling to the side. Very few got up and walked away immediately after.

"Do you mind if I use your bathroom?" I asked.

"Sure. Whatever." He didn't look at me. He'd walked over to the open window and was lighting a cigarette.

I closed the door behind me and fixed my smudged makeup in the mirror. I hoped I hadn't left too much smeared on the hotel's pillow.

I splashed water on some tissues and cleaned myself up. The last thing I wanted was to smell like sex when I saw Mister Five. Satisfied that I was presentable, I left the bathroom.

Mr. Anal was still smoking by the window, his back turned. I left the room without a word.

I was fifteen minutes late.

Usually, I would be prompt with a client. They were paying for my time, after all. But Todd hadn't given me much time and it gave me a little satisfaction to make Mister Five sweat. He'd told me to meet him at the 21 Club, a kitschy yet classy bar in midtown. If he was trying to impress me with opulent locations, it wasn't working. He was just coming across as desperate.

I approached the building, lined with miniature jockeys, and saw him standing outside. He glanced nervously at his watch and scanned the street. His eyes caught mine, and a relieved smile spread over his face. I had to hold my cheeks in place to stop myself from returning it. I didn't *want* to be happy to see him.

"Sorry about the predictable location," he said when I reached him. "I don't really know many places in the city."

"This is fine."

We walked inside and handed our coats to the check-in, then he led me to the bar and ordered us both drinks. A scotch for him and a cosmopolitan for me. He didn't even ask me what I wanted! The fact that I loved cosmos was beside the point.

"Would you like to sit somewhere private so we can talk?" he asked.

I nodded and allowed him to lead me to the back of the room and into a small round booth. I slid across the leather seat and folded my hands in my lap, waiting. He wasn't making eye contact; his eyes were scanning the miniature cars and planes hanging from the ceiling, and he'd run his hand through his messy hair several times since we'd arrived. I didn't know why he cared so much. So, you offended the prostitute? Who cares! He never had to see me again…unless he *wanted* to see me again?

"Thank you for agreeing to come," he finally said. "What happened last week…that was *not* how I wanted that night to go. *At all.*"

I nodded, and he let out a breath. He'd obviously been beating himself up over this. When I reached across the table and put my hand over his, his eyes shot up to meet mine.

"Look," I said. "You said something you didn't mean. It happens. And you didn't do anything wrong. I am a whore."

"No, you're not!" he countered adamantly. "I didn't even mean the words as they were coming out of my mouth. I've struggled so much with the fact that I keep booking a prostitute. That's not who I am. I hoped that if we just talked, spent some time together, I could convince myself that we were more than that. My anger was directed at myself. I'm so disgusted that I could say something like that to you."

"Scott, don't worry about it. I have sex with men for money. I'm pretty sure that's the definition of a whore. Look, it doesn't even matter. What you think of me *doesn't matter*. What we had was a business transaction. Harsh words were exchanged. It's okay for us both to walk away. I have other clients, and you can book another girl…or not…whatever you like."

His eyes burned with intensity as he stared at me.

"That's just it. I don't *want* to walk away. I feel something when I'm with you that I haven't felt in a very long time…maybe ever. I'm not ready to just walk away from it."

He'd said the worst word he could have possibly said, and I pulled my hand away.

*Feel.*

That was dangerous territory for me. I'd spent the better part of last night fucking myself back together after I'd let myself *feel* something. The worst thing of all was that I knew what he was talking about. I'd felt it, too. That damned connection.

"I'd like to keep seeing you on my visits to New York."

Those were the words I'd both been hoping for and dreading. I had a decision to make.

"But I don't want to pay you," he added. "I want to date you."

"I don't date," was all I think of to say in reply. "I fuck."

"We can still fuck." He smiled. "But just for the enjoyment of it. Like normal people do."

"Are you saying that I'm not normal? I know my lifestyle offends you, but I had hoped you might have a tiny bit of respect for me as a person. I wouldn't have a job if men weren't such horny pigs."

My voice had gotten louder than I'd planned, and a few people had turned to look at us. Scott slumped in his seat and said quietly, "I'm sorry, that was a bad word choice. But you know what I mean."

"I'm sorry, too. But the answer is still no." I hadn't been on a proper date in years. There wasn't a guy on the planet who could put up with dozens of other guys fucking his girl. It would never work out.

"No?" He looked deflated. "Without even giving it a try?"

I sighed. "Okay, let's do a hypothetical discussion. Pretend I just came home and you ask how my day was."

He shifted in his seat. "How was work today, dear?"

I smiled sweetly. "Pretty good. I fucked five guys. One shoved his cock so far up my ass that I don't think I'll be able to take a shit for a few days. Another guy was hung like a horse and had the stamina of the Energizer Bunny. Seriously, he just pounded into me for the whole hour."

Scott's face clouded, and he held up his hand so I'd stop talking. "All right, I get the point."

I gave him a sympathetic look. "Scott, if I'm being honest, then I have to say that I feel the same things you do. I would never have agreed to meet up with any other client after what had happened between us, but there's just something different about you. Regardless, the reality is that you couldn't handle my life. It would destroy you."

"I could learn to deal with it."

I knew that he wanted to mean what he was saying, but he couldn't.

"So, you're sitting at home, and I'm at work, fucking another man. You're fine with that? You're just reading a book or watching TV. You're not *at all* tearing your hair out because another man is touching me, kissing my body, thrusting inside me?"

He frowned. "I could get you a job at my company. You wouldn't have to do that work anymore."

"I don't do this because I *have* to. I like my job. It makes me feel strong and powerful and in control."

I could see he was fighting for us — for the chance of us. But I knew better. It would never work.

"I'm going to tell Todd that I didn't charge you for tonight because you came here with good intentions, but this is as far as it can go. Next week you can either book me for a quick fuck, or you can forget about me and move on with your life. Find a nice *normal* girl to settle down with. Just think about it."

I stood up to leave but he grabbed my arm. "I'm not ready for you to leave yet."

I raised my eyebrow. What else was there to say?

"Please, will you sit?"

I did, sliding back into the bench seat. He appeared to be thinking very hard. His eyebrows were knitted together and his fingers tapped rapidly on the table top as if he was playing a silent piano.

"You don't have to feel bad. This is just the way things are," I said.

"But they don't have to be. I *can* accept your life. I can tolerate you being with other men if you can assure me that you are as cold with all of them as you have been with me. If there is no emotional attachment, I think I could live with that."

"And if you can't and everything turns to shit?" That was my greatest fear. I'd been hurt before, and I wasn't ever going to allow that to happen again.

"Who says it would turn to shit?"

I laughed humorlessly. "Love always ends painfully. There is no other way."

He narrowed his eyes. "What would make you say that?"

I thought of Robert, weeping into my shoulder as his cum pooled on my leg. Needing the release and hating himself for it, because it broke his heart. I thought of myself three years before, curled up in a ball after seeing my college boyfriend, Nick, in bed with a red-haired slut from his sociology class. Never again. Not me.

"Love can only ever end in a breakup or death. There are no happy endings."

Scott pondered my words carefully.

"In a black and white world, that's very true. But think about everything you're missing in between. Do you not watch a movie because you know it has a sad ending? Or do you enjoy the movie and build up the strength to cope with the ending and move on?"

His words made sense, but I was afraid.

He grabbed my hands and looked into my eyes. "Please, just give me a chance to change your mind about love."

"You're delusional!" I laughed.

"I'm not saying that it's going to be easy but I'm willing to try if you are."

We stared each other down for several minutes. I was waiting for reality to set in for him, but he was being so stubborn. Finally, I threw my hands up in the air and sighed. "Fine. Let's give it a try, but I already know how it's going to end."

My stomach turned at the words as they left my mouth, and I wanted to curl into a ball and hide. Was I really ready to let myself become vulnerable to this man? A man who had called me a whore?

Scott was smiling. "Can I ask something?"

"Okay."

"I'd like it if you didn't see any clients when I'm in town."

"You want me to be *all yours* on Sundays?"

"Exactly. And if I decide to come to town midweek for some reason, that exception would apply then, as well."

I scowled at him and folded my arms over my chest. "I see what you're doing. In a few weeks, you'll tell me that you're moving back to New York and I'll have to give up all my clients."

He laughed, his eyes crinkling at the sides. "No. I'm not trying to trick you into anything. It's just, when I'm here, I want to know that you're with me and only me. When I'm out of town, I don't need to know what goes on. As long as it's only work."

"You've seen how hesitant I am about this. Do you *really* think I have emotional bonds with other guys?"

He smiled, a little relieved. "I guess not. But let's keep it that way."

"All right. I agree to your terms. When you're in town, then I'm off duty. I'll let Todd know."

Todd wasn't going to be happy. Weekends were our busiest times, and he usually had me fully booked on Sundays. I'd probably have to take a few more appointments during the week to make up for it.

"So, now that we're officially giving this a shot…and I'm in town… would you classify this as a date?"

I thought about his question. "I guess so."

"So, would it be out of line to kiss you at the end of the night?"

I was shocked. "What kind of girl do you think I am? Kissing on a first date?"

He laughed. I'd tried to play it off as a joke, but inside I was terrified. I'd gone so long trying to push my emotions down. I'd even spent last night fucking this man's cousin in order to put myself back together, and here I was just handing him my heart on a silver platter with a little sign saying "Break Me." *Stupid, Ally. Really stupid.*

And yet, when I looked into his eyes, I felt safe.

"Would you like to go for a walk? One thing that I love about coming to the city is the atmosphere on the streets at night."

"Sure."

He took my hand as we left the 21 Club, fingers laced together. I couldn't wrap my head around the fact that I suddenly had a *boyfriend*. Who *was* I, and where had Ally gone?

# CHAPTER THIRTEEN

People walked up and down the streets, arm-in-arm, laughing, and talking happily. New York was a wonderful place to be in when you were in love. I wondered if Scott and I would fall in love, if we would even make it that long. I tried not to get my hopes up.

My stomach grumbled loudly.

"Would you like to get something to eat?" he asked.

"Sure," I said, giving him a sheepish look.

We headed toward Time Square, and he bought us hot dogs from a vendor. As a local, this wasn't very exciting for me, but he seemed thrilled.

"Can I ask about your company?"

He smiled at me. "Of course. What would you like to know?"

"Did you really start it from scratch?"

"I did."

"How do you even do that? I mean, did you know how to publish books?"

He ran a hand through his hair. "Well, I've always loved literature. I can't write to save my life, but I love books. I knew I wanted to work in the publishing industry. I always thought it was going to be as an editor or maybe even an agent. But my parents had bigger hopes for me. If you knew them you'd understand. So, when I majored in literature at college, they made me take on a second major in business management."

"So you have a double degree?"

He nodded. "I didn't mind too much. The business classes were interesting, and I managed to apply a lot of what I learned to the publishing industry. When I graduated, I looked for jobs but everything I was offered…I don't know. Nothing really felt right. A friend of mine actually joked that if I couldn't find a job that suited me, I should just create my own. That idea stuck with me."

"And it was as easy as that? You just thought you'd be a publisher and you were? I always heard that the publishing industry was brutal."

He laughed dryly. "It wasn't easy at all. I took out a business loan and set up the company, but it was small, and I had no reputation to back me up. I nearly went bust that first year and only barely broke even the two years after that, but since then, the company has blossomed."

"Well, I'm impressed."

"I knew owning my own business would come in handy for impressing the ladies one day," he joked.

"And you're doing well enough that you can afford to fly in and out for meetings and have the rest of the time off?"

"Oh no! I work damn hard during the week, but I do it from home. Everything is done electronically now, so I'm never very far from my laptop."

"You said you live in Miami. I'm picturing you in some high-rise on the beach. Am I right?"

"Kind of. I have a penthouse apartment that overlooks Hollywood Beach. But I don't know if you'd call the building a high-rise. Where do you live?" he asked, once he'd taken the last bite of his hot dog and wiped his mouth with a napkin.

"In the Village. On the East Side."

"I'd like to see your place some time."

I hesitated. That was a dangerous thought. Could I picture Scott in my apartment? The truthful answer was *no way!* I was about to blow his comment off and change the subject when I reminded myself that if I was committing to this boyfriend thing then I might as well throw myself into it. Some parts of committing were uncomfortable.

"We could go there now if you like. I could show you a bit of my world?" There I went. Right off the high dive and into the deep end.

"Great! Should we get a taxi?"

"The subway is fine. It's not a long walk."

We caught the train and walked the extra two blocks to my apartment. We stood outside the door, and I jingled my keys for a few seconds.

"What are you doing?" he asked.

"I'm trying to warn my roommate that I'm about to come in. She often does things in the living room that should be kept private, if you get what I mean." That was only part of the reason. A sinking sensation had settled in my stomach, and I was trying to buy myself some time to think of a way to get Scott away from there.

His eyes went wide. "And you're okay with that?"

I shrugged. I usually just ignored her, but I had a feeling that it would be too confronting for Scott. Hesitantly, I slid the key into the lock and opened the door. My worst fears were realized.

"Fuck me!" Jamie screamed as she rode Adam.

They were on the floor in almost the exact position that Todd and Amy had been in the other night as I'd watched her audition. Yeah, Scott was never going to be comfortable in my world. The worms in my belly squirmed at the thought of exposing my life to him.

Scott's mouth dropped open as he watched Jamie bucking up and down. Adam was grunting loudly, and I wished the floor would open and swallow them up. Or me.

"Don't mind us!" I called loudly.

I grabbed Scott's hand and dragged him through the living room toward my bedroom. Jamie spun around, unashamed, and looked at us as she continued to ride without stopping.

"Ally! I thought you were going to be out all night. Wait, is that *Mister Five?*"

She let out a long moan when she finished speaking, and I practically pulled Scott out of the room. Once we were in my bedroom with the door closed, I collapsed against it.

"I'm so sorry about that!"

His eyes were huge, but he laughed nervously. "So that's your roommate?"

"That would be her. The guy is one of Todd's new recruits; I think they might be dating. His name is Adam."

"Does she work for Todd, too?"

"Yeah, that's how we became friends."

"Why did she call me 'Mister Five'?"

Shit! I'd hoped he had missed that. "Oh, well, the first time we met, you were my fifth client of the night."

He nodded and looked around the room, seemingly appeased by my explanation. As he studied my personal belongings, I suddenly felt vulnerable. Exposed. This was my safe place. I'd never brought a client here before. No—I had to remind myself that Scott wasn't a client anymore.

"I like your room," he said, sitting tentatively on the bed. "Um, do you bring many guys here?"

"Never. My bed is actually a virgin."

His eyebrows went up.

"This is my quiet space," I explained. "No boys allowed."

"And yet, here I am." He seemed very pleased with himself.

"Here you are."

"So, if you don't bring boys here and you don't date outside of work, when was the last time you were with someone who wasn't paying you?"

I thought hard. When I'd made the decision to try to make a relationship work, I'd decided the only way to do that would be to be brutally honest. Better he ran now than left me later for lying to him. Last night's activities flashed through my mind—I hadn't been paid for that, but I disregarded it. They were work colleagues. It didn't count.

"Not since Todd in college."

"Wait…*Todd?* My *cousin,* Todd? You fucked my cousin?"

*Shit.* I knew he wouldn't be able to handle it. We'd only lasted an hour.

"Um, yeah?"

"But you guys don't still…you don't still fuck now, right?"

"He wishes!" I said, laughing, then realized he probably wouldn't find that funny. "Sorry. No, Todd and I are just friends now. He's my boss. Last week, I watched him fuck a new girl and he watched as I fucked Adam to test him out but…" I trailed off when I saw the look on Scott's face.

I purposely left out the orgy the night before. It didn't even really count as sex. Todd had just given me some help, like a friend giving another friend a hug. A naked hug that ended in orgasm.

"What?" I asked.

Scott looked like he might throw up. "You've had sex with the guy who's currently doing your roommate?"

This was not going well. "Only once…twice, actually. But that's it."

He ran his hands through his hair and leaned back on the pillows. "Am I allowed to ask how many guys you've slept with?"

"Four."

He gave me a skeptical look.

"Four that I count. My sex number is only for guys who I've slept with willingly. I don't count clients."

"Who are the four?"

"Well, there's my high school boyfriend, Josh. We broke up in junior year. My senior prom date, Craig. My college boyfriend, Nick, and then Todd."

"So according to your counting system, we've never slept together."

I shook my head. "You were a client."

"And if you were to count up all the clients, what would your number be then?"

"You wouldn't want to know," I said with as much authority as I could.

"Why don't you try me?"

"I don't think so. What's your number?"

"Eleven," he said casually. "And I *do* count you in there."

Adam and Jamie were getting louder. This was the point that I would usually put on some music, but then Scott and I wouldn't be able to talk.

"Are they making you uncomfortable? We could go somewhere else?" I offered, pointing to the living room.

"I'm fine. I'd like you to answer my questions, please."

"Does it matter?" I asked.

"No. I'm not going to judge you. I know it's going to be a high number. I'm just curious."

I reminded myself *again* that I'd committed to being honest. What a pesky promise. I closed my eyes, feeling like that was safer. "About two thousand. I don't keep exact figures."

He was silent, so I opened one eye and peeked.

"All right." That was all he said. At least he hadn't run from the room screaming.

"So," I said, unsure where to go after my awkward confession.

"I was thinking—how does your bed feel about losing its virginity?"

"What?" I had expected him to be angry or repulsed, not thinking about sex.

"Well, seeing as you already call me 'Mister Five,' I thought I could earn that name for another reason. Make your list go *Josh, Craig, Nick, Todd*, and *Scott*." He ticked the names off on his fingers.

I smiled. "My Mister Five."

"Exactly. Let's see if we can show those two out there how it's really done!"

He grabbed me and swung me around onto the bed. I giggled and shrieked as I fell into the soft pillows. It had been a long time since I'd just had *fun* with a guy who wasn't Todd or my brother. Fun that was just for fun's sake. No payment required.

I sat on the edge of the bed and smiled up at him. It was strange how easily I'd been able to let him in. It was as if the decision had been made, and I couldn't turn my mind or my heart back to how I'd felt before. Scott wasn't a client. He was *mine*. And it terrified me.

He knelt down in front of me, smiling broadly. "I've been waiting to do this for two weeks."

It was hard to believe that I'd only known this man for that short amount of time. He'd consumed so many of my thoughts that it seemed longer.

His hands cupped my face and pulled me closer, and I realized he was about to kiss me. His eyes fluttered closed as his face approached, and I let him pull me in. It was the first time I'd kissed a guy properly. Ever.

I didn't count teenage make-out sessions because they were just all about tongue and grinding. I also didn't count drunken kissing in college because I didn't remember most of it. The kiss last night with Robert hadn't been about kissing him; it was more of a comfort.

And kissing Todd last night had been because I was broken—and very drunk.

This kiss was only about *the kiss*. It wasn't a precursor to sex or because I was so drunk that I didn't realize what was happening. This was just about kissing Scott.

Our lips touched and he was tentative at first. He started off with small pecks before pulling me in and tightening our embrace. I'd never realized how wonderful kissing could be. Our mouths moved together perfectly, fitting into each other like two pieces of a puzzle. It suddenly seemed ridiculous to me that our lips had never been joined before.

His hands held me against him, tangling in my hair, grazing my throat. He was all around me as we gasped for breath and exhaled into a glorious mixture of our desire.

I found myself glad that I hadn't done this with every guy. This was a special moment meant for *this* man. I couldn't give him my fidelity, but I could give him this. He was the only one who got my kisses.

When we finally broke apart, my head was spinning. Scott gave me a cheeky grin and chuckled as he crawled up the bed and leaned his forehead against mine. Our eyes were only inches apart and all I could see was icy blue. It was intoxicating.

"Let me into your heart," he begged in a whisper.

"I want to," I said. It wasn't a yes, but it was the best I could do for now.

The crescendo from the living room had died down, and I was relieved that they had finished. It was a bit like having porn in the background. Such a beautiful moment shouldn't be marked with that cheapness.

Scott rolled off and curled into my side, kissing up my throat and over my cheeks. I tried to unbutton his shirt, but his hand held my fingers still.

"I thought you wanted my bed to lose its virginity?" I asked.

"I do. Right now I just want to hold you though. Is that okay?"

He was still nuzzling against me. His breath on my skin sent shivers down my spine.

"Yeah."

He pulled me against his chest and held me tightly. It was nice. I very rarely felt close to anyone. My terror slowly started to melt away. Maybe I could do this.

"How do you take your coffee?" he asked.

"What?" I laughed. "That's random."

He chuckled. "It's just something that I was thinking about. I don't know anything about you, really. I want to know you."

"Milk, no sugar," I said, reaching my hand up to stroke his face.

It was the first time that I'd reached out to touch him in a non-sexual way, and his response was enthusiastic. He pressed his cheek against my hand and cupped his own palm over it, holding it against him.

"How would you feel about coming to Miami to visit me?"

"I'm sure we could arrange it. I'd have to let Todd know some dates so he can schedule around them."

Scott frowned, but didn't say anything. I wondered how hard it was for him to pretend like my job didn't bother him. Near impossible I would imagine. It set warning bells off in my head. He was *trying* to be okay with it, but it really did bother him. That was only going to get worse, not better. I suddenly felt suffocated in his arms. What was the point of letting myself care about him, get close to him, when I knew it wasn't going to work in the end? It was like setting myself up for pain. I might as well balance a brick above my hand and then watch it tumble down to crush my fingers. Not pulling away would be stupid.

I ducked under his arm and rolled out of his embrace. I sat up across the bed and hugged my knees to my chest.

"What's wrong?" Scott asked, alarmed and confused.

"I —I don't think I can do this," I stuttered.

Hurt shot through his eyes for a second, but he recovered quickly and put his hands up in a comforting pose.

"Ally," he said softly, crawling slowly toward me as if I was an animal that could bolt at any minute. "I'm not going to hurt you."

"You don't *think* you will. You'll try not to, but it will happen."

He sighed. "Are you not even willing to give it a try?"

"Why try at something you *know* you can't do?"

"Who says you can't do it? People fall in love and live happy lives together all the time. You just have to take the chance."

"*I* say that I can't do it. I know myself. I'm not capable of love."

What I meant was, *I'm not* worth *loving*.

He stood up and started pacing the room. "I don't believe you!"

"I'm sorry, Scott, I wanted to be able to be that girl for you, but I don't think I can. I can't be what you need."

"Ally," he said sadly.

I instantly switched back into my protective mode. It was easy, like flicking a switch.

"We can fuck if you want, so it wasn't a wasted trip here."

Scott looked like he'd been punched in the gut. "No! I don't want to *fuck* you!" he yelled. Suddenly he was back on the bed with his arms around me. "Shhh, don't cry," he whispered.

I hadn't even realized that I *was* crying. However, the salty drops sliding down my cheeks were proof enough.

"Ally," he whispered after a few minutes. "What happened to you?"

I opened my mouth to share something I'd never told anyone—how I had been irrevocably broken.

# CHAPTER FOURTEEN

*I ducked out of the rain and into the doorway. It was pouring, and I'd been lucky to get a bus from campus. I couldn't imagine how wet I would have been if I'd walked home. It was bad enough just running up the stairs from the street.*

*My professor had let us out early. He said he had a lot of grading to catch up on and gave us a chapter of the textbook to read to make up for cutting the lecture short.*

*That was fine with me. It was Nick and my two-year anniversary and I'd planned to cook him a special dinner. He'd been hinting around about marriage for the past few weeks, and I had a feeling that tonight was going to be the night he would propose.*

*I checked the mail, but there was only a telephone bill, which I left in the box. Bills could wait until tomorrow. Racing up the stairs to the third-floor apartment I shared with Nick, I mentally went through the menu I had planned to cook. It was going to take a few hours.*

*Nick had a lecture that got out at six p.m., so I had a while to get ready. I let myself into the apartment and dropped my bag on the counter, then went straight to the fridge and started pulling out ingredients for dinner.*

*A squeaking sound caught my attention. It was close, but I couldn't place where it was. I walked through the kitchen and living area and stood outside the bedroom door. The noise was coming from inside. Bed springs.*

*My stomach jumped into my throat and then plummeted. Part of me knew what I would see on the other side of the door, but I was still numb. I turned the handle and pushed the door open, but didn't take a step into the room. I didn't need to. From the doorway I had a front row view of the action.*

*Nick was lying on his back, on my side of the bed, and there was a woman riding him hard. Her body was long and lean, and her wild red hair was stuck to her back and breasts with sweat. They'd obviously been at it for a while.*

*"Shit! You're so good," Nick panted.*

*"Does your girlfriend fuck you like this?"*

*"Fuck no!"*

*His words were basically a grunt, but I made them out. I wanted to run or beat him to a bloody pulp, but I couldn't do either. I couldn't even move. I just stood there watching them as my heart shattered into a million tiny pieces.*

*I'd thought I would be engaged by the end of the night. What a joke!*

*"Ally?" Nick gasped, his eyes landing on me. "Oh, fuck!"*

*"It's Jasmine," the girl grunted. She obviously hadn't seen me yet.*

*"Get off!" Nick yelled, and pushed her away.*

*His cock—without a condom—slid out of her and fell against his leg. Bile rose up in my throat.*

*"Ally, honey, I thought you were in a lecture!" he said, like it was my fault he'd been caught.*

*Fury coursed through my veins and I ran at him, swinging my fists. He caught my hands easily.*

*"Calm down. This doesn't change how I feel about you," he said.*

*The red-headed bitch had casually picked up her clothes and was sneaking out of the room. I didn't care about her. Nick was the one who had ripped my heart out.*

*"So you've never loved me then?"*

*"Of course I do!" His expression implied that he thought I was being stupid. But I wasn't—if having sex with someone else didn't change his feelings, then his feelings couldn't have been very strong in the first place.*

*I couldn't look at him or listen to his voice anymore, so I fled the apartment.* Happy anniversary, Alison!

*Zach lived in a dorm on campus, so I ran there in the rain. I didn't want to sit on a bus and allow those strangers to see what Nick must have seen all along—that I wasn't worth loving. I felt like it was so obvious now.*

*Josh had cheated on me with the head cheerleader in high school, and now Nick had done the same. Obviously I wasn't the kind of girl that men could commit to. It couldn't be their fault. It had to be something wrong with me. I'd had two boyfriends, and they'd both cheated. I was the only constant.* I'm the problem. I'm the one not worthy of their love.

*I pounded on Zach's door and it opened slowly. Zach wasn't the one who answered it though.*

*"Todd, is my brother here?" I asked, gasping for breath.*

*"Sorry, Ally, he's out. Do you want to come in?"*

*I marched into the room and collapsed on their couch. Their dorm was small and always smelled like dirty socks. They each had a bedroom, and there was a shared kitchenette and living area. The bathroom was a communal room at the end of the hall.*

*"I'll get you a towel," he said.*

*I must have looked like a drowned rat. He handed it to me, and I dried myself slowly. I didn't care about being wet, but I was leaving a puddle on the floor.*

*"Are you all right?" Todd asked.*

*"No!" I choked out, and the tears came.*

*Todd looked like he didn't know what to do. I was sure he hadn't had to deal with many hysterical girls before.*

*"Do you want a drink?" he asked nervously.*

*I was about to say no, but suddenly a drink sounded like the best idea in the world.*

*"I'd love one."*

*Several shots of vodka later, I'd told Todd the entire story. He'd gone from furious and threatening to kill Nick for me to consoling and sympathetic. It was exactly what I needed at the time.*

*"You're much too good for him anyway, I've always thought so," Todd said, stroking my hair.*

*I knew his words were a lie. I wasn't good enough for anyone. If I was, men wouldn't cheat on me.*

"You're beautiful and sweet and funny. If I'm being honest, I've had a crush on you for a while now. Zach would kill me if he knew, but you're just such a great girl."

The words soothed my aching heart and before I knew it, I'd pounced on him. While we were kissing furiously, the pain went away.

I clawed at his shirt, removing it quickly.

"Fuck me," I growled in his ear. "Now."

Todd had had just as many drinks as I'd had, so he wasn't thinking clearly, and he didn't push me away. I had a feeling that if he had been sober, nothing would have happened.

"God, I want you," he replied.

That was all I needed to hear. He wanted me. Nick might not, but Todd did. Even if it was just for my body. I was wanted. I needed to feel that.

We ran into his bedroom and he dug around in his drawers, pulling out a box of condoms and throwing them on the bed. I was glad he was being smart, because I was way past caring about safe sex.

I pushed him down on the bed and removed his pants. His cock was in my mouth before he'd even taken a breath.

"Oh God!" he grunted as I sucked.

I glanced up at him with my lips wrapped around his dick and saw the look of desire in his eyes. It made me feel powerful. But it wasn't enough.

I threw a condom at him, and he hastily put it on as I pulled my shirt over my head. When he was ready, I crawled up to hover over his cock. I wiggled my hips and pulled my denim skirt high around my waist like a belt and pushed my panties to the side.

Todd's eyes were wide.

Then I sank down on him. His eyes almost rolled back in his head when I started to move. I felt so powerful.

Nick's words echoed in my head as I bucked up and down.

"Does your girlfriend fuck you like this?"

"Fuck no!"

I moved harder, proving him wrong.

"Fuck no!"

I rolled my hips back and forth, grinding onto Todd as hard as I could. He grunted and gasped as I moved.

"Fuck no!"

Nick's cruel words echoed in my mind again and again as I rode Todd. Pushing me forward, egging me on. I barely noticed the physical pleasure that my body was experiencing. It was there, but my mind was reveling in the emotional relief. With each stroke of Todd's cock, I was releasing Nick from my heart.

Each time Todd groaned with the pleasure that I was giving him, I felt powerful. I wanted to scream at Nick that I was *a good fuck*. But I couldn't, so I proved it to Todd instead.

"Jesus. Fuck!" Todd gasped. "Stop."

He grabbed my hips roughly and tried to hold me still. I hadn't even realized that he'd come.

"Sorry," I said, trying to pull myself back to reality.

I climbed off him, unsatisfied.

"What the fuck was that?" he asked, his chest rising and falling.

"Wasn't it…good?" I asked. My whole illusion began to crumble, and self-doubt clouded over me.

"Fuck no!"

Had Nick been right after all?

"Good?" Todd's voice was incredulous. "That was amazing. I didn't even know girls knew how to fuck like that."

Relief washed over me. Who needed a heart when you could get self-worth in less painful, less risky ways?

"Wanna go again?" I begged, needing to continue the power rush.

"Give me a minute," he pleaded. "You know, I have some friends who would pay a fortune for a fuck like that." He laughed at his joke, but I wasn't in the mood for talking. I needed to feel desired again.

His cock was lying limply in his lap, and I couldn't have that. I stroked it, coaxing it back to life.

"You're insatiable," Todd teased.

He leaned forward to kiss me, but I turned my head to the side. Kissing was too close to home, and I didn't want his emotions. Only his desire. He didn't seem to notice or care. His lips sucked on my throat as I climbed onto his lap again. He moved to roll us over so he could get on top, but I couldn't let him.

"Let me ride you," I whispered in his ear before sucking the lobe and grazing it with my teeth.

*He groaned and relaxed onto the mattress, giving himself over to me.*

*I used him like that, over and over, for almost two hours. Every time he came, I'd let him recover and then mount him again. It was exhilarating and by the fifth time I'd made him come, he was begging me to stop.*

*"I know I'm a college guy and supposed to be horny all the time, but you're just too much."*

*He laughed as I let my sweat-covered body fall against his chest. It was the most intense sexual experience I'd ever had. My body was aching and I felt raw, but my heart was still in tiny pieces.*

*"Seriously, Ally, you need to share your gift."*

Scott looked at me sadly as I finished the story.

"Sex isn't love," he said.

"I know. I don't want love. I tried to explain it to you before. Love only hurts you."

"Sex isn't power," he insisted.

"You're wrong," I countered. "You should see the look in a guy's eyes when I fuck him like he's never been fucked before. For those few moments, I'm in total control."

"Does it make you happy?"

"I don't know if *happy* is the right word, but it makes me feel good. The pain isn't there when I'm in control like that."

Scott pulled me into his embrace again and hugged me close.

"How do I put you back together?"

# CHAPTER FIFTEEN

I was roused from sleep by raised voices. Scott was curled against me and I looked around, shocked at the notion that we were in *my* bedroom. Yes, the walls were pale blue, and the bookcase held my favorite books and photos of my friends. It was definitely my room. There was a *man* in *my* room!

After I'd told him my story, I'd been too exhausted to keep arguing. Scott had refused to leave with our relationship status still undecided, so the compromise had been that we both sleep on it and pick up where we'd left off in the morning.

"Don't touch me, whore!" The harsh words from the other room forced me to get up.

"Just leave, Zach, tonight isn't a good night." That was Jamie's voice.

I walked out into the living room and saw Jamie standing in her underwear, her hair messed from sleep, her eyes puffy. Zach was standing on the other side of the room in jeans and a shirt. His face was bright red, and his features were hard.

"Zach, what are you doing here?" I asked.

His head whipped around to look at me and his expression darkened. He'd never looked at me with so much anger before. I automatically took a step backward.

"Ally," he said through gritted teeth. His whole body vibrated with fury.

I quickly ran to him and tried to pull him into a hug. He stepped out of my grasp and glared down at me.

"Zach, what is it?" I was starting to panic, too, and my voice was higher than usual.

"Tell me what you do."

"What?" I shook my head, trying to shake away the last of my sleepy haze. "I don't understand."

"Tell me what your job is," he hissed, and I finally understood.

"It sounds like you already know," I said flatly.

"I need to hear you say the words to me."

"Are you trying to embarrass me? To make me feel bad about myself? You don't need to. You have no idea how much I hate myself already, Zach."

"If you hate what you do then why do you do it?" he roared.

"I never said I hated the work. I hate *me*."

"Say the words, Ally."

"I fuck men for money and I love it. Is that what you want to hear?"

It was like we were children again, kids who were fighting over who got to sit in the front seat of the car. He'd always won those fights. I'd thought that he would scream back some sarcastic insult, but his face crumpled in pain. I wondered if a part of him had refused to believe what he already suspected or knew.

"I'm gonna fucking kill Todd," he said through gritted teeth.

"You're not going to say anything to him!" I demanded. "Todd has helped me more than you'll *ever* know. I'd be *nothing* without Todd."

There was no way Zach could ever understand how Todd had put me back together. How he had saved me from myself. I owed Todd a lot.

"How did you even find out?"

"What do you think Mom and Dad are going to say?" he yelled, blatantly ignoring my question.

It was my turn to be angry now. "You're not going to say anything to them. Do you hear me, Zachary?"

"You mean something like, 'Hey, did you hear that Ally's a whore?'"

"That's enough."

Zach and I both turned at the harsh voice behind me. Scott had appeared, groggy. His hair was extra messy, but his face was angry.

"Take that back," he said firmly.

"Who the hell is that? One of your *clients?*" Zach asked, looking at Scott like he was a cockroach.

"I'm her boyfriend."

I cringed at the word, and Zach's mouth dropped open.

"I wouldn't go that far—"

Zach cut me off with an angry bark of a laugh. "Her *boyfriend?* Ally hasn't had a boyfriend for years, unless you count the sham relationship she's been having with my best friend to hide her lies." He turned back to me. "Does *he* know what you do?"

"Yes."

Zach's eyes hardened. "Oh, right. So everyone knows but your brother. Fuck you."

Scott was across the room in a few seconds and right in Zach's face. "You're going to apologize to Ally and calm down, or you're going to leave."

"Do you want me to call Adam?" Jamie asked, looking nervously between the two men.

I considered it. If Zach and Scott started fighting there was no way that Jamie or I would be strong enough to pull them apart without getting hurt. But I didn't want to let it get that far.

"Let me try and calm them down," I said. "If that doesn't work, get him here quick."

Jamie ran to her bedroom, I guessed to get her cell phone, and I walked over to where Scott and Zach were staring each other down. They were a similar height and build; I couldn't pick which of them would win in a potential fight.

I stood right next to them with a hand on each of their chests, trying to push them apart.

"All right, let's all just try to calm down. Scott, can you give me a minute with my brother, please?"

"I'm not leaving the room. What if he tries to hit you?"

"I wouldn't hit my own sister, fuck-head," Zach spat.

"He won't hurt me. Please, just wait in the bedroom, and I'll be back in there soon."

Scott shot a warning glare at Zach before backing away. He left my bedroom door open, and I knew that he would be listening in.

"Zach, I know you're mad. I understand why, and I'm not angry at you. It's nice that you don't want this life for me, but please understand that I'm okay."

"You're better than this, Ally!" His voice had lost all of its anger now that we were alone. "Have you tried to do other work?"

"Zach, I like what I do. You don't have to like it, and I don't expect you to approve. What I do expect is that you'll still love me."

"Of course I still love you. This doesn't take away years of being your big brother. I just can't stand to think of guys treating you like trash."

I rested my hand on his arm, and he didn't pull away this time.

"They don't. I get treated very well, actually. Look, let's pretend that you don't know this. We'll go back to you thinking I work in a mail room."

He scowled. "It's not that easy."

"Can you accept it then?"

"I don't know." He sat down on the couch and fell back into the cushions. "I hate this. I don't want you to do it."

"I'm doing it for me."

"Are you so horny that you can't just have sex like a regular person?" He looked a little sick, but he must have been trying very hard to understand my motivations.

I laughed. If only he knew how little enjoyment I got out of the sex, he would never ask that question.

"Yeah, I'm a real horn-dog. My sexual appetite can't be quenched." He could hear the sarcasm in my voice, but he didn't laugh with me.

"I'm serious. Just get a good vibrator, or get that guy in your bedroom to do his job better." He threw his arms up in the air. "How does he date you and be all right with you fucking other guys?"

I sat down next to my brother and patted his knee.

"It's all very new, and he's not okay with it. He'd probably make the same arguments that you've just made if he thought I would listen. He just cares about me enough to try to overlook it."

As I explained Scott's motives to Zach, the words really sank into my own head as well. Scott cared about me. Why else would he be willing to put up with my job?

"Yeah, or he's just a sick pervert who gets off on his girlfriend fucking other men."

"No, he's trying to accept me as I am. Something I would hope you can do."

"If he thinks he can accept it, then he's a better man than I am," Zach said as he stood up and walked toward the door.

"What does that mean?" I asked after him, but he had closed the door behind him. "Zachary?"

His words spun through my head as I tried to make sense of them.

Strong arms wrapped around me and I jerked up, not realizing that Scott had sat down next to me.

"Are you all right?" he asked.

My heart ached from the rejection, but I nodded, not wanting to show Scott how weak I was. If my brother, someone who was bound by blood to love me no matter what, could walk away from me, then what hope did I have with anyone else?

"Your brother is an asshole," he said as he pulled me into an embrace.

"He just needs some time to adjust. It's a lot to take in."

I hoped my words were true. I didn't know what I'd do without Zach in my life. He was the only thing that made me a normal person. To him, I was a sister. To everyone else in my life, I was a slut. He was the only connection that I had to Alison, and without him, I felt like I might lose her altogether.

As much as I tried to keep her inside and locked away, I couldn't lose her. She was the real me, the person who I wished I could be again. She was the only hope left in my life.

"You don't need him if he's going to treat you like shit."

I knew the words were meant to be encouraging, but I *did* need Zach in my life. Alison was weeping inside me, but I held my own tears back. I wasn't going to let them out. Scott couldn't see how weak I was. I needed to be strong.

"I want you to fuck me now," I whispered, asking for what I knew would put my wall back up.

"Now?" he asked, incredulous.

I started kissing his neck, running my tongue over his throat, and nipping at his Adam's apple.

"Ally, I really don't think this is the best time."

He held my shoulders firmly and detached me from his throat.

"It's the *perfect* time. Don't you want me?" What was the good of having a boyfriend if you didn't get regular sex?

He pulled me into his arms and cradled me against his chest. "Of course I do. I just don't want our first time together as a real couple to be angry sex."

I sighed in frustration and wondered if I could call Todd for a job. Surely he had a few clients who would be interested in a late night meet-up. Then I remembered that I wasn't supposed to see clients when Scott was in town. I couldn't have sex *with* Scott, and I couldn't have sex with anyone else *because of* Scott. This wasn't working out already.

He grabbed my hand and pulled me back to the bedroom. "Come on." He closed the door and sat next to me on the bed. "Have you thought at all about what we talked about last night?"

"I haven't really had the time. We fell asleep, and then Zach was here."

He nodded. "Okay, well think about it now."

He turned my own trick against me and started pressing soft kisses along the inside of my wrist, working up to my elbow. He watched me out of the corner of his eye and smirked as my eyes fluttered closed.

"If you can handle the realities of 'us,' then I think it could work."

He chuckled. "And if I *can* handle those realities, where do you see this going?"

"I don't know." My voice came out as a whisper. His lips had completely climbed my arm, and they traveled up my neck and over my chin until his face hovered right in front of mine.

"We would be great together," he said softly.

"We could be," I agreed reluctantly.

I could feel his warm breath, taste it in my mouth. I wanted to lean forward and kiss him, but as I moved, he leaned ever so slightly back, keeping a small distance between us.

"And I want you all to myself," he said, his voice deep and husky.

"You're the only one here right now."

He sighed. "I want that to be enough for me."

I stroked his face and ducked my head down so I could look into his eyes.

"Scott, I'm agreeing to give this a try. Please don't push me too fast. I'm doing the best I can." It seemed like every time I gave him an inch, he immediately wanted a whole foot.

"You're right," he said and gave me a crooked smile. "So, you're my girlfriend?"

I hesitated and bit my lip as I tried to calm my racing heart. It was time to step up, and I decided that if I didn't do it now, with this man, would I ever? "I guess I am."

It actually felt good to say the words; I didn't think it would. I thought it would terrify me, but looking into his face and seeing the happiness in his smile, I was filled with a quiet confidence.

"What are your plans for this week?" he asked, stroking his fingers through my hair as we lay in my bed.

"Just work," I said, shrugging my shoulders.

"How would you feel about taking some time off and spending the week with me in Miami?"

I cocked an eyebrow and smirked at him. "Remember earlier when I said you were going to trick me out of working? It's already happening."

He laughed. "No, I just want to start our relationship off right. I thought we should spend some time together. Really get to know one another."

"Todd won't let me. I'm fully booked this week. Maybe in a few weeks."

Scott frowned and grabbed his phone.

"Who are you calling at three a.m.?" I asked.

"My cousin."

"Scott, don't."

Todd must have picked up the phone because Scott smiled at me and leaned away when I tried to grab his cell.

"Cuz! What's wrong with you? Oh! Yeah, he was here, too. I wanted to let you know that Ally's going to be going out of town for the week. Yes she is. She's coming to Miami with me." There was a long pause. "I don't care about her other bookings. There are a million other prostitutes in New York. Todd—Todd! He wants to talk to you." Scott handed me the phone.

"Hey," I said with an apologetic tone.

"What the fuck, Ally? I can't just cancel nineteen appointments." Todd's voice exploded through the phone.

"I know. I told Scott to wait a few weeks."

Scott shrugged unapologetically.

"How much has he offered to pay for the week? At least if we make some good money it won't be a total loss."

"Um…"

"Ally," Todd said in a warning tone as if he knew what was coming.

"Here's the thing: Scott won't be paying for me anymore. We're kind of dating."

There was silence on the other end of the phone for a few seconds, then Todd swore loudly and hung up.

"So, I think he's mad," I said, handing Scott the phone.

"He'll get over it. He was already in a bad mood because Zach yelled at him. We'll talk to him about it again in the morning."

"You shouldn't have called him. This is my *job* you're messing with. My livelihood. You know, how I pay my rent and eat?"

I didn't want to have a fight with Scott on our first night as a couple, especially after how emotional the night had already been, but I wasn't going to let him come marching in and start controlling my life.

He gave me a guilty smile. "I'm sorry, Ally. I'm just so used to always getting my way. I promise to be more considerate in the future." His lips and hands moved over my skin and sent shivers down my spine. My body was screaming for him.

"Can we get to the sexy time now?" I asked, my anger pushed aside.

"Ally," he said, using the same warning voice that Todd had used on the phone.

"I want you inside me, Scott. Please."

He groaned as if my words caused him actual physical pain, but he was smiling.

"You make it incredibly hard to be a gentleman."

"Does that mean you'll let me suck your cock?" I batted my eyelashes at him, and he laughed again.

"You are a devil, woman!"

I crawled across the bed on my hands and knees and pushed him back against the pillows. He didn't object when I reached for his pants. It looked like I was going to get my fuck after all. Having a boyfriend might just work out.

I pulled his underwear down to his knees and stroked his cock a few times, feeling it grow in my hand. This was what I needed. Seeing him get hard because of *my* touch was so empowering.

His eyes were locked on my mouth as I licked the head and sucked on just the tip. His gaze was clouded with desire. It made me want to climb on and ride him right away, but it wasn't time for that yet. He hissed when I took him completely into my mouth.

There was a familiar clicking sound behind me, but I ignored it, too focused on Scott.

"Fuck!" he said.

I'd only just gotten started, and he was already swearing under his breath. I was about to pat myself on the back when he pushed me off and pulled a pillow over his crotch.

"What's wrong?" I asked.

He was staring over my shoulder, so I glanced back.

Todd was standing in the doorway, furious.

# CHAPTER SIXTEEN

"**A**re you all right?" I asked, momentarily distracted from the fact that he'd barged into my bedroom by the dark bruise that was swelling his left eye shut.

"Oh *this?*" he asked, waving toward his face. "A little gift from your brother."

"I can't believe this is happening. How did he even find out?"

"I couldn't give a fuck how he found out. Talk to me about *this*." He pointed between me and Scott, and I was brought back to the reality of the situation. A minute ago, I'd been throat-deep in cock.

"Todd!" I shrieked. "Get out of here!"

"Oh, give it a rest, Ally. I've seen you blow guys before, including me."

I glanced back at Scott, who was frowning, but I didn't have time to make sure he was all right. Todd was already pacing the room.

"So, you're dating?"

"Todd, can't we talk about this tomorrow?" Scott asked.

"Some family you are! Stealing my best girl, destroying my business."

"Stop being over-dramatic!" I scolded. "He hasn't stolen me from anything."

"So you're still working for me?" He tried to keep the angry mask on, but I could tell that he was relieved.

"Of course! Nicole had a boyfriend when she first started working for you."

"Which didn't work out," he reminded me.

"We're going to make sure this works out," Scott piped in.

Todd seemed placated, but he was still pacing.

"So, you'll be gone for a week and then you'll be back on my books?"

"Except when I'm in town," Scott spoke again. "If I'm here, then she's mine."

"Sundays are one of the busiest nights!" Todd protested, raising his voice.

"Work around it," Scott said firmly. "Ally's already agreed."

My neck was starting to hurt from turning from one to the other as they fired words back and forth. Todd was pissed, but he looked at me for conformation, and I nodded.

"I'm all yours to book out as you please any night that Scott's *not* in town."

Todd sighed and leaned against the wall. "I guess that can work. And you're really okay with that? I mean, she does some nasty shit." His question was directed at Scott, but it was me who answered him.

"You're not helping, Todd. Is there something else we can do for you?"

"You could let me watch you guys?"

I knew he was only joking, and I rolled my eyes.

"Get the fuck out!" Scott said, not laughing, and pointed at the door.

"You're going to be a lot less fun now," Todd said to me, pouting.

"I'll be just as fun, but Scott will be the one enjoying it."

"If I get any reports back from clients about you not fulfilling your job, we're going to talk about this *arrangement* again."

"Okay, Todd. But it's not going to be an issue. I promise."

He mumbled something about having to make a million phone calls and then left.

"Where were we?" I asked.

Scott smiled and removed the pillow. His cock was completely limp. I gave him a sad face.

"Hey, it wasn't going to hang around with my cousin in the room talking about you sucking his cock."

"Were you upset by that?" I asked.

"I can't say it was my favorite thing to hear, but I wasn't surprised."

"What *would* be your favorite thing to hear?" I asked seductively, taking his cock in my hand.

He thought for a moment and then frowned. "I don't want to tell you."

"Why not?" I asked, a little hurt that he didn't want to share.

"I know my audience." He laughed and pulled me in. "I hope I'll hear it one day."

I tried to let the matter drop as he kissed me, but I couldn't help that it tickled the back of my brain.

He was slowly removing my clothes, kissing the skin as it was exposed. I forced the thought out of my conscious mind. If Scott thought it would upset me, then it was best left unsaid. If I wanted to have him inside me tonight, I couldn't break the mood again. But I would have to for one other detail.

"Condoms are in my bag."

"We don't need them," he said, continuing to kiss me.

"Yes we do!"

"Ally, we're a couple. I'm not sleeping with anyone else, and I'm sure you always use condoms at work, am I right?"

"Always," I said.

"And you're on the pill?"

"Of course."

He smiled and continued to kiss me, but I put a hand against his chest. "Scott, I've never had sex without a condom, and I'm not starting tonight." He sat up and looked into my eyes. I wasn't sure what he was searching for but after a moment he nodded and reached onto the floor for my bag. He reappeared with a condom between his fingers and quickly slipped it on his already-hard dick.

"Thank you," I said, crawling across the bed to him.

I put my hands on his chest and tried to push him back so he was lying down again, but he grabbed my wrists and held them tightly.

"Let me be in control," he whispered.

It went against my very nature to let the man be in control. I had to have the power.

"I can't."

"Please trust me. I won't hurt you."

"Please don't push me, Scott. I'm doing the best I can."

His eyes bored into mine and I could see his silent request. *Trust me.* I wanted to. I didn't want to be the closed-off girl who couldn't let anyone in. I wanted this for myself.

I let my muscles relax, and he smiled when he felt me give in. I'd done the submissive thing with clients before, and I was sure I could do it for Scott.

He kissed my mouth again, which still was an exciting novelty for me. I ate him up eagerly, enjoying the feeling of his tongue. He was lying flat against my body, and he pressed one knee between my legs, edging them apart. I allowed his exploration, and soon his legs were between mine.

I could feel him at my entrance and I wanted to push down, to engulf him, but he'd asked to be in control, so I stayed still, waiting for him to move.

"I'm going to make love to you, Ally," he whispered before sucking my earlobe into his mouth.

I gasped as he entered me slowly, sheathing himself all the way to the hilt, and then rocking his hips back and forth in a slow rhythm. He was barely moving in and out, just rubbing us together.

His mouth was on mine again. I couldn't help it, my hips started to move with his, causing more exquisite friction.

"No, go slow," he said, pulling back to look into my eyes. "There's no rush."

"I need to feel it," I begged.

"You will. *We* will. Just enjoy this, baby."

His hips started their agonizingly slow movement again, and I almost cried in frustration. The slow burn was like torture. Beautiful, blissful torture.

Every part of our bodies was touching, and I'd never been in such an intimate embrace. I could feel him everywhere. Our legs were twined together, his torso was gliding over mine, and our arms wrapped around each other. Even our lips were connected, kissing softly as we rocked together.

"Ally," he breathed out.

"Faster," I begged.

He shook his head. "Just feel me."

He didn't speed up, but he did move his hips in and out a bit further, giving me that amazing pulling sensation. I tried to buck my hips to meet his, but he held me down on the mattress.

"There's no rush," he whispered in my ear.

"How can you stand it? I feel like I'm going to explode!"

He chuckled. "That's the whole point. Imagine feeling like this for an hour instead of just ten rapid minutes."

He was right. I'd conditioned my body to think of sex as a fast thing. Get in there, make him come, and then get out. I always thought that the orgasm was all that mattered. Get to it as fast as you can. But the buildup was just as important. I could see that now.

It was like I was having sex for the first time all over again. I'd never had slow sex before. In high school, it was always over quickly. Even though I had loved Nick and thought of what we did as making love, I could see now that it wasn't. Nick only cared about his own release, and as soon as he was done, we were both done…apparently. And with Todd, it was only ever hard and fast.

*This*, with Scott, was a new experience. Apart from the fact that his cock was inside me, I couldn't even relate the two acts together. The movements and sensations were completely different.

The slow burn built inside me in a way that made me feel like a pressure valve. I was going to burst if it kept mounting. Scott's hips were still moving slowly and deliberately, but every second or third thrust they would spasm a little, and I wondered if he was having as much trouble with our slow pace as I was.

My heart raced, and because his chest was flush against mine, I could feel his heartbeat, too. Our bodies glistened with sweat even though we were hardly working.

I glanced at the clock and saw that he'd been inside me for nearly twenty minutes. Normally we'd have been finished and onto round two by this time, but Scott didn't even seem close to being done with me.

"I want you to roll over," he whispered, nipping along my jaw.

He pulled out and I grabbed at his shoulder, wanting to pull him back in. I felt cold and only half myself after having him so close.

"Roll onto your side, Ally."

I did as he asked, curling my legs up. He lay behind me and spooned me, kissing the back of my neck as he entered me again. I'd thought we were in an intimate position before, but that was nothing compared to how we were now.

He thrust a little faster now, but we didn't lose any of the intimacy of being face-to-face. His hands had free rein over my body now that he wasn't lying on top of it, and he took full advantage. He sucked and nipped at my shoulder as his hands roamed over my stomach and breasts, pulling me closer to him.

"Fuck!" I breathed out as his hips pistoned.

"Don't swear this time."

"Why?"

"Swearing makes it cheap. We're not fucking so there's no need for the word."

I concentrated on other things I could say that would let him know how good I was feeling, but now that I'd been told *not* to say it, all that was running through my head was *Fuck! Fuck! Fuck! Fuck! Fuck!*

I was so conflicted. The sensation inside me was so intense that my body was begging for him to speed up and move harder, faster. But my mind wanted to allow the body to feel that good for as long as possible, and so I kept control of my hips.

I stayed as still as I could, allowing Scott to move and thrust as he wanted to. It was one of the hardest things I'd ever done. The instinct to climb up and ride him until my body exploded in bliss was overwhelming. The only thing that held me back was the knowledge that as soon as the orgasm hit, it would be over. And I wasn't ready for that.

"God, Ally, it feels so good inside you." His voice was husky, and it sounded like he was getting close.

"I want to ride you," I begged.

My muscles were starting to cramp from trying to hold them still, and I needed to stretch them out, to feel like I was contributing to what we were doing.

He groaned, and I smiled when I remembered how much he loved to see me above him.

"Slowly," he warned.

He rolled onto his back, and I settled myself on top of him, sinking down as slowly as I could. He closed his eyes and let out a soft hiss between his teeth. He was definitely close.

I didn't move up and down like a usually would; I wouldn't be able to stop myself from speeding up if I did that. Instead I just rocked my hips, moving him inside me without the in and out motion.

He grunted and stroked his open palm down over my breasts and stomach. I reached my arms up over my head, enjoying the pop of the joints in my back and shoulders. With my muscles looser, I could enjoy the internal sensations so much more.

"God. Yes," I moaned, holding in the "Fuck!" that tried to escape.

Scott's eyes were only half open, and he gazed up at me with a lazy smile. His eyes were filled with lust. I'd never seen anyone look as handsome as he did in that moment with his tousled hair and flushed cheeks.

He gasped. "You're so beautiful. I could watch you ride me all night long."

I gave my hips a quick buck in response to his words, and he grabbed them firmly, holding me still.

"Don't make me roll you over again," he warned, but his eyes were joking.

We'd been at it for over half an hour now, and I was ready to burst into flames. Everywhere our skin touched was like fire, and I wanted it to consume me. I would willingly welcome a burning death if this was the way I would go.

His body jerked beneath me, and he let out a soft grunt. "I'm so close."

"Me too."

He reached up and pulled me down so I was lying on his chest, the opposite of the position we'd started in. His lips captured mine, and he kissed me hungrily.

I couldn't stop my body from moving faster over his as the pleasure built, but he didn't hold me back this time. He was craving the friction just as much as I was. It was enough to bring me right to the brink.

"I'm going to come," I cried into his mouth.

"Mmm, enjoy it, baby."

I cried out in joy and arched my back as the orgasm exploded inside me. My muscles convulsed, and I was aware that Scott was shuddering beneath me, his whole body shaking.

"Yes, yes, so good," he groaned.

The waves of release in my body were not like any other orgasm I'd experienced. They felt amazing, but it was more than that. It wasn't just a physical release. My heart was glowing in my chest, and the usual dark feeling that came along with sex wasn't there. There was no need to feel powerful or strong. In fact, I was fragile and vulnerable in Scott's arms…and I *liked* it.

"Oh my God," I said once I'd been able to catch my breath.

I was sprawled across Scott's chest, which was rising and falling quickly with his own recovery.

"That was perfect," Scott said with a smile.

He kissed the top of my head and then tilted my face up so he could reach my lips. We kissed for a long time, just as slowly as our earlier movements had been. Not for any end result, just to be connected to each other. Scott and I had made love, and it was beautiful.

# CHAPTER SEVENTEEN

"**A**lly."

I heard my name being whispered and felt a soft hand on my shoulder.

"Ally."

I opened one eye. The room was still pitch dark, so I groaned and rolled away from the voice. A low chuckle rumbled near my ear. "Wake up, sleeping beauty."

"Leave me alone," I grumbled.

Suddenly the warm cocoon of blankets was ripped away, and I was left shivering on the bed.

"What are you doing?" I demanded, trying to give Scott an evil glare while keeping my eyes closed.

"You have to get up. We have to leave for the airport in a few minutes."

"A few minutes?" I stared at the clock and saw that we only had about half an hour to get to the airport or we'd miss the flight to Miami. "Why didn't you get me up earlier?"

I jumped off the bed and ran to the bathroom. Scott laughed as he followed me, mumbling something about trying to wake me up for fifteen minutes.

The bathroom light burned my eyes as I brushed my teeth and combed my hair. There was no time for makeup or a shower. My only consolation was that at this early hour, hopefully the other passengers would look as dreadful as I did.

I spent the taxi ride to the airport dozing on Scott's shoulder. I only really woke up when we got to the check-in line and I realized that I didn't have a ticket. Scott had only invited me to Miami a few hours before.

"Good morning, sir. May I see your I.D.?" the lady asked.

Scott handed over some paperwork and smiled at the woman.

"I'll need a second ticket as well, please," he said politely.

The woman clicked her false nails on the keyboard in front of her and frowned.

"I'm afraid that business class is sold out on your flight. I can offer you a second ticket in economy class," she offered.

"That's not acceptable." The look on Scott's face reminded me that he'd said he was used to getting his own way.

"I'm sorry, sir."

"It's all right, Scott. I don't mind traveling in coach," I said, but he ignored what I'd said.

"There *are* several economy class seats available, Mr. Walker." Her fingers tapped nervously on the keyboard waiting for him to make a decision.

"Fine. I will swap my business class ticket and take two economy seats."

She typed on her keyboard again and then looked up at me.

"Your name, ma'am?"

"Alison Mitchell." I handed her my driver's license, and she entered my details into her system.

The irritation disappeared from Scott's face for a moment, and he looked at me with wonder. He mouthed my full name and smiled.

"You'll make the final call if you hurry," she said, handing us our boarding passes.

We raced through security and made it to the gate just in time to board. We took our seats at the very back of the plane and were airborne before my tired brain really caught up to the fact that it wasn't curled up in bed anymore. What a morning!

"How long is this flight?" I asked.

Scott was shifting in his seat and pushing the buttons on the console. He did not look happy.

"What's wrong?" I asked, forgetting my earlier question.

"Don't these go back further?" he asked, pushing the button on his armrest so the chair tilted back slightly.

I shook my head.

"That's it?" he said. "It's still completely upright. I thought they'd recline a little bit more than *that*."

"Have you only ever flown business class?" I asked.

He smirked. "Maybe."

I laughed.

The plane took off and once the seat belt sign turned off, I reclined my chair and tried to doze.

After having late-night visits from both Zach and Todd, and then the lovemaking, I'd barely had an hour of sleep. I drifted off easily, but kept being woken up by the chair moving and loud, annoyed sighs from next to me. Finally I gave up and turned my head, watching Scott as he contorted his body in the chair.

"Can't sleep?" I asked.

"These chairs are impossible."

I rolled my eyes and put my seat in the upright position again. Scott accidentally kicked the seat in front. "Sorry," he mumbled to the person seated in front of us.

"Hey," I said, reaching out to take his hand. "What's up with you? I've never seen you like this."

"I wanted to take you on a special holiday, show you a good time and…It just hasn't started out all that well."

I smiled. "Scott, I've never been to Miami before, so this is special for me."

He digested that and then smiled. "I wonder if we can get something for breakfast. I could use a coffee." He stretched up to look over the seat in front.

"You know what would make this even more special?" I asked wickedly.

He turned me eagerly, obviously wanting to make me happy.

"I'd like to join the Mile High Club," I whispered. My words hung in the air for a second. I wasn't sure if he had heard me.

"You naughty girl." He chuckled.

"Are you interested in membership?"

Scott's face went serious, and he looked up over my shoulder. I spun around to see a flight attendant smiling politely at us.

"Can I get you anything to eat or drink?" she asked.

"Two coffees," Scott said automatically.

"Of course, sir." She poured our drinks and moved to the row behind us.

Scott sipped his coffee and watched me out of the corner of his eye.

"You're thinking about it, aren't you," I teased.

"Thinking about what?"

"About taking me against the sink in the tiny bathroom."

He choked on his coffee and wiped the drips that had fallen onto his shirt. I drank my coffee in larger gulps than usual and then, without saying a word, I folded up my tray table, unfastened my seatbelt, and stood. I looked down, winked at Scott, and walked to the bathroom.

Just as I went inside, I quickly glanced back over my shoulder to make sure he'd seen which stall I entered, and sure enough, he was meerkatting over the row of seats. I counted to ten in my head and just as I finished, there was a soft knock on the door. With a cocky smile, I opened the door quickly for him to slip inside.

"What if people see that we're in here together?" he hissed, locking the door.

"Then they'll be jealous."

Scott was still tense.

"Look, if you're not comfortable, we'll just go back out to our seats and try to get some sleep," I offered. "But last night you showed me what it was like to make love, something that is comfortable for *you*. Now let me show you what is comfortable for *me*."

I stroked my hand down his chest and started rubbing his groin through his pants.

"And what might that be?"

I leaned in, nibbling along his jaw until I reached his ear. "Taking risks."

He nodded slightly, and I took that as approval to move forward.

"This is going to be quick and intense. Don't even take off your clothes," I whispered.

Six frantic minutes later, I slipped through the door, opening it only enough to fit through in case someone was standing right there and could catch a glimpse of Scott still inside.

Luck was on our side, because there was no one waiting to use the bathroom, and most of the people were dozing, reading, or had headphones on. Only one or two people glanced up as I walked past, but none of them gave me much notice. Only the elderly lady sitting opposite me smiled as I sat down.

I settled into my seat just as Scott stepped out of the bathroom. I made a mental note never to play poker with him; his "straight face" was terrible. He blushed a deep red and practically ran back to his seat.

"Don't be embarrassed, dear," the older lady said once he was seated next to me. "If my husband and I had looked like you two, we would have enjoyed coitus every chance we got."

Scott flushed even more, and I offered her a polite smile as I gently patted his arm.

# CHAPTER EIGHTEEN

Scott walked through the automatic doors as if it was the most natural thing in the world to walk from clean, air-conditioned air into a wet blanket. The Floridian climate was thick and damp, and I felt like it swallowed me up. I was just starting to feel like I could breathe properly when we pulled up outside his condo.

I wasn't sure what I expected Scott's home to look like, but it certainly wasn't what was in front of me. I'd always pictured him in a high-rise apartment with sleek, modern furniture and neutral colors. That couldn't be farther from the truth.

The condo was in a multi-story building, but it wasn't all glass and metal like I saw it in my mind. It was covered in warm terracotta bricks, surrounded by palm trees, and right on the beach. The inside was just as surprising. Scott lived in the penthouse which took up the whole top floor. The longest wall in the apartment was one huge bookcase which led to a kitchen that was all modern appliances and granite counters. The furniture was polished wood, and everything was in warm shades on the red spectrum. It reminded me of a sunset. The room smelled like cedar oil and cinnamon. The entire back wall was floor-to-ceiling windows that overlooked the ocean. Both the sky and the water were so clear that it was almost impossible to see where they joined. It was just one huge expanse of blue.

"Welcome to your new home for the next week…or however long you want," Scott said, dropping our bags on the couch and waving his arms around.

"It's amazing!"

"Would you like to have a nap? We haven't had much sleep," Scott asked.

I *was* tired. My body was exhausted, but my mind was racing. I walked over to the wall of windows and looked down at the beach. The sand was as white as snow, and small waves crashed onto the shore, creating a foamy border between the sand and the water.

"Can we go down to the beach?" I asked.

"Whatever you like," Scott said. He was smiling at me as I stared out the window.

I changed into my bikini and some denim cutoffs, and Scott brought two towels from a closet.

The sand crunched like snow under our bare feet, almost squeaking as we walked over it. The breeze coming off the water was refreshing and cool enough to combat the humidity.

"I could spend the entire week lying here," I said, breathing in the salty air and spinning around on the sand.

"I certainly hope not. I have plans for you that definitely need four walls and a bed."

I laughed. "I'm sure people have sex on this beach all the time."

"Not likely. This is my private beach. This stretch—" he held his arms wide "—is the property of the penthouse apartment."

I looked back and forth along the shore and noticed that on both sides of us, the beach was packed. Surfers, swimmers, volleyball players, families picnicking and tanning were everywhere the eye could see, except around us. We were alone.

"You have your own beach?" I gasped. "What else about you don't I know?"

He smiled and put his hands in the pockets of his cargo shorts. He looked so comfortable, and I wondered how much of his life would be a shock to me. So far everything else had been unexpected.

"Well, I have a boat," he offered with a slight shrug.

"Is it a yacht?" I asked.

"A speed boat. Have you ever been in one?"

"The only boat I've ever been on is the ferry to New Jersey. Does that even count?" I laughed.

"That's like comparing a fifteen-year-old arthritic Saint Bernard to a greyhound!"

"Ah. But they're both dogs!" I said, proud of my logic. "I can't believe you own your own beach. If no one else is having sex here, then we should give it a go."

"No way. I did the plane thing because nobody could see us. This is way too exposed." His voice was firm.

"We'll see. I have a feeling that I'm going to get you naked out here before the week is done."

He held out his hand for me to shake. "Challenge accepted."

I laughed as we shook. I knew I was going to have to use all my skills, but I was determined to have him on the beach before I went back to New York.

"I can't believe you can cook!" I said, wishing it wasn't bad manners to lick my plate so I could devour all the sauce. I ran my finger along the plate's rim and popped it into my mouth with a sheepish smile.

Scott grinned and cleared my plate from the table. "I'm glad you enjoyed it."

"Let me clean up. It's only fair."

I followed him to the kitchen. When I cooked, the kitchen looked like a bomb had gone off, but all of his counters were clear of pots and pans.

"No need," Scott said, placing our plates into the full dishwasher. He pressed a button and turned to me with a smile. "All taken care of."

"So we're free to do other things?" I kept my voice innocent, but he saw my underlying intent.

"Want to watch some TV?" he asked.

"Not really."

I wrapped my arms around his waist and got up on my tiptoes, leaning in to kiss him. Scott pecked my lips and then my forehead before reaching behind himself and removing my arms, placing them carefully at my sides. I cocked my head.

"Want to read one of the new manuscripts I'm considering offering a contract to?" he asked.

He moved past me and soon emerged from his office with a stack of papers.

"Will you sit with me?" he asked, settling on the couch.

I sat and curled my legs underneath me. He passed me half the papers and began to read the ones still in his hands.

"What do I do?" I asked.

He glanced up. "Just read. When you've finished, let me know if it's worth buying."

I loved reading. I actually spent a lot of my free time with my nose in a book, but that wasn't what I'd had in mind for my first night at Scott's house.

"Don't you have people who do the reading for you?" I asked, putting the papers on the sofa next to me.

"Of course. But acquiring new material is one of my favorite parts of this business, so I like to read some of the manuscripts myself. You're right though; most of the submitted manuscripts are read by the acquisitions team."

I snuggled into his side and traced patterns on his chest with my fingers.

"You're not reading." He didn't look up from the manuscript.

"I'm not in the mood," I said honestly.

"Want to turn the TV on?"

I sighed. "No."

Scott's eyes quickly scanned a page, then he put his papers down and turned to face me. "What's wrong?"

"There's nothing *wrong*. I just thought new couples weren't supposed to be able to keep their hands off each other."

Scott laughed. "Trust me—I plan to have my hands all over you for a great portion of this week, but there's more to relationships than just sex, Ally."

"I know there is."

"And I have to keep up with my work."

"I know that, too." I felt like a sulking child, and I wished that I'd never brought it up. "Sorry."

Scott pulled me into his lap.

"You have nothing to be sorry for. The truth is that I was hoping we could have a night without sex. I should have told you that was my plan instead of just hoping you'd pick up the hint."

"You *don't* want to have sex?"

"It's not that I don't want to. Sex is all we've had up to this point, and that's not necessarily a bad thing, but we need to have more than that or we won't work. We don't have to read, but let's spend some time together with our clothes on."

"Maybe a walk on your beach?" I offered.

Scott laughed. "Not a chance."

"Oh!" I realized he must have assumed I was trying to make good on my challenge. "I didn't mean for sex. I just thought it would be nice to have a moonlit walk. You can do a lot of things in New York, but a nighttime beach walk isn't one of them."

Scott kissed my forehead and helped me to my feet. "That sounds perfect."

The moon was reflected on the water, making it look like two silver orbs mirroring each other. I took a deep breath of the salty air.

"It's so beautiful out here," I said.

Scott's hand slipped into mine and he led me down to the shore. The warm, foamy water lapped at our bare feet.

"Yes, it is." He picked up a handful of white sand and threw it at the water. It scattered and fell like raindrops, making a soft hissing sound.

I waded out until I was ankle-deep, but Scott didn't move forward with me, so I couldn't go any farther without letting go of his hand, which I didn't want to do.

"Come in with me?"

"We're not wearing bathing suits."

"No one is around. The water feels great."

"Ally," he warned when I reached to pull my shirt over my head.

"Come on, Scott. Play with me." I reached down and splashed water in his direction.

Dark spots spread over his shirt. He swore and stared down at himself with his mouth open. I froze, unsure if he was actually angry. I really didn't know him well enough to gauge his reaction.

"You're in so much trouble!" He laughed and yanked me backward where he caught me in a tight embrace.

"You'll pay for that," he whispered in my ear.

Before I could reply, he ran, pulling me along with him into deeper water, and dunked us both. I gasped for air, but Scott was laughing when he emerged.

I swam away from him and floated just out of his reach. "I thought you didn't want to swim."

"My priorities changed," he said, shaking his head and spraying me with water from his dripping hair.

"Well, you do know it's war now," I warned.

"I'm terrified."

"Oh, you should be."

He surged forward and pulled me toward him, locking his hands behind my back.

"So you got what you wanted—we're swimming. What now?" His eyes were gray under the moonlight. My heart swelled as I gazed upon his face.

I leaned forward and kissed him. He wasn't expecting me to move with such force, and we both floated backward through the water.

"Ally, don't," he said, breaking off the kiss.

I could feel his erection against my leg, so I knew he was turned on. Frustration swelled up inside me.

"Why?" I demanded.

"Someone could see us."

I let go of his neck and allowed the water to move us apart.

"There's nothing wrong with kissing, Scott. It's not perverted, it's fucking normal."

"Hey, there's no need to be angry," he said, reaching for me.

I let him pull me in but didn't wrap myself around him.

"Don't be mad. You're right, there's nothing wrong with kissing." He wiped some wet hair that was stuck on my forehead.

"I'm not mad. It just feels like you're not that happy to have me here."

"I'm *so* glad you're here with me. It feels right to have you in my world. I never want you to go back to New York."

I smirked. "Never, huh?"

His eyes darkened, and he kissed me. He tasted like salt from the ocean. I laughed when he nibbled my bottom lip and along my jaw up to my ear.

"Never," he whispered.

"Let's just focus on right now." I was trying my best to do the girlfriend thing even though it went against my core being, but talking about *forever* was a bit much for me.

"Okay." He pressed an open-mouthed kiss to my throat. "Right now I want to take you back to my bedroom."

We made love again that night. It was slow and sweet, just as it had been the night before in my bed back home.

By the time the weekend arrived, all we'd done was lie on the beach, shop, read, and eat. It was lovely and relaxing, but not the sex-filled tropical escape that I'd imagined. We'd made love once every night since I'd arrived and then fallen asleep in each other's arms. It was slow, passionate, and blissful, but I was craving something more. It seemed that Scott didn't want to just *fuck* anymore. Physically, I was completely fulfilled with Scott. I'd never had so many orgasms in my entire life, but there was something primal that I wasn't getting from our encounters.

As we lay in bed on my fourth night in Miami, curled together in sheets that were bathed in moonlight, I broached the subject. "Are you happy?" I asked.

"I'm about as happy as I could be," he said, pressing a soft kiss to my forehead.

"And the sex…is that okay?"

"Ally." He laughed, tilting my head up to look at him. "You can't seriously be doubting your skills."

"I just want to make sure you're satisfied. If you wanted something more, you could tell me."

"I am blissfully satisfied."

I chewed my bottom lip. Maybe I should just let it drop. I could get my more primal needs met by my clients.

"Wait, are *you* not satisfied?" he asked, sitting up and causing me to slide off his chest and onto the pillow.

"What? Oh, yes!" I assured him a little too adamantly.

"Ally. The truth, please."

I let out a defeated sigh and sat up as well.

"It's not that I'm *un*satisfied, it's just that I'm used to sex being more…I don't know…desperate?"

"Desperate?" He raised an eyebrow, and his forehead crinkled.

"That's probably the wrong way to describe it. Maybe 'energetic' is a better word. Do you move so slowly because you don't feel the passion to go hard and fast?"

I could hear the insecurity in my voice, and I hated that I was making myself vulnerable. I wished I'd just kept my mouth shut.

"Honey," he whispered, pulling me into his arms. "I don't want to fuck you hard and fast every time we have sex. Sometimes I want to love you, slowly, for hours. It's a good thing."

"All right," I said, but I wasn't convinced.

I knew men's sexual appetites, and no guy had ever paid me for slow sex before. If that was what they wanted or craved, then surely I'd have had a few guys fuck me like that. Hard, fast, intense. That's what men wanted.

"You don't like making love to me?" I could hear the hurt in his voice.

"Of course I do! I guess I just miss the other kind of sex, as well. It doesn't always have to be soft and slow, you know — I like it when you want me so much that you can't control yourself."

"You want me to lose control, huh?" His voice had taken on a gravelly quality, and there was a glint in his eye that hadn't been there a second ago.

"I'd like you to want me that much."

He grabbed me roughly by the shoulders and pushed me back onto the bed, crushing me beneath him.

"How's this?" he asked, kissing my neck.

I giggled and squirmed beneath him. "It's good."

He bit my shoulder, and I squealed in surprise.

"Is this what you want?" he murmured against my throat before trailing his tongue along my collar bone.

I froze. I didn't want him to do anything that he didn't want to do.

"Is it what *you* want?" I countered.

He propped himself above me on his elbows and looked into my eyes.

"I want to make you happy."

"How happy?" I asked, sensing an opportunity.

"As happy as possible."

I grinned. "Let's go out to the beach," I whispered.

His smile dropped, and I knew that I'd pushed him too far.

"I'm not comfortable doing that," he said.

"How about we meet in the middle?" I asked.

"Ally, I don't think having sex in the middle of the street or in a parking lot is a good idea either."

"How about on the balcony?"

"The balcony?"

"It still has all the benefits of being outside—the fresh air, the moonlight—but we can't be seen." I couldn't believe the idea had never occurred to him.

"How do you know that we can't be seen?"

"We're on the top floor of the building."

"I guess that's all right," he said thoughtfully.

We were both still naked from making love earlier, and the moonlight made his skin shine like silver as I took his hand and led him out the glass double doors onto the balcony.

"Isn't it nice out here?" I asked.

A light wind came off the ocean and a million tiny stars sparkled above us.

"Can you feel the breeze on your skin?" I asked.

He closed his eyes and breathed in the ocean air, his chest expanding and then falling slowly as he exhaled.

"I could bring a chair out," he said.

"We don't need a chair. All we need is each other…and this."

I flicked a condom at him and walked over to the railing and turned my back on him, enjoying the view. I felt him approach from behind and press his chest against my back.

"It's so beautiful," I said.

He hummed, kissing the back of my neck. He wrapped his arms around me and stroked over my bare belly and down between my legs. I gasped as he found my clit and trapped it between his thumb and index finger.

"You want this?" he asked huskily.

"Yes," I breathed.

"You want me to fuck you."

"Yes."

"Say it."

"I want you to fuck me, Scott."

He growled in my ear and roughly pulled my hips back so I was leaning on the railing. His hand pushed my head forward and then stroked all the way down my spine. I eagerly spread my legs.

"Fuck me," I begged.

He slammed into me without warning and shoved me against the railing. I cried out from shock and pleasure as he thrust inside me. This was not making love. He was moving hard and fast and my legs were already starting to feel boneless.

I braced my body and looked out at the waves crashing on the beach as he moved.

"You like this? Is this what you want?" he grunted.

"God, yes! It feels so good," I cried, not bothering to try to be quiet.

A sea bird squawked somewhere below in reply. In the far distance on the public beach, I could see the silhouette of a couple walking hand-in-hand, but they were so far away that I knew there was no way they could see us.

Scott moved his hands from my hips and placed them on the railing on either side of my body, pinning me between him and the barrier. He groaned and thrust furiously.

"Fuck, Ally." He leaned over me and bit my shoulder again, trailing his tongue down my back.

His left hand abandoned the railing and grasped at my breasts; it was cold from the metal and my hard nipple stiffened more at his touch. The loud slapping of his hips smacking against my ass echoed around the balcony and off the glass wall of his bedroom like a round of applause, encouraging us along.

His hand, now warm from my skin, slid down my body from my breast, over my stomach and between my legs. He rubbed my clit frantically, sending me over the precipice I was balanced on.

"Yes, fuck!" I yelled as my orgasm exploded and my legs almost gave out. I was sure that if Scott hadn't been pinning me upright, I would have sank to my knees.

His hips jerked wildly as he came, roaring his release into the night. He collapsed onto my back, and I became aware of how sweaty we were. Out of the air-conditioned bedroom, the humidity had swallowed and drenched us.

We were both breathing heavily, and I enjoyed the cool sensation of the metal and glass against the front of my body. He pulled his softening cock out and kissed the back of my neck.

"Was that *satisfying?*" he asked smugly.

I laughed and turned to face him.

"Consider me more than satisfied. See, fucking isn't so bad, is it?"

"Fucking definitely has its good points," he agreed, grinning.

"And outside is nice," I prompted.

"When nobody is around to watch."

We both leaned on the rail, still naked, and looked out over the ocean. The temperature was dropping, and the breeze was starting to have a chill to it. Out of the corner of my eye, I could tell he was watching me, and I turned to face him.

"What are you thinking about?" I asked.

"I was just thinking of telling you something, but I have a question first."

"Okay."

"Do you hate the slow, sensual sex?"

"No!" I assured him. "I enjoy it very much. I just *also* enjoy the urgent, passionate sex we just had. I think participating in both regularly would be the perfect combination."

He nodded, smiling slightly. The moon reflected off his hair, making it more golden than usual, and his eyes were almost silver in the pale light.

"You wanted to tell me something," I prompted.

He bit his lip nervously and cupped his hand to my face.

"Please don't freak out," he whispered.

"I won't." Despite my pledge, I my stomach tightened.

He smiled down at me, and his eyes radiated love. *Oh!* Suddenly I knew what he was going to say. I tensed, hoping that if I was prepared, I could contain my reaction, but as I looked up into his eyes, I didn't feel panicked — or anything negative at all. My mouth dropped open in surprise because I couldn't wait to hear the words.

"No, please let me say it," Scott said, obviously mistaking expression. "I think I'm in love with you, Ally. Well, I know I am. I love you."

Despite the cool air, warmth rushed through my body.

I tried to say it back, I *wanted* to say it back, but I found the words hard to get out.

If I said those words, there was no taking them back. I was in this all the way, no turning back.

Scott's eyes sparkled with anticipation, reflecting the starlight from above. When I looked at his face, I knew that I loved him. I could trust him. He wasn't going to hurt me.

"I…I love you, Scott," I said softly.

"You don't have to say it if you're not ready," he said, but I could see the huge grin that spread over his face, radiating pure joy.

"No, I want to say it."

"I want you to say it."

"I love you," I said again, testing the words in my mouth.

Scott turned out to the beach and leaned over the railing. "*She loves me!*" he yelled out into the night, and his voice echoed off the surrounding buildings.

He scooped me into his arms, and we went back into the bedroom.

# CHAPTER NINETEEN

Saturday morning, we ate breakfast on the balcony and watched the early morning surfers.

"So, it's your last day here. What would you like to do?" Scott asked.

"I don't know. I think I've done everything."

"You've hardly done anything!" he protested.

"I've shopped so much that I think I'm going to get charged for excess baggage, and my tan is so dark that my family may no longer recognize me," I joked.

He looked out at the water.

"Would you like to go out on my boat? I haven't taken it out in a few months. We could go north to Pompano Beach."

"I can't wait to try out your *greyhound!*"

He hadn't been wrong about the boat being fast. My hair whipped around my face, stinging where it hit my skin and eyes. I struggled to grab it all and secure it in a loose bun high on my head to keep it out of the way.

We raced across the water, bouncing off the waves like we were hovering over the surface. The wind was so loud that, combined with the roar of the motor, we couldn't really talk to each other.

On our left, the coastline sped past us in a blur, and on our right there was nothing but open water. I held on and took in the tropical paradise until he docked the boat and tied it up.

"Your hand, m'lady," Scott said, offering to help me off the boat.

After all the bouncing on the water, my legs were a bit unstable on the ground, but Scott was more than happy to support me as we walked up to the beach. He had a small cooler in his hand and pulled out two Coronas, handing me one.

We sat on the sand under the shade of a coconut tree and drank our beers, watching a group of people playing volleyball. The players were actually pretty talented, diving and yelling as they played.

"I didn't realize there would be so many people here," I said.

"Are you suddenly shy?" Scott had removed his shirt and was sitting with his hands stretched out behind him so he could look up into the sky.

"I'm not, but you are. How are we supposed to fuck?"

He laughed and looked around to see if we were within earshot of everyone. "As wonderful as that would be, and as much as I desire you every minute of the day, we don't have to fuck *all the time*."

"But a day *with* sex is better than a day without."

"Who said we had to have a day without sex? We will have lots and *lots* of sex tonight."

I rolled my eyes. "You know what I mean."

He moved over so he was lying next to me in the shade.

"Trust me. The sight of you in that bikini is driving me crazy, but I want to spend some time with you. No sex. Just time together. Okay?" He leaned in and kissed me.

I sighed and rolled onto my stomach so my tan would be even. I had hoped that our time on the balcony the night before had loosened Scott up a little, but it didn't appear that anything had changed.

In the afternoon, we walked hand-in-hand up the beach and waded through a rock pool that we discovered. Scott's good mood was ruined when a crab decided that his big toe looked threatening, and it clamped its claw on.

I squealed as I tried to grab for it, and its slippery shell was hard to grasp, but after a moment of wrestling with the crustacean I managed to yank it off and drop it. It scuttled away and disappeared behind a rock. Scott swore at it.

"Are you all right?" I asked, bending down to inspect his toe.

"It's fine."

"No, you're bleeding!"

"Let's just go home," he grumbled as he hobbled back over the rocks to the beach.

The sun was just starting to set and the sky was turning pink on the horizon. The wind had picked up, and the ride back was so choppy that I started to feel seasick.

When we finally staggered back to his apartment, we both showered, but neither of us felt any better. My nausea was made worse by the sound of the crashing waves through the window, and Scott was limping. We both ended up watching TV on the couch, not even touching.

So much for the romantic last night together that we'd planned.

Our flight back to New York was very different than the trip to Miami. Scott had booked early enough to get both of us business class tickets, but his mood was very low. He'd barely spoken all morning and had stared out the window for most of the flight. When I reached to hold his hand he moved it at the last second to scratch his leg and then held it in his lap, out of my reach.

"Is everything okay?" I finally asked once we'd collected my bags from the carousel.

"Fine."

I let him continue to stew in silence until we reached the line of people waiting for taxis. Then I pulled him aside and looked him in the eye. "Scott, what is it?"

He let out a defeated sigh. "I don't want to be back here."

"You only have a four hour meeting." I laughed, relieved that his issue didn't have anything to do with me.

"No, I mean I don't want *you* to be back here. I'm going to go to my meeting and fly home and you'll be here, fucking other men."

A few people's heads turned in our direction, so I pulled him farther away from everyone, behind a coffee kiosk.

"Why is that suddenly a problem *now?* You weren't worried about that yesterday."

"Yesterday I still had you safely in my bed."

"Scott," I said in what I hoped was a consoling voice. "I love you." Each time I said the words they came easier. I found that I actually enjoyed saying them.

He pulled me into a tight hug and rested his chin on the top of my head. "I love you."

"Please don't worry. The other men only get my body. You get my mind, my heart, and my soul. Those are only for you."

He frowned.

"Are you greedy?" I teased, trying to make him smile. "You want everything?"

He tried to smile but couldn't hold it. "I just want you to myself. The thought of other men touching you makes me sick."

"So don't think about it. Lots of people have long-distance relationships, and they're hard, but they can work if you really want them to. If you really love each other."

"Those people aren't fucking around."

"Neither am I! I'm *working*." I was getting sick of having the same conversation. Either he was going to accept the situation or he wasn't. There wasn't a halfway here. It had to either be the bed or the beach. There was no balcony this time.

"I know. I know." He ran his hand through his hair and then back down, scrubbing over his face. "I'm doing my best to be okay with this."

"Come on. Let's not ruin our last few minutes together. Please don't be sad."

He glanced at his watch and nodded. "I do have to get going. My meeting starts in an hour."

We rejoined the taxi line and waited, holding hands but not talking until we reached the head of the line. I tried to make Scott take the first cab that appeared, but he assured me that he would prefer to see me off, so I climbed inside the car. I quickly lowered the window and knelt on the seat so my torso was sticking out the window.

"I love you. I love you. I love you," I said, pulling him against the car door to kiss him.

He smiled against my mouth, and I was glad that we weren't having a sad goodbye. It would only be a week until I saw him again, but I had to admit that there was a sick sensation in my stomach at the thought of one hundred and sixty-eight long hours without him.

When I walked in the front door and dropped my bags on the floor, Jamie jumped up off the couch and tackled me with a hug.

"You're home!" she cheered. "How was it? I bet it was amazing!"

"I had a great time."

She pulled me over to the couch and ran to the kitchen, appearing a second later with a bottle of champagne. She popped the cork and offered me the bottle. I took a long swig and then gave it back.

"Tell me all about it," she gushed.

I told her about my week with Scott and she asked lots of questions, making me give explicit details about every aspect of the trip, including our adventure on the balcony. To Jamie, there were no boundaries between friends.

"I like your skin this tanned. What color would you say you are so I can ask the tanning studio for it?"

I looked down at my arm and shrugged. "Miami bronze?" I joked.

"I think that's actually on their list!"

I unpacked my bag and looked around. It was still my bedroom, exactly the same as it had been a week ago when I'd been Ally the prostitute. Single Ally. Broken Ally.

But everything inside me had changed so dramatically that it felt strange to be back here. I realized that I'd held onto *Ally* for so long that I'd let her become who I was. I'd grown so used to keeping Alison locked away that I'd almost forgotten how to let her out.

But Scott had set her free.

I missed Scott. It was the only thing I could think of that could be the cause of the ache in my chest and the hollow pit in my stomach. I'd been home for one day and already my body craved his.

"Why are you so mopey?" Jamie asked as she sipped her coffee.

"I'm not moping."

She laughed. "You're pouting right now. Look at that bottom lip."

I straightened out my mouth and shrugged my shoulders.

"Oh, I get it. You miss your boy. You've got the love aches."

"I don't have the *love aches*," I lied.

"You need to get laid. When has Todd got you back on the books?"

"Tonight."

I couldn't tell her that the thought of having sex with other men turned my stomach.

"Perfect. Go and fuck that love out of your system. By the time you get home tonight you'll be saying, 'Scott who?'"

"Yeah." I laughed, but it wasn't genuine. I didn't want to forget about Scott. What had happened to me? A few days in a topical paradise in the embrace of *that man* and suddenly Alison was in control.

"You're right," I said, more adamantly. "I just need a good fucking."

My cell phone rang, and Scott's name flashed on the screen. I went to my bedroom and closed the door before answering.

"Hey, you," I said.

"Hey, yourself." He sounded tense. Something was wrong.

"How are you?"

He let out a long sigh. "I miss you like crazy."

I smiled. "Me too."

"Are you working tonight?" The tension in his voice increased.

"Yeah, I have two appointments."

I wanted for him to say something, anything, but there was only silence on the other end of the phone.

"What are you up to tonight?" I asked, trying to keep the conversation going.

"I might fly to New York," he said nonchalantly, but I could feel an undercurrent of something else.

"Scott," I warned.

"I know, I know. I promised I'd be okay with it, but it's hard, Ally. The thought of some other guy, *two* other guys, touching you — it's going to drive me insane."

Pain burst in my chest. I could hear the words leading toward the inevitable breakup conversation. I'd been so stupid to think that I could have a relationship. I'd *known* that Scott wasn't comfortable with my work. Had I thought he'd just suddenly be fine with it? I was stupid if I had.

"So, you're ending this." It wasn't a question. I knew it was true. I tried to keep my voice hard and level while my heart started to crack. The pain was coming, and I was terrified.

"No! I don't want that. I'm just saying that this is hard for me."

"It's hard for me too."

He snorted in disbelief, and my jaw tightened. As if I wanted dozens of men touching me when I was aching for only *his* hands, *his* lips. The pain that was blossoming in my chest started to harden like ice and turned into anger.

"I could be there in a few hours." His voice was soft, tentative.

"Don't you *dare* show up at my door tonight," I threatened. "We made a deal before I agreed to any of this that you wouldn't stop me from working."

"I *know*, and I want to stand by that, but I just need to see you."

I exhaled heavily. "Scott, I've just taken a week off work. I can't ask Todd for more time off if you come into town. I have responsibilities."

"I wish your responsibilities weren't to fuck other men."

"And I wish I were a multimillionaire with an apartment in Paris, but life isn't like that."

"Your life *could* be like that. I could buy you a French apartment."

"Don't be ridiculous! You've only known me a few weeks."

"Ally, I love you. I know we haven't known each other very long, but I believe that you're the girl I'm meant to be with. I want to share everything I have, everything I *am*, with you. That includes my money."

"No."

Silence. I glanced at the clock and saw that I only had thirty minutes to get to my first appointment. I didn't have time for an argument.

"Can we talk about this later? I really have to get going."

"To work?"

"Yes. I have to go to work. I don't want this to be a fight. Please."

He didn't say anything.

"I'll talk you later, okay? I'll call you when I get home," I said.

"I don't want you to go." His voice was as cold as ice, and it sent a shiver down my spine. I'd never heard him talk like that.

"I'll call you later." I hung up the phone before he could say anything else. There was no point continuing the conversation, because we were never going to agree, and I was beginning to see that he wasn't going to back down.

# CHAPTER TWENTY

Just as I stepped into the lobby of the hotel, my phone rang. Scott again, of course. It was his fifth call since I'd hung up on him and left home. This guy couldn't take a hint. I switched my phone to silent, something I usually never did when I was working in case Todd called. But I couldn't have Scott calling all through my appointment.

I avoided the expectant look of the receptionist and walked straight past her to the elevators. My call sheet said that my client, Theo, was in room 1217. I stepped into the elevator and pressed the button for the twelfth floor. The phone vibrated in my bag, and I tried with all my strength to ignore it. Finally, it stopped. I grabbed it and switched it completely off.

I pictured Scott's face when the call went directly to voice mail and my chest tightened. If he thought this wasn't hard for me then he was crazy.

I found the room and rolled my shoulders a few times before knocking. A red-haired guy, probably in his late twenties, opened the door and grinned.

"Theo?" I asked.

"Yes. Are you Ally?"

I smiled. "It's nice to meet you."

He stood in the doorway staring at me.

"Can I come in?" I asked.

"Oh! Sure." He stepped aside and closed the door behind me.

I could feel the nervous energy coming off him in waves. Poor guy. To help him relax I took my iPod out of my bag and put on some slow, seductive music.

"How are you tonight?" I sat on the end of the bed and crossed my legs, bouncing my foot.

He swallowed visibly and stayed by the door. "I'm…good."

"Why don't you come sit here by me?" I coaxed, patting the duvet.

He walked robotically over and sat on the other side of the bed, as far from me as he could get. That wasn't going to work! I slid along the length of the mattress until I was right next to him. He swallowed thickly again and kept his gaze locked on the floor.

Theo smelled of bar soap and toothpaste and I appreciated that he'd cleaned up before I'd arrived. Many men weren't so considerate.

"Hey there," I whispered, running my fingers gently up his thigh. His leg jolted but he still didn't look at me. "There's no need to be nervous. I'm here to make you feel good. There's nothing to be scared of."

His eyes shot up and met mine. I could see hope, longing, and desire burning inside. His eyes were a different color, bright green, but something about the deep emotions that were bubbling just underneath the surface reminded me of Scott's blue ones.

I shook my head and kept my gaze lower, away from his eyes.

"Do you have something for me?" I asked.

It was so much easier when guys had the money ready or slipped it into my hand discretely. It made me feel less like I was selling myself.

"Oh!" He shot off the bed and grabbed his wallet off the bedside table, riffling through it. He handed me a wad of fifty dollar bills, all perfectly flattened and turned in the same direction. I wondered how long he had spent counting and arranging it.

"Thank you." I slipped the money into my bag and dropped it on the floor by my feet. Now we could get down to it.

I reached for Theo's hand and pulled him onto the bed beside me again.

"So, Theo, how did you picture our time together?"

The hesitant ones were always trickier to read. Sometimes they were hesitant because they weren't very experienced, or because they were shy. If I was too dominant, I could freak him out. But then there was the other type, the quiet but deadly kind. They were hesitant because they wanted you to fulfill some fetish or fantasy, but they didn't know how to ask for it. If I had to guess, I'd say Theo fell into group one, but you could never be sure.

"Um, sex? If that's okay?"

I smiled. Definitely shy.

"Can do, sugar." I slid off the bed and knelt between his legs, pushing them slightly apart.

His eyes were wide as he stared down at me, but I tried not to look up into them in case I saw Scott staring back at me again. The last thing I needed was to be thinking of Scott while I sucked another man's dick.

I thought of my phone right next to me on the floor. How many times had he tried to call since I'd switched it off? Was he sad or angry that I was working? I had no way to know. And it pissed me off that his emotional state bothered me.

I pushed Scott out of my mind. I was here to service Theo. He deserved my undivided attention; he'd paid for it. Scott had paid for me, too. I ran my hands up Theo's legs and cupped his crotch. He was as hard as stone, and his whole body jerked at my touch.

I undid his pants and he lifted his hips, allowing me to pull the jeans and underwear down to his knees. His cock was on the smaller side of average, but I could work with it.

"You're so pretty," he blurted out as his cheeks flushed.

"Thanks." I gave him a warm smile and leaned forward, licking the tip.

He let out a groan that I suspected was more about the idea of what I was doing than any real sensation — I'd barely touched him. But it motivated me to keep going. I cupped his balls and rubbed them between my fingers as I stroked his cock with my other hand.

"How do you like it?" I murmured, kissing up the shaft to the head.

"Just what you're doing is great," he said through gritted teeth.

The expression on his face told me that he was close to coming. I'd seen it a million times and I knew it well. But I'd barely even started, so I second-guessed myself.

He was breathing heavily and grunted when I slipped the head into my mouth and ran my lips down the shaft. His hips spasmed, and I let him piston in and out of my mouth. On his fifth thrust, he came without any warning, and I gagged because I wasn't expecting it. He'd only been going for a minute—the gold medal goes to Theo, The Quick-Draw Kid.

Normally, I would have worked him up until he was about to blow and then finished him off with my hand. I didn't make a regular habit of swallowing client's cum. I forced it down my throat, trying to avoid the shudder that threatened to rip through me. I hoped that Todd had done a thorough background check. I'd have to get an STI check ASAP. My brain went through damage control scenarios.

"You're amazing," Theo sighed.

I came back to the moment, pushing my panicked thoughts away. There was nothing I could do about that now, and I was still on the clock. I just needed to rinse out my mouth. I smiled up at him and stood up.

"I'll be right back," I promised and went to the bathroom, closing the door.

I cupped water into my mouth with my hands and swirled it around before spitting it out. I gargled another handful back down my throat and rinsed again. Good enough.

Once I was back in the bedroom, I noticed that Theo hadn't moved at all. He was still sitting on the edge of the bed with his pants around his knees. He smiled at me.

"Can I touch you now?" he asked.

The rest of Theo's appointment went by in a flash, literally. We had sex three times, and I still got out of there before my hour was up. I'd never met a guy who came so fast in my life. But at least he was satisfied. Four orgasms within an hour—some might say he was lucky.

He showed me to the door and watched me with sappy eyes as I got into the elevator. Soon I was speeding uptown on the subway to my next appointment. I turned on my phone and scrolled through the calendar, looking at the details. *Karl, 36. House call.* I turned off the phone again without looking at the missed calls or text messages. I'd deal with them when I got home.

I walked along the strip of brownstones, the smell of the steam coming through the grates making me gag. It was a nice area, otherwise.

I found the address that Todd had given me and walked up the stairs to knock on the door.

The most gorgeous guy I'd ever seen answered. He was broad-shouldered and had thick blond hair, a square jaw, and perfect white teeth. In fact, he looked a little familiar.

"Hello." His voice rung with a strong accent—Russian or eastern European of some sort. Suddenly it hit me—he was the model from a car company advertisement on television. A minor celebrity.

He wasn't the first celebrity I'd serviced. Several of Hollywood's finest had booked me when they were in town, but I never told anyone. Jamie didn't even know. They'd given Todd fake names of course, but they couldn't hide their faces when I'd shown up at their doors. Bookings with famous people usually came with a form to sign for non-disclosure and a silence payment on top of the agreed fee. Plus, there was the added incentive that it was cool seeing them in a movie and knowing what their "come face" looked like.

The contrast between Karl and The Quick-Draw Kid was laughable. I couldn't have had two different clients if I'd tried.

"Please, come in," he said, his accent making me smirk. It reminded me of the Count from *Sesame Street*.

The house was nicely furnished. There was a fireplace in the living room, crackling invitingly. The scent of wood smoke filled the room.

"For you," he said, bowing slightly and placing a thick white envelope in my hand. "There is a little extra for your confidence."

"My confidence?" I asked, confused.

"Er, excuse me…privacy?"

"Oh, confidentiality?"

"Yes." He smiled. "A little extra for your confidentiality."

"Of course. It's our little secret."

He nodded in thanks and poured two glasses of red wine. He handed me a glass and took a sip from his own.

"I like the sex with me on the top. Then I want you on the top. That is all."

He was straight to the point, so I put my glass down on the coffee table and waited to see if he wanted anything else.

"Whatever you'd like is fine with me." It sounded like tonight would be one of my easier nights.

He raised an eyebrow. "Anything?"

"I'm here to please you."

He considered that for a moment, a cheeky smile forming on his lips.

"Will you give me the blow?"

"A blow job?"

"Yes, I would like very much if you licked on my penis."

I flashed back to Theo's cum squirting into my mouth and shivered. I wouldn't let that happen again.

"Of course. I'd love to suck your cock."

His smile grew, and he undid his belt and dropped his pants to the floor on the spot.

"You like?" He wiggled his hips and his flaccid cock bounced around.

He was tall and broad so I expected all of him to be big. That wasn't the case. His cock looked to be a similar size to Theo's, if not smaller.

I bit my lip to stop from laughing. I couldn't wait to tell Jamie about this one.

"Very nice." I licked my lips and stalked toward him. "Would you like to go to the bedroom?"

"Right here is better. I like the fire."

"I like it too," I said.

"I would very much like to see your naked body."

"Would you like me to strip, or would you prefer to undress me?" It was impossible to tell what guys preferred, so I always liked to offer several alternatives.

"I will remove your clothing, please."

I stepped up and pressed myself against his body. He smelled like cologne and cigarettes. His hands were smaller than I was expecting, but I guessed it made sense considering the other small appendage he had which was growing hard against my side. He removed my shirt quickly and unfastened my bra.

"Your breasts are very nice."

"Thank you?" I said, not meaning for it sound like a question, but it did.

He bent down and removed my pants. It was all so mechanical and I couldn't work out if he was nervous, which he didn't *seem* to be, or if he was just not very experienced. But surely someone as attractive, and semi-famous, as him would have bedded more than his fair share of the ladies — right? Perhaps not, considering he'd booked a prostitute and had a tiny cock.

Once I was completely naked, he removed his own shirt, kicked off his pants, and sat on the couch.

"Now, lick on the penis." He pointed to his lap and then relaxed back on the couch and closed his eyes, waiting for me to start.

I stood still for a moment, trying to work out what to do. He was acting very confidently, but also as if he had no idea what he was doing. It couldn't all be the language barrier, could it?

Deciding it didn't matter, I knelt on the floor and took his cock in my hand. It was definitely smaller than Theo's. When I made a fist around it, I could grasp the whole shaft at once with my fingers touching my palm. I tried to move my hand but there was nowhere to move! Deciding the only way I could give him any friction would be with my mouth, I leaned down and captured him between my lips. He let out a loud exhale.

I pushed my lips all the way down to his groin and he didn't even hit the back of my throat. This was going to be the easiest blow job ever. No gag reflex issues. I sucked and bobbed my head up and down a few times but kept an eye on his face so he didn't surprise me like Theo had.

He stayed perfectly silent as I worked on him, and his head was tilted back so I couldn't see his expression. I hoped he was enjoying it, but there was no way for me to tell. Deciding to check, I pulled him out of my mouth and smiled up at him.

"Does it feel good, baby?"

"Ooh, is so nice."

I took that as a positive and got back to work. He was a bit more vocal after that, grunting and breathing heavily. He leaned forward and ducked his hands under my chin to grasp my breasts.

"I like your nipples very much."

I held the laughter inside and kept sucking. His hips were bucking now, a good sign, and soon he was practically panting.

"I come! I come!" he grunted and at lightning speed I moved my head out of the way just as a stream of cum squirted from the tip.

I rubbed him with my hand as best as I could with the little I had to work with until he was lying breathless against the cushions.

"Now, we fuck." He didn't wait to recover or to thank me. I didn't really expect thanks; the money was all the thanks I needed, but most guys would usually show some appreciation. "Lay on the floor."

So I did. He'd already told me what he wanted—him on top and then me on top. Easy.

I grabbed a pillow from the sofa and a condom out of my bag on the coffee table and handed it to him. I got comfortable as he settled himself over me like he was going to do a pushup. I spread my legs for him and he sank down.

"You ready? I put it in now."

I didn't know what to say to that. Of course I was ready. That's what I was here for!

"Okay," I said.

He slid up my body a little and then started moving back and forth at a feverish pace. I took a moment to process that he was thrusting. I couldn't feel anything at all down there. I could feel his weight pressing down on me and his chest sliding along mine but as far as where it mattered, he could have been a Ken doll.

Thinking that we must just be lying at a strange angle, I tilted my hips up and wrapped my legs around his waist.

"Ooh ya!" he said, obviously enjoying the tighter sensation, but I still felt absolutely nothing.

This had never happened to me before. In more than two thousand men, I'd never experienced *nothing*. He continued to move over me, grunting and groaning. His eyes were scrunched up, but as far as I could tell, he was enjoying himself.

"*Da! Da!*" he gasped as his movements sped up.

It dawned on me that I was just lying there like a dead fish, not moving or making a sound. It didn't matter if I felt anything; I had to make him *think* I was enjoying myself.

"Mmm, your cock feels so good," I moaned and started rocking my hips.

"*Da!*"

I hoped that he would come soon. As much as I tried to stay in the moment, Scott kept creeping into my thoughts. I wondered how many times he'd called, and if he hated me now. All I wanted to do was go home to bed and cry. It had been a horrible night, and I knew I'd have a mountain of angry voice messages waiting for me.

"Ooh, is so good, is so nice. I come!" He collapsed on top of me. I couldn't tell if he'd pulled out of me or if he was still inside. If I hadn't experienced it for myself, I wouldn't have believed it was possible.

"We go again?" he asked after a moment.

"Me on top?"

He smiled. "Yes! I want to see your nipples."

It amused me that everything he said was just slightly off. I got the idea of what he was trying to say, but it was still funny. I hoped that by being on top, and in control, I would be able to feel him this time.

We rolled over and I straddled his lap. To his credit, his cock was still hard so I quickly changed the condom and then slid down on it right away.

He hissed between his teeth.

I swiveled my hips around, trying to feel him inside me, but still there was nothing. I slid up and down, but I was worried that he would fall out if I went up too far, so instead I just rocked my hips back and forth. I could feel the friction against my clit as I ground on him, but inside there was no sensation at all. I may as well have been grinding into the seat of a chair. It was unbelievable, and not in a good way.

His hands moved up my stomach, and he kneaded my breasts and pinched my nipples, licking his lips and staring up at me with hooded eyes. I was glad that he was enjoying himself, that was all that mattered really, but it was still strange.

"You like my penis?" he asked.

"Oh yeah! You feel so good inside me," I moaned, pulling what I hoped were expressions of pleasure.

"Mmm. I keep you for another hour. We do more sex."

I stopped moving and rested my hands on his chest. Another hour of this? No way!

"I'm sorry, I have another appointment after this," I lied, pouting and looking disappointed.

"Oh." He frowned. "I book you tomorrow?"

"Sure. Tomorrow is good," I said.

He smiled, satisfied, and jiggled my breasts in his hands.

"Fuck my penis," he instructed.

I went back to my grinding and made a mental note to tell Todd to give Mr. Model to another girl when he called to rebook.

Half an hour and a round of doggy-style later, I was back on the street and trying to hail a cab. I shook my head as I thought about my night and marveled that even in doggy-style, when the guy is usually as deep as he can get, there was barely any sensation for me. Maybe there was something wrong with me? Maybe Scott had broken me with his *lovemaking*.

But no. I hadn't had an orgasm with Theo, but I'd at least been able to feel him inside me. The only thing I could put it down to was that Mr. Model's cock was just so small. Poor guy.

Once I'd climbed inside a cab and told him my address, I pulled out my phone and readied myself for an onslaught of messages. The phone beeped repeatedly for a full minute as they all came pouring in. There were fourteen missed calls from Scott, a missed call from Todd, and four voice messages. I was a coward, so I called Todd back first.

"Cherry pie," he said cheerfully when he picked up.

"When my client from tonight calls you to book me again for tomorrow, tell him that I'm fully booked and give him to one of the other girls." I decided to tell him that before I forgot.

"Easily done. You *are* fully booked tomorrow. I couldn't give you to him anyway."

"Okay, just don't let him talk you into switching my bookings around. You've done that before."

"All right, I think Jamie has a free slot tomorrow. Fill her in when you get home."

"Okay, I'm on my way there now."

"You tired?"

"Why?" I asked, already knowing what he was going to say.

"I have another guy if you want him."

"What's the job?"

Normally I wouldn't have taken on another client so late at night, especially after the night I'd had, but if I went home then I'd have to listen to Scott's messages, and I wasn't ready to do that just yet. I needed to escape a little bit longer and more fucking was the only way I knew how to do that.

"No fetish. Vanilla sex. He asked for my best lady."

"I'll take it. Text me the details."

"Good girl." I could hear the smile in his voice.

We hung up and a second later a text messaged arrived with the address.

"Change of plans," I called to the driver.

Fifteen minutes later, I was walking into a motel near Times Square, hoping for a decent fuck. The Quick-Draw Kid and Mr. Model had done nothing for me, and I really needed some hardcore fucking to get my head on straight.

The whole taxi ride I'd told myself not to think about Scott, but in saying that over and over, I'd really been thinking about him the whole time. Oh well, another hour before I had to listen to his messages.

I went up to the room and knocked. A man in his mid-thirties opened the door and smiled at me.

"You must be Ally. I'm Kyle. I hear you're the best in New York."

"I like to think so," I said, giving him a flirty smile.

"I'll let you know in about an hour." He winked at me and closed the door.

I walked into the room and placed my bag down by the television. Arms wrapped around my waist from behind and warm, wet kisses trailed along the back of my neck. So, straight into it then.

"Your money is just there," he whispered before sucking my earlobe into his mouth.

I grabbed the money off the top of the TV and slipped it into my bag.

"Show me why you're worth seven hundred dollars," he growled in my ear.

That was more like it. I could tell that I was going to get fucked until I couldn't stand. It was exactly what I needed, and my body sizzled with anticipation.

I spun in his arms and pushed hard against his chest, shoving him backward onto the bed. I removed every piece of his clothing and stroked his cock until it was rock hard. He laughed and looked up at me with lust-filled eyes. Slowly I stripped for him, teasing when it felt right, but letting him know that my body was his to play with.

"Fuck, you're sexy," he whispered.

"You like my tits?" I squeezed them for emphasis.

"Yeah."

"You like my ass?" I spun around and wiggled it.

"Mmm."

I slowly crawled up the bed, slid a condom down his shaft, and then lowered myself onto him.

"You like my pussy?" I squeezed my muscles on his dick and smiled when he let out a soft groan.

"Fuck, yeah!"

"*This* is why I'm worth seven hundred dollars."

And without another word, I rode him hard. I planted my hands on his chest. It felt so good to be stuffed with a big cock; it stretched me and filled me the way a cock should.

His eyes never left my bouncing breasts as they swayed over his face. His hands moved down to my hips, guiding me.

"I hope you're in for a long fuck, because I can last awhile."

I smirked. "Good."

A nice long session was exactly what I needed. The lovemaking had been nice, but there was no control in it, no power. I liked it hard and fast and passionate. I liked to sweat and feel my heart pumping in my throat. I loved that frantic feeling when you would give anything to be able to move faster and harder, but your body was limited by human speed and strength. It was a blissful frustration that I craved.

I fucked him as hard and for as long as I could, and when I felt myself starting to tire, I shifted positions and rested my arms back on his thighs. I continued to buck my hips and even felt an orgasm coming on. Not a rip-roaring, stars-exploding-behind-my-eyes type of orgasm, but a physical release all the same.

I let all the tension and frustration I'd felt about Scott flood through me as I came, and I yelled out a throaty, "Fuck yes!" as I clamped down on his cock.

"You're beautiful when you come," he groaned.

I stopped moving as I enjoyed the sensations flowing through my body.

"My turn," Kyle said, flipping us over.

I lay on my back and let him pound into me while I caught my breath. He was chanting something softly to himself that I couldn't make out, but I didn't ask him what it was. I didn't need to know.

I kept my eye on the clock, something I always did out of habit, and noticed that we'd been going for thirty minutes and he hadn't come yet. I'd had guys last a long time before, and he'd told me that he could last awhile, but he wasn't showing signs of even being close.

I squeezed my muscles tightly, milking his cock from the inside. It was a trick that always worked, and when I used it, guys would come within four or five more thrusts. Kyle groaned and leaned his head down on my shoulder.

"Fuck, you're so tight," he breathed, but he kept going.

I watched each minute tick by with growing curiosity. I tried bucking underneath him, squeezing my legs together, moaning and groaning—which most guys loved—but nothing made him come.

I could feel that I was getting dry and a bit raw. I wasn't sure how much longer it would be until he actually started hurting me.

"Your hour is almost up, sexy," I mewed in his ear after fifty minutes.

"I'll pay for a second hour," he grunted. "I've still got a way to go."

"What? Is something wrong? Can I do anything to make it feel better for you?"

He stopped moving for a second and stared down at me.

"Feel better? Honey, you're the best fuck I've had in a long time. I'm not going to let this feeling stop until I absolutely have to."

"Oh."

He started thrusting again.

"Do you mind if I just grab some lube out of my bag?"

He laughed but didn't stop moving. "I thought you were supposed to be the best fuck in the whole city. Don't tell me you can't handle it."

Pride bubbled within me. *Of course I can handle it. I'm Ally Fucking Mitchell!*

"Oh, I can. I just like a slippery ride." I kept my voice cocky, trying to let him know that he wasn't getting to me.

In compromise, he spat on his fingers and rubbed it into my pussy. It wasn't perfect, but it was better than nothing.

# CHAPTER TWENTY-ONE

More than an hour later, I hobbled home. My pussy was raw, and I was utterly exhausted. Once he was half-way through his second hour with no signs of stopping, I finally offered to just suck him off. He came quickly once he was in my mouth, and I took great pleasure in spitting the cum back onto his stomach. He'd loved that, thought it was kinky or some shit. Whatever. I was just glad it was over.

I had a hot shower and applied some lube to my raw skin. Not that I was planning on having any more sex that night, but I needed the chafing to heal as quickly as possible, so I wanted to avoid more irritation.

As I dried off and dressed in my bra and boxer shorts I tried to keep thoughts of Scott and all his messages out of my mind, but it was impossible.

My phone mocked me as it flashed from my night stand. Another call from Scott. It was nearly two in the morning, so the fact that he was still trying to call meant that he wouldn't go to sleep until he spoke to me. With a sigh, I picked up the phone.

"Hi," I said, in a tired voice.

I could hear the relief in his voice when he spoke. "Oh thank God! I was starting to think something had happened."

"I'm sorry I didn't call back. I haven't even had time to listen to your messages yet. I literally just got home and had a shower."

"Big night?" he asked. I knew he wanted his comment to come across as a lighthearted joke, but I could hear the pain in his voice.

"You don't want to hear about it," I said. "I'm really tired. Can we talk in the morning?"

"Too tired from fucking other men to talk to your boyfriend?" The sneer was unmistakable now. He wasn't even trying to hide it anymore.

"Don't twist my words. I'm tired, and I'm not in the mood to fight."

"Who's fighting? I just wanted to know how your night was."

"Fine! You want to know how my night was?" He didn't say anything, so I continued. "My first client was a young guy with a quick-draw problem. I was sucking him off and he came so quickly that I didn't have time to pull my mouth away. Then I had a guy whose cock was so small that I couldn't even feel it inside me. I was going to go home, but Todd gave me a third client. That guy fucked me for almost two hours before he came, and now my pussy is raw and sore."

There was silence on the other end of the phone, but I could almost feel his fury radiating out of the earpiece.

"Fuck," he breathed out in a disgusted tone.

"Don't get all pouty now," I spat. "You wanted to know."

"I *don't* want to know."

"Scott!" I said through clenched teeth, totally frustrated.

"I wish there wasn't anything *to* know."

"Well, get over it. It's my job. I don't ask you for a play by play of your work day."

"Because I'm not fucking other women in my business meetings."

"You could be for all I know. I never ask."

"You'd be okay if I fucked other women at work?"

"If it was your job. If I'd known it was your job *before* I'd decided to get into a relationship with you, then yes, I'd be okay with it."

"Oh, so if I decided to become a male prostitute, you'd have no problem with that."

"Unlike you, I have the ability to detach emotionally during sex."

"Oh, I'm well aware of your ability to detach from your emotions."

I was seething. Scott sighed loudly, but neither of us spoke. I thought about just hanging up the phone, but then pictured the hurt that would be on his face. It softened my rage.

"Look, I don't want to fight with you. I know that my job is hard for you, and that's why I don't want to talk about it. Telling you the details is like rubbing salt in the wound. Can't we just ignore it and talk about other things?"

"Like what, Ally? It's a pretty big fucking elephant staring us in the face, waving its trunk around under my nose."

"We had plenty of things to talk about last week. I was still a prostitute then."

"Not in practice. You were here with me, not with anyone else."

"I knew this was going to happen. I *knew* you wouldn't be able to handle it."

"I don't need the 'I told you so' speech. This is where we are now. Let's work it through."

"Fine. Tell me how I can make this better," I said through gritted teeth.

He was quiet for a moment and then he said, "Don't get mad."

"I won't." I had a pretty fair idea about what he was going to say anyway; it wouldn't be a surprise.

"I want you to quit your job."

I closed my eyes and let the words wash over me, trying to contain my anger. I'd been expecting it, so I tried to brush it off and stay calm.

"And how would you propose that I earn a living?" I asked, proud of the control in my voice.

"With *any* other job in the whole world. I could easily get you a PA job in my company."

"I don't know anything about publishing or administration."

"Fine," he said evenly. I was quite proud of how civilly we were speaking about this. "What job would you like to do?"

I wanted to say, "Prostitution!" just to annoy him, but decided to be mature.

"I don't know, Scott. I started working while I was still in college and I've never done anything else."

"Well, think about it. You can do anything you want."

"It's late. I'm tired from work, and I'm not in a great mood. Future planning is not really high on my priorities right now."

"Okay, why don't you take some time to think about it and get some sleep."

"Thanks."

"I'll see you tomorrow."

"Wait, what?"

Scott chuckled into the phone. "I told you I have a ticket to New York."

"I thought that was when you were going to come and drag me away from work."

"It was. But I miss you, and since I already have the ticket, why not come and see you?"

"Because I have to work tomorrow!" I yelled. All thoughts of sleep were suddenly gone.

"We had a deal that you wouldn't work when I was in town." He sounded smug.

"No!" I was so angry that I stood up and started pacing the room. "I told you that you couldn't just start spending all your time here to stop me from working. You promised me that you wouldn't trick me."

"I'm sorry, Ally, but I'm not going through another night like tonight. If you're not going to stop working, then I can't do this."

There. He'd said it. We'd both been thinking it, but I hadn't been brave enough to say it out loud. We were over.

"Fine. Then I guess we're done." My voice was icy cold and hard as steel. I hung up the phone before he could say another word.

The phone rang again instantly, but I sent it to voice mail and threw my phone across the room.

"Fucking men!" I yelled into my pillow.

I could feel Alison sneaking out of her box with her tears and her broken heart, but I wasn't going to let her control me. Every man on the planet could go to hell as far as I was concerned.

*Fuck them all. Fuck Scott Walker.*

I wasn't going to let the pain take control of me. *I* was the one in control.

I needed Todd.

My phone rang again, but I left it where it was on the floor and walked out the door.

"You okay, babe? I heard yelling," Jamie said, poking her head around her bedroom door.

"Everything's just fine," I said.

I left the apartment and walked the few blocks to my brother's apartment and knocked on their door. No answer. I used both fists, banging in a quick rhythm until I heard footsteps inside. Todd answered. His hair was a mess and his eyes were only half open.

"Hey…wait, what's wrong?" he asked, going into manager mode as soon as he saw the murderous expression on my face.

"Where's Zach?" I asked, walking inside and slamming the door.

Todd took a few steps back to allow me into the room and shrugged his shoulders. "I don't know. Since he yelled at me about hiring you, I haven't seen him."

The sister part of my brain set off alarm bells, and I told myself that I'd try to call him first thing in the morning. There was nothing I could do to find him at two a.m. What I *could* do at two a.m. was fuck myself better.

"I need you. Right now," I said.

"Huh?" Todd rubbed his eyes and stifled a yawn.

"Don't play games with me," I said as I pushed him down onto the couch and ripped the shirt over his head.

"Um, shouldn't we talk about this, Ally?"

"No!"

I got to work on his pants, throwing them onto the floor. He wasn't hard but I knew that I could change that. A few rough pumps of my hand and he was growing stiff. *So predictable.*

I dug around in my purse for a condom and threw the packet at him so I could strip down.

"You know what I want," I said.

He sighed, and I was worried for a moment that he was going to push me away. Didn't he want me either? But he didn't disappoint. He rolled the rubber down over his dick and gave me a warm smile.

"Come here, sweetheart." He held his arms out, welcoming me.

I straddled his lap and mounted him. I immediately started bucking in his lap. I was sore and achy from the chafing, but I deserved the pain. It was what a *whore* deserved.

"Open your eyes, Ally. Look at me," Todd asked.

Annoyance bubbled through me as I lifted my lids. I just wanted an anonymous fuck. I didn't want to feel the guilt of using my friend. I didn't want to look into his eyes, but he was forcing it on me. His pupils locked with mine.

"You're so beautiful," he murmured.

Something in my chest cracked, so I rode him harder, trying to push the painful feelings away. All that mattered was his cock sliding in and out of me. My feelings could go to hell.

"Yes!" I breathed, letting my head fall backward as I moved.

"I love you, Ally."

My head snapped up and glared at him. *That* wasn't part of the deal. I wanted to feel needed, desired. I needed to fuck my loneliness and inadequacy away. I'd never wanted *love.*

"Don't!" I warned.

"I'm trying to help you," he murmured between grunts. "Plain old fucking isn't going to heal you."

"Be quiet. Just fuck me," I begged.

His eyes were sad, but he didn't say anything else. We fucked silently, but he wouldn't let me close my eyes. Each time they slipped closed, he would stroke his thumb across my eyelid, coaxing them open again.

Staring into his eyes, I could see the pain it caused him to do this for me. The sacrifice of his own feelings. I knew that Todd did genuinely care about me. He wasn't *in* love with me; he wouldn't have been able to send me off to other men if that were the case, but I wasn't surprised to hear he loved me in some way. I just didn't want to hear it. I didn't want to know that it hurt him to help me. It burned down deep inside.

I collapsed on his chest, not even close to fulfilled, but utterly exhausted. His torso rose and fell as he caught his breath, and he hugged me to him.

"Are you finished already?" he asked.

I shook my head and tilted my neck back to stare into his eyes again. I'd never really noticed much of a family resemblance between

Scott and Todd. I believed they were family because they both told me they were, but now, post-coital, I could see the same hooded eyes, the same smug half-smile.

I pushed away from him and sat up, my mind suddenly clear.

"What's wrong?" he asked.

"Nothing. I have to go."

"Did I help?"

"More than you know," I replied as I threw my clothes on.

I left him lying naked on the couch and walked out into the deserted streets. The odd taxi would drive by, but essentially I was alone.

Tonight, staring at Todd's face, I knew for the first time that I couldn't keep doing what I had been doing. Fucking my problems away hadn't worked, and it was never going to.

Scott's words echoed in my head as I walked. I *could* do whatever I wanted. I was still young. I had my whole future ahead of me. I wasn't going to let Nick-the-ex have any more power over me. Enough was enough, and it ended tonight.

I wasn't sure why it was so clear all of a sudden. It was as if fucking Todd had flicked a switch in my brain, and now I couldn't turn back. I'd thought that I was moving on by sleeping with thousands of men, that I was the one in control. I wasn't wallowing at home because my boyfriend didn't love me. But I'd been wrong. Nick had been the driving force behind every blow job, every fuck. My anger at him had defined me and taken over my personality. No more!

The neon lights of a twenty-four-hour store burned across the street, and I went inside, deciding to make the first change of many for my new life. I went to the glass stand that was filled with cell phones and signed up for a new phone and a new number. Todd could have his phone back; I didn't want it, or his job, anymore.

With the small piece of technical freedom in my pocket, I walked home and let myself inside. Walking in the crisp air had really cleared my mind and I knew what I had to do.

# CHAPTER TWENTY-TWO

I packed all night. I didn't have many personal belongings, another side effect of my issues with commitment. When Jamie emerged from her bedroom around noon, I was sitting in the kitchen combing through a newspaper. Despite not sleeping at all, I felt invigorated and motivated to get my new life started.

"Anything interesting happening in the world?" she asked as she poured a cup of coffee.

I took the pencil I'd been chewing out of my mouth and bit my lip. I wasn't sure how she was going to take my decision.

"I'm actually looking at the apartment listings."

Jamie quirked an eyebrow as she blew on her steaming coffee.

"Abandoning me, huh? Mister Five buying you a big penthouse on Fifth Avenue?" She laughed, but her eyes were guarded. She could tell something was off. We knew each other well enough for that.

"Actually, I'm not seeing Scott anymore. I'm not going to be seeing anyone."

Jamie's eyes narrowed, and she put her coffee down on the counter. "What's going on?"

"You know that something's not right with me. I use sex to hide from my emotions."

"So does everyone on the planet!"

"Not like I do. I just wonder if there is more to life for me than fucking hundreds of faceless guys."

"*He* talked you into this, didn't he? I knew having a real relationship was going to screw with your head."

"No! This isn't about Scott. It's about *me*. I'm not happy with my life, Jamie. I thought I could fuck my problems away, but it never works. I'm sick of using Todd as my crutch, he deserves better than that, and so do I."

"So that's it, you're just going to quit and live a normal life with tea parties and one sexual partner for the rest of your life? That's not you, Ally."

Her words stung more than I thought they would.

"How do you know, Jamie? Maybe I would be perfectly content being a housewife. I don't know because I've never even given a normal life a chance."

"I don't have to give living in Antarctica a chance to know that I wouldn't like the cold. Inside, you're a working girl and you always will be. Just like me."

"You're wrong."

"Fine. But don't sit there and tell me that you aren't going to miss the sex. I give you a week before you're on the phone to Todd begging for some cock."

She flung her hair over her shoulder and stormed out of the room, slamming her bedroom door. I cringed and stared at the newspaper. I hoped she wasn't right. If sex was the only thing I was good at, then what kind of life would I have without it?

I thought about being a fifty- or sixty-year-old woman, wrinkled and gray-haired and still frequenting hotels. Would guys even pay for me when my body let me down?

How much longer did I have in the industry anyway? Maybe fifteen good years before I was classed as a "mature escort"? That might be the life Jamie wanted, but I didn't.

With a new-found determination, I went back to looking at apartments. I had a nice savings account, but I hadn't saved enough to buy my own place yet. Two years and two thousand men, and I'd only saved about half of what I'd need to buy something in this city. I had no other option but to rent.

I knew that Todd was looking for a new roommate since my brother had moved out, but living with him would defeat the purpose of moving altogether. I may as well just stay with Jamie. I needed a completely new start away from my old life.

Thinking about Zach made me wonder where he was. Had he found a new place to live? I decided to try to call him. I hadn't heard a thing from him since he'd found out about my secret life.

Unsurprisingly, his voice mail answered.

"Zach, I know you're angry and that you don't want to talk to me, but please call me back. I quit working for Todd and I'm moving into a new apartment. I'm going to start fresh with a whole new life. I'd really like my brother to be a part of it. I'm even looking for a roommate if you're interested. Please, just give me a call on *this* number. I gave my old phone back to Todd."

I hadn't given Todd the phone back yet, but I would. That was a conversation that I wasn't looking forward to. If Jamie was mad, then Todd was likely to go supernova.

I decided that it was better to get it over and done with before I lost my nerve. I grabbed the old cell phone and walked to Todd's apartment. He opened the door, his expression wary.

"How are you today?" he asked.

I sat down heavily on the couch. "I'm feeling much better. I'm really sorry about last night. I won't happen again. I promise."

"You know I'm here to help when you need me. But the way you deal with your pain isn't good for you. Maybe you should see a therapist or something."

"A therapist?" I asked.

"Not that you're crazy or anything!" he said, back-pedaling. "Just someone to talk with."

"No, I'm not offended. I actually think it's a great idea. I need to deal with my issues."

Having someone professional to help me talk through my feelings was a good idea. I needed to make some changes, and a therapist would really help me succeed in my new life.

"Oh, well that's great!" Todd said, but he still watched me cautiously.

I had the phone in my hand, twisting and turning it, building up my strength to hand it back.

"So, Todd," I said, "I wanted to talk to you about my job."

He cocked his head to the side and stared. "Don't tell me you want *more* time off. You only just got back from a week away."

"No, I don't want time off." I cringed when he visibly relaxed. "I'm… I'm quitting."

He stared blankly at me, but slowly, very slowly, I could see the furious reddish tinge creeping up his throat.

"Did my cousin ask you to fucking marry him?" he exploded, shooting out of his chair.

"What? No! We actually broke up. I'm doing this for *me*."

Todd paced the room, scrubbing his hands over his face.

"Are you giving notice or this just a straight 'fuck you, Todd, I quit!'?"

I'd known he wasn't going to like it, but it still hurt that he was so angry with me for wanting to make my life better.

"It's neither. This is just me saying that you've been a great support for me over the years, and you're one of my best friends, but I need to make some changes in my life. You just told me to see a therapist because I'm so messed up. This work is just enabling my behavior."

"I get it," he said, sighing and collapsing on the couch. "But I don't have to like it. I want you to be happy, I *do*, I really do. I just wish that working for me made you happy."

I slid up next to him on the couch and took his hand.

"Honey, you know this isn't about you. Working for you *has* made me happy, but now I have to do something for me."

"You're my number one girl."

"I know, but I think Jamie is more than capable of being your new number one. And you've got Amy now."

"You really broke up with Scott?" he asked, changing the topic.

I nodded and bit my lip to stop the tears I'd been holding back since the night before. He wrapped me in a tight hug, and I knew without a doubt that our friendship would survive.

"Hello?" I said into the phone.

I'd stupidly given Todd my phone back without transferring my contacts over to the new one, and now I didn't have anyone's number. So I had no idea who was calling.

"Is it true?"

"Zach!" I said, relief flooding through me.

"You really quit?"

"Yes, it's true."

"What happened? One of those assholes didn't hurt you, did he?"

I smiled. Even when he was angry at me, he was still my big brother. "No, Zach. I'm fine, I promise. We have a lot to talk about. Can we do it in person?"

"Gino's in twenty?"

"See you there."

I hung up the phone, grabbed my purse and keys from the counter, and walked the four blocks to Gino's diner. Zach and I had found it when we'd first moved to the city and had frequented it so often that Gino knew us by name.

I opened the door, and I was accosted by the smell of coffee and bacon. The scent of pure happiness. I breathed it in.

"Ally! Good to see you, hon. Zach's in your booth."

"Hi, Gino," I called over my shoulder to the elderly Italian man behind the grill.

Zach smiled when I walked over, and I slid into the leather booth next to him.

"What are you doing?" he asked as I squeezed him hard.

"Hugging my brother."

"No, I mean why are you sitting over here? It's weird."

He had a point. The majority of people would sit opposite each other, but I just wanted to be close to him.

"Shut up and order me a coffee," I said, ignoring him.

"Gino!" he said. "Two coffees."

"Coming right up!" Gino called back. He appeared a moment later with two steaming mugs.

"So, tell me what happened," Zach said once Gino had left us alone.

"Nothing bad," I assured him. "It just wasn't what I wanted for myself anymore."

"Well, I'm glad to hear that. I just don't understand why you wanted to do *that* in the first place."

I rested my hand on his. "It's a long story, and there are a lot of details that you won't want to hear. I thought it was making me happy and, for a while, it was good for me. It's just not good for me anymore."

He nodded.

"How did you even find out?" I asked. "I saw the shiner you gave Todd. Did he accidentally let it slip?"

Zach shifted in his seat and cleared his throat.

"That story has some details that I don't think *you* want to hear. Just believe me when I say that I found out from an unexpected but reliable source. And Todd deserved it. I can't believe he kept that from me for years. Some friend."

"Don't be too hard on him. I'm sure he thought he was doing me a favor by keeping you in the dark."

"It wasn't up to *him* to tell me what you did."

"No. I take full responsibility."

"How can I trust you now, Al?"

"Zachary. You're my brother. You know me inside out and back to front."

"I thought I did."

"You *do*. That job wasn't who I was. It was just what I *did*. No one knows me like you."

Zach drained his coffee cup and looked me square in the eye.

"You're done with that job? For real?"

"Yes."

"Then I'll forget about it. I'll never bring it up again. But if you ever go back to that work, I will kick the ass of anyone who tries to hire you. Got it?"

I smirked. "Got it."

"Well, now that that's over, you said something about looking for an apartment?"

"Yeah. You interested in moving back in with your little sister?"

He rubbed the top of my head. "I guess so. I've been staying with Mom, so I'd like my own apartment again. Just don't nag me about my dirty towels."

"Well, don't leave them on the floor and I won't have to."

"I like my towel on the floor."

"Really?" My voice rose with exasperation.

Zach laughed. "This is going to be great! Now we just have to find the new Mitchell Manor."

"Are you sure about this, babe?" Jamie asked as she helped me carry the last box out of my room.

"I'm sure. I'm actually excited to try something new."

"So, is this goodbye?"

I took the box from her, placed it on the table, and pulled her into a hug.

"Not forever," I promised. "Just give me a little time to get settled and make the changes I need to make."

"Is this the last of it?" Zach asked, appearing in the doorway and pointing at the box.

"Yeah, that's the last one," I called back over my shoulder.

He scooped it up and left the apartment, taking it to load up with the rest of my belongings on the moving truck. I turned back to Jamie and put my hands on her shoulders.

"You're the number one girl now. You've earned it, and you'll be great."

She gave a half-nod and smiled sadly. I hated to see her like that. I wanted her to be happy for me, so I decided that I needed to make her laugh.

"One last squeeze before I hit the road?" I asked.

She snorted and giggled as she thrust her chest out. I grabbed her breasts and jiggled them a bit. "They really are perfect."

With one last hug and one final glance around the apartment, I turned to leave. Just as I got to the door, I turned to wave to Jamie. She was still smiling.

"Your ass looks fucking hot in those jeans!" she said and then wolf-whistled.

In Jamie-speak she'd just told me that she loved me. Our friendship would survive the changes in my life. I was sure of it.

She closed the door, and I stared for a moment longer before I turned and walked out onto the street. Zach was standing awkwardly by the truck as Amy chattered at him.

"Ally!" she squealed and ran over to me.

She'd changed her hair again. The blue that it had been the last time I'd seen her was still in place, but there were silver-gray streaks through it now. She really had a sense of style all her own.

"Moving in right away, huh?" I asked. "Not even letting my old room get cold."

"You're not mad are you? Jamie said it would be okay."

I smiled. "Of course it's okay. I'm glad you and Jamie will have each other. Don't let her get too wild, okay? You might need to be the voice of reason sometimes."

Amy frowned. "And what about you? Are you going to have someone to look after you?"

"I have my brother. I'll be fine."

"You know we're all here if you need anything."

I hugged her again. "I know. And I'm here for you too. If it gets too hard or you want to make a change, just call me okay?"

"I'll remember."

"Ally, we really have to go. We've only got the truck for another two hours."

"I'm coming!" I called to Zach.

"Sorry about Zach finding out," Amy whispered as she gave me one last hug and then ran up the stairs into my old building.

Wait—what did *Amy* have to do with Zach finding out?

"Why were you so weird around Amy?" I asked once I was seated in the cab of the moving truck.

"No reason. I wasn't weird." The words spilled from him a little too quickly.

"Zach, I know you well enough to see when you're not comfortable. You had the same look on your face when Kristy Morgan tried to kiss you at summer camp."

Zach cringed at the memory, but kept his eyes on the road.

"Is it just because you know what she does now?"

"No." His ears had gone bright red, something that only happened when he was embarrassed.

"Okay, spill it," I demanded.

He clenched his jaw, but let his shoulders drop. "Amy was the one who told me what your job was."

Amy's whispered comment suddenly made sense.

"When did you and Amy ever talk one-on-one? Was she visiting Todd or something?"

"Ah…Yeah, that was it."

I smelled a lie. "Just tell me already!"

"You *really* don't want to know."

"Zach, you're starting to piss me off. This isn't a good start to us living together."

"Fine. I booked Amy."

"You…*booked* her? As in, for a *job?*"

His ears burned brighter.

"Well, I didn't know I was booking *her*, specifically. She showed up at the door, and I thought it was a mistake, and then she told me what you did."

There was a lot going around in my mind. First, I wanted to laugh at how shocked he must have been when he opened the door and Amy was standing there. Then it dawned on me that for her to show up, that meant he'd booked a prostitute. My brother having sex, *paying* for sex, wasn't something I wanted to think about.

"You didn't…I mean, you guys just talked, right? She didn't *service* you? Actually, don't answer that. I don't want to know."

"No, you don't."

"Ugh! Gross!" I cringed and turned away from him. I coughed deliberately. "*Hypocrite*."

"What does that mean?" he asked, his voice higher than normal.

"Just that you have such a double standard. You freak out over *me* being a call girl when it's fine for you to book one?"

"You're my *sister*, Ally."

"No shit, Sherlock!"

"Well that's all that needs to be said. I don't want my baby sister fucking guys for money. End of story."

"But it's okay for you to pay to have sex?"

"Let's just drop this. Obviously, it wasn't my most shining moment."

"Gladly."

I wasn't naïve enough to think my brother had never had sex, but I didn't want to *know* about it.

After we'd unloaded the boxes, Zach returned the truck he'd borrowed from work while I started cooking our first dinner as roommates. It was refreshing to be starting new. Unpacking and choosing new homes for my belongings was cathartic. Zach brought a six-pack of beer home with him and neither of us spoke of Amy, my old job, or Todd for the rest of the night.

The gym smelled like sweat, rubber, and chlorine. I ducked through the doors and quickly scanned the room to make sure Jamie wasn't around. It wasn't that I didn't want to see her—I missed my best friend, but I was ashamed.

After not working for nearly a month, I'd already dipped into my savings. The truth was, until I found a job, I would have to cut back on some of my usual luxuries, including my gym membership.

I approached the counter and rang the bell. Jeremy, the manager, came out of his office.

"Ally. You can go straight through, no need to sign in," he said.

"Actually, I needed to speak with you."

He seemed intrigued and waved me into his office. The room was small and had pictures of a younger Jeremy in bodybuilding outfits.

"What can I do for my favorite client?" he asked, leaning back in his chair.

I cringed and put my membership card on his desk.

"I need to cancel."

Jeremy frowned. "Are you not happy with our service?"

"No, that's not it at all. I'm just not working at the moment, and I need to cut back on my expenses."

Jeremy chewed his lip and rocked the chair back and forth.

"So if there's a form I need to fill out or something—"

He held up his hand. "Maybe we can work something out."

My skin crawled at his words. I'd never hidden my profession from Jeremy, but I hadn't advertised it either. I prayed that the next words out of his mouth wouldn't be about paying him in *services*.

"I'm opening a new gym in Philadelphia and half of my staff is being transferred there. So, I'm looking to hire some new people to replace them. You've worked out here enough to know the machines and many of the clients. What do you think?"

I was stunned. I blinked as I processed his unexpected words.

"Your membership would be part of your employment," he added.

"Don't you have to have qualifications to be a personal trainer?" I asked.

"Yes. But you could be an assistant while you get certified. You could work with one of the trainers, help people with the machines, spot the lifters, collect the towels from the pool."

It sounded easy enough. I could certainly use the work, and if there was a course provided, there would be an opportunity to build a career. But Jamie and probably Amy would be working out regularly.

"Would it be possible to only work night shifts?" I asked.

"Sure. Most of my staff prefers to work during the day, and I always struggle to have enough people on at night, so I usually end up doing it. It would be very convenient for me if that suits you."

"It does." Jamie always worked out during the day. If I could work around her schedule, I wouldn't have to face her until I was in a better place in my life.

Jeremy rummaged under his desk and then threw me a polo shirt with the gym's logo.

"You start tomorrow night. Six o'clock. I'll have all the paperwork ready for you to fill out."

He pushed my membership card back across the desk to me.

"Thank you, Jeremy. Seriously, this means a lot to me."

I blinked into the bright sunlight when I left the building and walked down the street. My new life was falling into place. I'd made up with my brother, found a new place to live, and just landed myself a job doing something I enjoyed. The fact that I saw Scott's face in my dreams every night and thoughts of him plagued me during the day seemed less worrisome. I didn't need a man. I was creating a new life all on my own. But that didn't stop me from missing him.

# CHAPTER TWENTY-THREE

"**A**lison Mitchell, the doctor will see you now."

I smiled at the receptionist and walked down the hall. The walls were white, and there was a white door at the end of the hallway. There was no art on the walls or posters advertising support groups.

I knocked and someone called out, so I opened the door and walked inside. The office was all white, as well. White walls, white furniture. Even the computer was white.

A woman with graying hair and pointed features stood up and walked over to me.

"You must be Alison. I'm Dr. Wyatt, but feel free to call me Gillian. Please have a seat," she said, indicating the day-lounge.

I sat on the cool white leather and crossed my legs. Gillian sat opposite me with a notebook and a pencil.

"What can I help you with today?" she asked.

I swallowed and uncrossed my legs.

"Um, I've been making some bad choices in my life, and I want to make some changes."

"I think that's very brave of you, Alison. You've taken the first step, and that's great. Can you tell me a little bit about the choices that have led you to this point in your life?"

I launched into my story. Her pencil flew furiously across the page as I told her about my whole romantic history with Nick, working for Todd, and finally the influence that Scott had in my life.

She nodded as I spoke but never interrupted. She just let me vomit out my words until I was done.

"It sounds like you've experienced a lot of pain and developed a mechanism to deal with that hurt. There's nothing wrong with that; it's a very human response. Some people turn to drugs. Your drug of choice was sex. It's actually quite common."

"So can you cure me?" I asked.

She laughed and put her notepad down on the small white coffee table.

"Only you can fix yourself, Alison. But in quitting your job, you've taken the first step. Coming to see me is another step in that journey. You're moving in the right direction. I have a few questions for you, if you don't mind?"

"That's fine." I shifted on the lounge.

"First of all, would you like a coffee? I'm dying for one."

"That would be really good, actually."

She got up and walked over to a side table and came back carrying a silver tray with two cups, some milk and sugar, and a small pot of coffee. We each made a cup, and then Gillian sat back down. She curled her legs up under her and blew the steam from the top of her cup. The atmosphere was much more relaxed, and I almost felt like I was just sitting and talking with a friend.

"Okay, now for the tough questions." She gave me another smile. "Won't you miss the sex?"

My mouth dropped open, but I tried to recover quickly from my shock. I had not expected that question from my therapist. Jamie? Yes. Dr. Wyatt? No way!

"I don't know. Maybe?"

"I think the answer is that you definitely will. And who wouldn't? Our bodies are genetically programed to crave sex. It's the biological urge to carry on the species. But it's more than that for you. It's become an addiction, something you use to silence your pain. What are you going to do the next time that pain comes?"

I took a sip of coffee to give myself time to think. "Well, the past few days I've been working out at the gym more than usual."

"That's a good way to release some of your frustration, but I think you might need something more. Your body is used to having sex almost every day. For hours. Going from that quantity to nothing is going to be a shock to your system. I don't think cold turkey restraint is the answer for you."

"You want me to keep fucking? I may as well have kept my job!"

"No. Anonymous sex for money is damaging to you. Sex in general is a wonderful thing that I think people should indulge in more frequently."

I looked Gillian over, really seeing her for the first time. Her body was tight and lithe for her age, and her features were pretty. The casual way she sat exuded confidence. I could see her enjoying her sex life, and I envied her.

"Sex isn't the bad, dirty thing that people make it out to be. It's a normal human function that brings pleasure. You abused and distorted it into a power game. But the act itself is not evil."

"I experienced that with Scott," I said. "I just don't think I'm ready to do that yet."

She nodded. "Tell me—why do you enjoy sex?"

"It makes me feel powerful. The fact that I can make a man so vulnerable that his knees shake makes me feel strong."

"All right. Do you know why most people love sex?"

"Because it feels good?"

"Because it feels fucking amazing, Alison. That moment when your toes curl and your back arches off the bed, when you have no control over the moans that escape your lips or the blood rushing through your body…For that short time, you're in heaven. I think you need to re-educate yourself about the physical pleasure of sex."

"If I'm not working or dating someone, how do I do that?"

"You need to learn to love yourself."

"You mean like masturbation?"

"Yes that. But also emotionally. When you truly love yourself, you won't degrade your own body with meaningless sex. You're right though; masturbation will be an excellent tool for you. Get to know what makes *you* feel good. And when you're ready, you can learn how to share your body in a loving way with someone else. We're almost out of time, so I'd like to give you some homework that we'll talk about next time."

"Okay."

"I want you to have at least one orgasm every day. More if you like, but at least one. Experiment with trying different stimuli until you discover what turns your bones to jelly."

I left Zach watching TV in the living room and closed my bedroom door. I had some homework to do that definitely had to be done in the privacy of my bedroom. The session with Gillian that afternoon had been informative, and I was relieved that she hadn't judged me. I'd worried about that.

I looked at the bed and sighed. I was actually quite inexperienced at masturbation. When you had three sexual partners almost every single day, there wasn't really much need for it. Masturbation was a common part of my work, but I was always putting on a show or getting myself off while watching others. I'd very rarely felt the desire to touch myself for no other reason than just the pleasure. But I was excited to give it a go. It had been a while since I'd had sex and my body was practically buzzing with anticipation.

I turned off my lamp, throwing the room into darkness, and got undressed. I lay back on my bed and started rubbing my breasts. It seemed like the best way to start. My nipples tingled and grew firm as I grazed my fingernails over them and kneaded the surrounding flesh.

I kept my left hand stroking my nipple and let my right hand slide down over my stomach and into my folds. I was surprisingly wet already, and I guessed it was because of my sex drought. My legs spread open, and my hips bucked when I touched my clit. I ran my finger over it again and closed my eyes.

Warmth spread through my body as I started to rub the small nub in constant circles. I didn't really know if there was a right or wrong way to do this, but I didn't really care because it felt good, and Gillian had wanted me to feel how good sex was.

"Yes," I hissed softly as the sensation in my clit began to build. It was a different feeling than when a cock was inside me. This was like a shot instead of a whole drink. Intense and fast with double the bang.

My soft, natural moans weren't forced like when I was with a man. These weren't moans to let him know that was a good spot, or to help arouse him. These were just pure pleasure being expressed from my body.

My hips rocked against my hand, and I dipped my fingers lower, sliding them inside myself as my thumb found my abandoned clit. My fingers didn't feel like a cock, not even close, but it was still nice.

Just as I started to build up a steady rhythm, it was all over. Bright lights flashed behind my eyes and my back arched off the bed. I could hear the blood rushing in my ears as the ecstasy of orgasm burst and radiated all over my body.

When I opened my eyes in the dark room, I was covered in sweat and breathing heavily. And I was smiling.

"So, you've been coming to see me for six weeks now. I think it's time we did a mini review and see where to go from here. How are you finding your new life?" Gillian asked.

I shifted in the leather chair and gave her a smile.

"I think I'm getting used to the different routine. The gym that I've been going to for years had a trainee personal trainer job opening, and I got it. I'm enjoying the work, and I'm studying to get my PT certification. They're also opening a new branch in Philadelphia, and they've asked me if I'm interested in working there as a full-time personal trainer. It would mean another move, but it would be a great opportunity."

"How would you feel about moving again so quickly? You've only just settled into this apartment with your brother."

"Yeah, he's a bit put out at the thought of finding a new roommate. It was really nice for us to be living together again. We're a lot closer now. I think Mom and Dad liked to know that we were looking out for each other, you know?"

She nodded and jotted something in her little notebook.

"But you think moving is the right decision for you at this point in your life?"

"I don't know if it's right, but it's terrifying and exciting. Two months ago I knew exactly what my life was, but now I could be living in another state, meeting new people, being a different me."

Gillian smiled warmly, leaned forward, and removed her glasses. "What's wrong with the old you?"

I shifted uncomfortably in my seat. "She was a whore."

"She was a woman in a lot of pain."

"Who channeled her pain into whoring. I know you're trying to make me see my past differently, but I lived it. I know what I did."

"Do you regret that life?"

That pulled me up short. I'd always tried to live a life of no regrets.

"No, I don't regret it. It was something that I needed to do in that period of my life, but I'm not that girl anymore."

"Complete personality transformation takes a long time, Alison. You can't change your core being in a few short weeks."

I frowned. "Are you saying that I'll end up going to go back to prostitution? That I can't escape it?"

"Not at all. I think you've done amazingly well to move on as quickly as you have. I just want to caution you about being overly confident. It's only been a few weeks, and there is still a long road for you to travel."

I chewed on my lip as I processed what she'd said. I'd been so sure that I'd put all that behind me.

"Can you honestly say that you still don't miss the sex?" she asked, leaning back in her chair.

Heat crept over my cheeks. "You know, six weeks is the longest I've gone without sex in years."

"And how are you coping with that loss?"

I laughed. Gillian and I had spoken about my prostitution a lot when I'd first started seeing her, but the past few sessions had been more focused on building my new life.

"With a lot of masturbation."

Gillian cleared her throat and sat up a bit straighter. "Is that satisfying you?" she asked, pen poised.

"It's a completely different experience. The sex I used to have wasn't about orgasming for me. I very rarely came with my clients. It was about the power of giving pleasure to someone else and feeling in control. That was what made me feel good. I have a lot more orgasms now, but I've lost that feeling of control and power."

"How do you think you could compensate for that? It was a core part of who you were for a long time, and you'll need to fill that void if you don't want to relapse."

"Well, I suppose I get the adrenaline that I'm missing from working out."

She nodded and jotted down a note in her pad. "And the control?"

"I guess I don't need it anymore. The craving that I had wasn't to control *everything*; it was more to prove to my ex-boyfriend that I was desirable. I knew that he had no idea what I was doing, but in my mind I was proving a point. I don't feel the need to prove that anymore. I couldn't care less about him."

Gillian smiled. "You've come a long way since we first met, Alison."

"Thank you," I said, taking a satisfying breath.

"If you're really serious about moving to Philadelphia, then I'll get a list of therapists I can recommend for you to see there."

"I'm serious. I feel like it's the right step for me."

"All right. Well, I'll see you the same time next week. Keep up the good work."

# CHAPTER TWENTY-FOUR

"I've made up my mind. I'll take the job!" I said as I walked into Jeremy's office at the gym.

"Fantastic! How soon can you be down there to help with the set-up?"

"How does two weeks sound?"

"Great! I'll do the transfer paperwork today and let them know to expect you in a couple weeks. You're not going to regret it, Alison. You'll love Philly!"

"Thanks for the opportunity, Jeremy. I'm actually really excited about moving and getting a fresh start."

I left his office with a huge grin on my face and took a seat at my station. One of the regular clients, Greg, came over and leaned on the counter.

"Alison, care to spot me?"

"Sure. I'll just get a towel. Go set yourself up."

Greg was attractive. He was the classic tall, dark, and handsome, and I'd seen him head home with several of our female members. Classic ladies' man.

I grabbed a towel and a water bottle and walked into the weight room. Greg had set himself up on one of the machines and was adding weights to the bar. I mentally calculated the total he was lifting and made a note to challenge myself more when I trained.

He lay back on the bench, and I stood behind him. I wasn't sure if I would be much help if he dropped the bar; there was no way I would be able to lift it off him, but at least I'd be close by to call for help.

He started his reps, and I watched him in the mirrored wall.

"You're looking good tonight," Greg said through gritted teeth.

"You should be concentrating," I scolded.

He finished his reps, put the bar back in its cradle, and then sat up, taking the water I held out to him.

"It's impossible to concentrate when you're standing there looking so sexy."

"Greg…"

"Have a drink with me tonight?" he asked.

"I don't get off work until late." I thought that was the kindest way to let him know I wasn't interested.

"Even better. We can skip the drink. No need for bullshit. You're hot, I'm hot. Let's fuck."

I coughed and stepped backward.

"That's very flattering, but I'm not interested."

"Come on, I'd blow your mind. You look like a girl who loves a good fuck."

If only he knew how true his words were. My resolve faltered. It would be so easy to go home with him. He wasn't the kind of guy who had second dates, so I wouldn't have to worry about strings. I could just have my desires satisfied and walk away.

I was enjoying the masturbation, but it wasn't the same as a good hard fuck. If I was being honest, I really did miss it.

And Greg would be good. He looked at me with the confidence of a guy who knew he could turn my bones to jelly. For a moment, I almost took him up on his offer.

"Really, I'm not interested."

"You married? I'm very discreet. No one would know."

"No, I'm not married. I'm just trying to be more respectful with my body."

He cocked an eyebrow, but I held my resolve.

"Your loss," he said finally, then walked out of the room.

He was probably right. It wasn't any setback to him. I was certain that he would find another girl to satisfy him, and I would be home alone.

I took a deep breath and reminded myself *why* I was doing this. The breath came out slowly, and I was proud of myself. I'd have to remember to tell Gillian how I'd beaten temptation.

I left the weight room and saw that there was a girl who was pushing random buttons on a treadmill but not getting anywhere. I jogged over to her.

"Hi, I'm Alison, can I help you out with this beast?"

The girl gave me an appreciative smile. "Thanks. I can't figure out how to make it incline. I just moved from San Francisco and even though I love New York, it's so flat here. I miss hill running."

I pushed a few buttons, showing her how to adjust the controls, and then left her with her iPod and her machine-made hill.

"You are one tough girl to track down," a male voice said behind me. I froze. I knew that voice. My mouth automatically curled up into a smile, but I bit my lip back into submission before turning around.

"Scott," I said, trying to keep my voice flat. "What are you doing here?"

"You work here."

"Yes. But that doesn't answer my question." I put my hands on my hips. I wasn't in the mood for games, especially from him.

"Yes, it does." He smiled down at me, looking me over as if I was a bottle of Gatorade and he'd been wandering through the desert for a month.

"Okay, let me rephrase. What do you want?"

"Ally, can we talk please?"

"It's Alison," I said a little more harshly than I'd intended.

He cocked his head to the side and gave me a curious look. "Alison."

I dropped my arms and rolled my eyes, making a show of my frustration. "Fine. Follow me."

I led him back to the staff changing rooms and then locked the door so we wouldn't be disturbed.

"This better be important!" I barked. "I'm working."

"You look good in Lycra."

I glared at him, letting him know that my outfit wasn't what we were here to discuss.

"All right, all right," he said with a sigh, holding his hands up in defeat. "I wanted to see you. I've spent weeks tracking you down."

"How *did* you find me? I moved, changed my phone number, and I haven't even spoken to my old friends."

"I hired someone," he told me unapologetically.

"You *investigated* me?"

"Well, you didn't really leave me much of a choice, Ally…son." He lengthened my name when he saw my eyes narrow.

"Your choice was to forget about me and move on, like I have."

"That wasn't an acceptable option for me. Look, can we please just talk and not fight?"

"What is there to talk about?"

"I have a question."

"You had me investigated and then flew all the way to New York to ask me a question?"

"It's a very important question."

I folded my arms across my chest, bouncing my hip. "Well?" I asked after he was silent for a while.

"Todd told me that you quit your job. Your other job."

"That's not a question," I pointed out.

"I know. I just wanted to make sure it was fact before I asked."

"Yes. I've quit that job."

His body visibly relaxed. "Okay, then. Why did you cut me off? We could have been together this whole time."

A rush of air left me as if I'd been struck in the gut, and I took a step back. Didn't he understand? Couldn't he see why I had to be on my own? Surely he would have known how many times I'd wanted to call him, to talk to him.

"Because I couldn't do it for you," I stammered.

His brow creased, and he stepped toward me with his hand extended. I backed away again.

"I don't understand," he said.

"I couldn't change my life for *you*. I had to do it for myself. I had to want it, not feel like I'd done it for anyone else."

"Did you do it because of me?"

I opened my mouth, but couldn't find the words to say. I wanted to scream that of course I'd done it for him. That I couldn't bear the thought of having another man touch me after I'd fallen in love with him. I also wanted to yell at him for being so egotistical. Not everything I did revolved around him and his wants. It was *my* life, and I'd made changes to have the life I wanted to live. The reality of the situation fell somewhere in the middle of those extreme thoughts.

"You were the catalyst, but I wanted the change."

He started to walk toward me again, and I automatically stepped away from him. My back hit the wall. I was trapped. He didn't stop his advance until he was only a few inches from me. The smell of him was overwhelming and brought back the memory of waking up on silk sheets and looking out the window into the flawless blue sky of Miami.

"Ally," he whispered.

"Alison," I choked out.

My body was failing me. I'd been so strong for six weeks. Denied every attempt to contact him, and denied every advance from a man. I'd worked my body hard at the gym to release the build up of sexual tension and, despite all that, I was about to melt at his feet.

"I don't care what you call yourself, I just want to be near you."

"You're pretty close right now," I said.

He smiled. "I could be closer."

"Not much closer."

"Is that a challenge?" He took a final step and pressed his body against mine. His arms encased me, and he rested his forehead against my own.

"Please don't make me leave," he begged.

"This is a staff room, so you'll have to leave eventually."

"Ally," he scolded.

I laughed, my body vibrating against his chest.

"God, I've missed you." He breathed against my throat as his mouth traveled over my skin. He kissed all the way up my jaw, but hesitated, hovering over my lips. "Can I kiss you?"

I bit my lip, thinking about the answer. My body was screaming for him. Each pump of blood from my heart was full of burning desire for the man holding me. Looking up into his eyes, I nodded.

His lips were on mine in an instant, hard and full of longing. He tasted like cinnamon and I opened my mouth, deepening the kiss.

His body fell against mine, pushing me hard against the wall. Just as I'd remembered, we fit together perfectly. All I could hear were his gasps for air between kisses and the rush of blood through my body.

He was clutching at my crop top, trying to get his hands underneath but couldn't.

He chuckled against my lips. "You might look sexy, but this outfit is impossible!"

Without thinking, I reached between us and pulled the top over my head, leaving my breasts free. He groaned and grasped my exposed skin before crushing his lips to mine once again.

His hands were rough and desperate. I wanted him so badly that I didn't think I could ever get enough of him touching me. I reached down to his zipper, but my hands froze. I'd been so strong for so long. I couldn't just throw it all away now. No matter how much I wanted to, I couldn't do it.

"Scott," I gasped, pulled away. "Don't."

He froze and pulled away, breathing heavily.

"You're right. We have a lot to talk about. When I saw you, I just couldn't keep my hands off you."

It was quite ironic that he was *now* having the response to being close to me that I'd wanted when we'd started dating. I pushed him away and quickly walked to the other side of the room so I wouldn't be tempted to kiss him again.

"You'd better go." I tugged my shirt on, and he nodded.

I showed him out and quickly scanned to make sure everyone was working out happily. I couldn't see anyone who looked like they needed help, so I kept walking to my station at the front desk. Scott followed closely behind.

"When do you get off?" he asked.

"We close at nine, and then I have to help pack up the equipment. I should be home by ten."

"Is it okay if I stop by later so we can talk?"

"Talk, huh?" I said with a laugh.

"Well, talk *first*." He winked.

"Just talk," I said.

He gave me a curious look, obviously wondering if I'd had a personality transplant.

I grabbed one of the gym's business cards off the counter and scribbled my new address on the back. He raised an eyebrow when he took it from me.

"I moved," I explained.

"New roommate?"

"Yep."

"Does your new roommate have sex in the living room like Jamie did?"

"Geez, I hope not. I wouldn't want to walk in on that. He's not exactly my type."

Scott's eyebrows raised up almost into his hair. "You live with a *guy?*"

"Oh, yeah. He's really handsome, and I've seen him naked loads of times. We used to shower together, but not anymore. It was getting kind of inappropriate."

I held back a laugh as hard as I could. Scott obviously didn't expect me to be talking about when Zach and I were children.

"I don't think I like this guy."

"Well, I was moving quickly, and I didn't have a lot of time to be picky about roommates."

"Hmm."

Just then, Jeremy walked out of his office and glared at Scott. "Alison, I need you to help me with this email."

"Sure, what can I do?"

"Can you give me an exact date for relocation?"

I glanced at the desk calendar and counted the days. "How about the seventeenth?"

"Great. And will you need a car when you get there? You can lease one through the company if you want. Philly doesn't have the same extensive public transport as New York, but there are busses."

"Thanks. I'll think about it. Can I let you know tomorrow?"

"Sure. I'll send these papers off then."

He shot Scott another look that clearly said, "Let my staff get back to work!" and then went back into his office.

"You're moving to Philadelphia?" Scott's eyebrows shot up. "Were you going to tell me this?"

I waved at two guys as they walked in and swiped their membership cards. Once they were gone, I glared at Scott.

"Before half an hour ago, I wasn't talking to you."

"Hey, Alison."

I waved as more people came to work out and greeted me on their way by. "Can we talk about this later? I'm supposed to be working."

Scott held up the business card I'd just handed him, and gestured, "I'll be *here* at ten tonight."

"Alison, can you come in here for a minute?" Jeremy called from his office.

"Coming!" I called loudly, then said to Scott, "See you later."

I left him standing at the counter. When I returned, he was gone. It was such a busy night at the gym that, unbelievably, I was able to forget about Scott. Jeremy was surging full-speed ahead with the plans to transfer me to Philadelphia and even had me looking at apartment listings online during work time.

After all the equipment was organized and I'd said goodbye to everyone, I made my way home. Scott was leaning against a light pole outside my building.

"You could have waited for me inside," I said as I approached.

"I didn't want to talk to your shower buddy," he admitted with a cheeky grin.

I laughed and unlocked the front door. "Come on, he won't bite."

Scott followed me in and looked around the living room. I tried to see the room from his eyes and embarrassment swelled within me. The secondhand couch and brick of a television mocked me.

"I know it's not much, but we moved in really quickly and have only been here a few weeks."

"I like it," Scott said. "It feels homey."

While I was trying to work out whether Scott was genuine or just trying to make me feel better, Zach walked out of his bedroom.

"Oh, it's *you*," he said to Scott. "I thought we got rid of you."

"Zach!" I scolded.

Scott smirked at him and then smiled at me. "I get the naked shower comment now."

I smiled back while Zach looked at us like we were speaking Chinese.

"Did you bring home any food, sis?"

"Sorry. The store was closed by the time I left work," I said.

"There's a twenty-four-hour one just two blocks over!"

"I have company. Why don't *you* go?"

Zach rolled his eyes as he grabbed his wallet off the coffee table. "You want anything?"

I looked at Scott, but he shook his head. "We're good," I said to my brother as he left.

"Can I see the bedroom?" Scott asked.

"I don't know if I trust you in a bedroom," I teased.

"Me? You were the one who jumped me in the locker room!"

"As if! You couldn't get my clothes off fast enough!"

He put his hands up, palms facing me. "I think it's fair to say we were both to blame."

I chewed my lip to keep from smiling. "All right. Truce."

"So, the bedroom?"

I showed him through the apartment, giving him the grand tour and ending with my tiny room. It was about half the size of my bedroom in the old apartment, but all I needed was a bed and bookcase and I was fine.

"Homey," Scott said again.

"What you meant to say is *small*."

He sat on the bed and bounced the springs with his hand, testing it. "So, Philadelphia?" His tone was casual, but I knew he was nervous about my answer. His eyes and jaw were tight.

"Yeah, where they have cheesesteaks and the Liberty Bell?" I replied.

"Cute. I'm *trying* to have a serious conversation here."

I sat down on the bed and folded my legs under me. "Okay, talk."

"Why?"

"I got offered a job there."

"What's wrong with your job here?"

"What does it matter where I live?"

"I thought what happened tonight at the gym meant something for us. I thought we were both on the same page," he said.

"Please, enlighten me."

"I still love you, Ally, and I know you love me too. I can see it. We work so well together, and our chemistry is off the charts."

"I still don't see what my job has to do with this. You live in Florida, so what does it matter if I'm here or Philly?"

"Because I come to New York every week. I never go to *Philly*." He said it like it was a dirty word.

I took his hands and grasped them tightly. "I don't really know what you want from me. You didn't want me to be a prostitute and I'm not. Now you don't want me to work in the gym?"

"No, it's not that. What I really want is for you to come live in Miami with me. You could work for my company—at least at first until you find something you like better. Maybe another gym down there. Or, even better, not work at all if you don't want to."

"Seriously? I'm not a damsel in distress. I don't need a knight to come and save me and put me in his ivory tower, even if that tower does have amazing ocean views. I *want* to work. I want to earn my own money and take care of myself."

We glared at each other.

"You can't stare me into submission, Scott. I'm taking the job in Philly."

He smiled. "I forgot how stubborn you can be."

"I prefer *determined*."

"You're right. You are determined, so I'll come to you."

I shifted in my seat and slid away from him.

"Scott, I don't want this to come out the wrong way, but I'm doing really well on my own. I kind of want this move to be mine, *for me*."

Scott frowned. "I wasn't imagining that back at the gym, was I? You kissed me back," he said.

"I know I did. I do still care about you, and one day maybe there will be a chance for us to be together. I'm just not ready for that right now. I'm making some major changes to my life and to who I am. Maybe you won't even like the new me."

"Tell me about the new you. I can't think of any change you could make that would stop me from loving you."

I smirked. "Alison is strong without needing to be in control. She respects herself and doesn't need men in her life to give her a sense of worth."

Scott held up his hand for me to stop.

"I like those things, and I fully support them. But you're still a human being, and humans need companionship. We need love and affection."

"I agree. I do have those needs. I'm just fulfilling them differently now."

"Please don't try to pull the whole all-a-woman-needs-is-chocolate bullshit."

I laughed. "No. I'm satisfying my own needs now. I'm not saying I'll never be with a man again, because I know that's not the case. But it won't be until I'm emotionally ready."

Scott smiled, and his eyes lit up. "I never thought I'd be so happy to hear a woman say she didn't want to have sex with me. That's a *huge* change for you, Ally."

"It is. You have no idea how much having you here is testing my resolve. If you were in Philly too, I wouldn't stand a chance. Please, Scott. I'm not saying no. I'm just saying *not yet*."

"I can live with *not yet*. Would it be all right if I visited you sometimes, though?"

"And we can talk on the phone," I said.

"So, long distance."

"I'm willing to give it a try if you are."

"I'll take any chance you're offering. Up until a few hours ago, I still thought I might never see you again."

I moved closer and gave him a tight hug. "I'm sorry this meeting isn't what you hoped it would be."

"It's better," he mumbled into my shoulder. "Except for the very first night we met, sex hasn't been what I wanted from you. *This*, having you in my arms and knowing that you care about me. It's what I want."

"I *do* still care about you. I've actually thought about calling you every single day. I almost did so many times."

"I wish you had."

"It wasn't the right time then. Maybe it's not even the right time now."

"Ally, there never *is* a right time. Life doesn't work like that. Something is always going to stand in the way. You have to take each opportunity as it comes and make the best of it."

"You're right," I said, stifling a yawn.

"You're tired. I should get going."

"How long are you in the city?" I asked.

"I had only planned to be here for the night. I have a flight back in the morning. I was planning for a worst-case scenario, being that you didn't want to see me. But I can change that if you'd like me to stay longer."

"I would, but I won't have much time to spend with you. I'm working all week, and I'll be packing and helping Zach find a new roommate."

"Okay. You said I could call you, though?"

"Yes. I'd like that."

I gave him my new phone number and then walked him to the door.

"This isn't goodbye," I said. But it certainly felt like it. My stomach churned, and my heart clenched.

"I'll call you tomorrow," Scott promised.

"You'd better."

I leaned up and gave him a soft kiss. I wished he never had to let go.

"I love you," he mumbled.

"I love you, too, Scott."

We shared one last kiss, and then he walked to the curb and hailed a cab. He turned back to give me a wistful smile as he got into the car, and I waved until the brake lights were out of sight.

# EPILOGUE

*Six Months Later*

"**Y**ou're doing great, Colleen. Give me ten more, and then we'll cool down."

"Thanks, Alison," Colleen gasped between crunches as I sat on her feet.

I counted her down from ten and then helped her stretch.

"Great job. See you next week!" I said.

Colleen waved as she headed toward the locker room. Her flushed face and heaving chest let me know that she'd had a good workout.

"Alison! Can I see you in my office please?" Jeremy's voice came over the loud speaker.

I jogged through the gym to the office, knocked on the door, and then stuck my head inside.

"You wanted to see me, boss?"

"Quick. Come inside and close the door."

Anxiety burst inside me. What could Jeremy need to talk to me about with the door closed? Perhaps he'd decided that I wasn't working out and he needed to let me go. What would I do then? Would I have to move back to New York? I'd only just settled into my routine in Philly. The streets were beginning to feel familiar and

I'd finally found a coffee place that made my latte exactly how I liked it. Moving back to New York would be a step backward.

My shoulders slumped at the prospect of calling Zach and asking if I could stay with him until I could find a place of my own. And I'd thought everything had been going so well.

"Don't be nervous," Jeremy said. "You haven't even opened it yet." He held up an envelope, and I stared at it, puzzled.

"What is it?" I asked.

"Just open it."

I walked slowly across the room and took the envelope from him. It had an official emblem on the front that was familiar, but I didn't place it until after I'd ripped it open. Once I knew where the letter was from, the anxiety I'd felt earlier fluttered back to life and made my hands shake.

"Do you know what this says?" I asked, glancing up from the envelope to Jeremy's face. He looked just as nervous as I felt.

"No idea."

I sucked in a breath and pulled the folded piece of paper out. It crinkled as I flattened it. The typed words on the page blurred together, and I almost couldn't read them. This was worse than thinking that Jeremy was going to fire me. At least if that had happened I could have gotten a job at another gym. If this letter held bad news, then I'd be looking for *another* new career.

"You read it!" I said, throwing the paper across his desk.

Jeremy grabbed it up and scanned the page, his lips spreading into a huge smile. His eyes flashed with pride as he put the letter down and smiled at me.

"I knew you could do it."

"Shut up!" I jumped around the desk and grabbed the paper to read for myself.

I scanned the page three times, reveling in the words.

Dear Ms. Mitchell,

It is our great pleasure to inform you that you have satisfactorily completed all units toward your diploma and certification in personal training science. We wish to invite you to enroll in further study...

I squealed and hugged Jeremy, who wrapped his arms around me and swung me in a circle. "I knew you could do it."

"So," I said. "What now?" I was eager to continue the forward momentum of my new life.

"That's really up to you. You have a permanent PT position here, and if you decide to continue with a higher level of study, then we'll support that. The gym would benefit from having a nutritionist on staff."

I stared down at the letter again, my cheeks starting to ache from the huge grin.

Jeremy laughed. "Why don't you take off early today and celebrate."

"Are you sure?"

"Yeah! You've earned it."

"Thanks, Jer. You're the best!"

I practically skipped out of the gym. I stopped off on my way home and bought a bottle of champagne. It was the same brand that Scott had served me the first night we'd met. I'd been right in my assumption that it was expensive, but passing my certification was worth the splurge.

I wondered what Zach would say if I asked if I could come home for the weekend and sleep on his couch. I was enjoying Philadelphia, but hadn't managed to make too many friends outside of work yet. To celebrate, a Saturday night dancing with people I cared about at my favorite club, Lavo, was in order. I could even ask Jeremy to have Monday off and spend Sunday night with Scott in his usual room at The Plaza.

It had been two weeks since we'd seen each other, and I missed him terribly. Our nightly phone calls just weren't as fulfilling as I'd hoped they would be when I'd suggested the long-distance relationship.

Thinking of Scott made me miss him even more, and as soon as I got home, I put the champagne bottle in the fridge and took the cordless phone to the couch. I dialed, but his phone went straight to voice mail. He was probably on a work call.

I waited until the champagne was cold, then poured a glass. "Here's to me!" I said to no one in particular and took a sip of the bubbly liquid.

The phone rang, and I answered it on the first ring, expecting it to be Scott calling me back.

"Scott!"

"Better. It's *me*." I could practically hear the smile on my brother's face.

"Hey, Zach. How would you feel about your little sister sleeping on your couch this weekend after a night at Lavo?"

"I'd feel pretty awesome about it." We both laughed. "Seriously, you're coming home? It's been months."

"I know. I haven't been ready to go back, but I want to celebrate with you."

"What are we celebrating?"

"Your sister is a certified PT."

He cheered a man-grunt that I was pretty sure meant he was happy.

"So, we're on for the weekend?" I asked.

"You bet."

"Great. I'll stop off at Mom's on my way to the city. She's been nagging me to visit more."

"She just worries about you, Al."

"I know. I'm just nervous because I think I'm going to tell her the truth about my life."

"Shut the fuck up! Don't you dare."

"Why not?"

"Do you want her to have heart failure?"

"No, Zach. Of course not," I said flatly. "But she's my mom and I want her to know me. She hasn't known the real me for years. I miss talking to her about things, and now that I'm settled in my new life, I'm hoping she'll take it well."

"It's your funeral. Just ease her into it, and if she starts to freak out, promise me you'll stop talking."

"Don't worry, I don't plan to go into graphic detail."

The call waiting beeped.

"I think Scott's calling me back," I said.

"See you on the weekend then. Oh, and Al…"

"Yes?"

The call waiting beeped again.

"I'm proud of you."

"Thanks, Zach."

He hung up, and I switched to the waiting call.

"Hello?"

On the line I heard a long exhale. "I've missed your voice."

I laughed. "You spoke to me last night, Scott."

"It feels like forever ago."

I moved through the apartment and curled up on the couch, ready for a long conversation. "How was your day?" I asked.

"I miss you more today than I did yesterday," he said. "I think I need to come visit you soon."

"I'd really like that."

"Good. How was *your* day?"

I squirmed in my seat as excitement bubbled in me again at the thought of my news. "My day was awesome! I got a letter—"

"Wait. Don't tell me now."

"Why not?" I asked, wondering why he wouldn't want to know my news. Scott was *always* interested in what I had to say.

"Tell me after you've answered the door."

"What?"

Just then there was a loud knock.

I squealed and ran to the door, pulling it open. Scott was standing on my doorstep with his cell phone pressed to his ear and a huge grin on his face.

I dropped the phone and threw my arms around him.

His hands cupped the sides of my face as he pulled me in for a long kiss.

"It's so good to see you," he breathed.

I felt the same way. My chest was lighter, and joy swelled within me, for no other reason except that he was standing in front of me. As if I was suddenly whole.

I grabbed his hand, pulled him into the apartment, and kicked the door closed. He spun us around, pushing me into the hard wood as he pressed himself against me and kissed me again.

"Yes," I moaned when he began trailing his mouth down my throat. He hadn't shaved that morning, and his stubble scratched my skin.

He froze. "No," he said, pulling back.

"Why are you stopping?"

"I'm not going to push you more than you're ready for. I didn't come here for *this*. I just wanted to see you."

He pulled away and ran his hands through his hair, and I followed him into the living room. It felt good to have him in my apartment, as if he belonged in my private space. He sat down on the couch, settling back into the cushions as I chewed my lip.

He'd been so patient with me. Six months of kisses, above the clothes petting, and *no sex*. I wasn't sure how he was restraining himself, but he was, for me.

That was the moment I decided that enough was enough. I loved Scott. I had Ally well under control and hadn't felt her presence for a long time. I was *me*. I was strong. And I wanted the man I loved to be able to touch me.

"So, your news?" he asked, excited.

"That doesn't matter right now." I stalked across the room.

He raised an eyebrow at my expression. "What are you doing?" He slid farther back into the couch.

I stood in front of him and reached out my hand. He reluctantly laced our fingers together.

"I love you, Scott."

His eyes softened. "I love you, Alison."

"Make love to me," I whispered.

Scott chuckled nervously. "Don't tease me," he warned.

I sat on his lap and pressed soft kisses along his jaw. "Who's teasing?"

"Alison…Don't you think we should talk about this?"

"I'm sick of talking," I said honestly. "All we've done for months is *talk*. I'm ready, Scott. I swear."

"Say it again."

I stood up and tugged on his arm. He allowed me to pull him to his feet and moved with me a few steps toward the bedroom. He was still cautious, but I could see desire there as well.

"I want you to make love to me," I purred.

Scott's expression changed to one of pure joy, and he swung me up into his arms and carried me into the bedroom. He laid me gently on the bed and pressed the length of his body against me.

"I thought you'd never ask."

# ACKNOWLEDGMENTS

There are so many people who helped this book find its way into your hands. And I am eternally grateful to each and every one of them. To all the staff at Omnific Publishing, who have been so professional and supportive of this story. Elizabeth, Lisa, Traci — thank you. To my hard working editors who helped develop Ally and Scott into real live people in my head — Colleen and Sarah. There is as much of you both in this story as there is me. What a team we made! Also, to the first person who critiqued this work and believed in the characters, Jenn Owen. You fanned my flame and I'm extremely grateful.

To my two dear friends, who kept this story a secret for everyone around us — Bree and Mikahla — I owe you both, big time. Thank you for reading multiple drafts, helping with tough plot points and listening to me sulk when the characters weren't doing what I wanted them to do. You both know I adore you.

To my mom, who I wasn't going to tell about this story. Thank you for not being too shocked when you heard the plot line. I asked you not to read this book, so if you're reading this now — naughty! But, I'm honored that you support my writing, no matter what I write about.

To my aunt, and friend, Saylor. Thank you for being my confidant, my champion and my hero. I wish I were as strong, inspirational and brave as you.

And finally, the most important thank you of them all. To you, the person reading this book. Thank you, thank you, thank you. I hope you enjoyed Ally's journey. And I wish you all a Scott Walker of your own.

# ABOUT THE AUTHOR

Joy is a fiery redhead who takes full advantage of the Australian lifestyle, sunning herself on tropical beaches and flirting with handsome lifeguards. She loves cats, books and chocolate, and of course the male physique. Joy started writing as a teenager and never stopped, although she writes about much more mature topics now. You can often find Joy browsing the shelves of her local bookstore or researching her favorite city, New York, in preparation of fulfilling her lifelong dream to live there one day.

＊—ய—＋Young Adult＊—ய—＋

The Ember series: *Ember* & *Iridescent* by Carol Oates
*Breaking Point* by Jess Bowen
*Life, Liberty, and Pursuit* by Susan Kaye Quinn
The Embrace series: *Embrace* & *Hold Tight* by Cherie Colyer
*Destiny's Fire* by Trisha Wolfe
The Reaper series: *Reaping Me Softly* & *UnReap My Heart* by Kate Evangelista

＊—ய—＋Erotic Romance＊—ய—＋

The Keyhole series: *Becoming sage (book one)* by Kasi Alexander
The Keyhole series: *Saving sunni (book two)* by Kasi & Reggie Alexander
The Winemaker's Dinner: *Appetizers* & *Entrée* by Dr. Ivan Rusilko &
Everly Drummond
The Winemaker's Dinner: *Dessert* by Dr. Ivan Rusilko
*Client N° 5* by Joy Fulcher

＊—ய—＋Paranormal Romance＊—ய—＋

The Light series: *Seers of Light, Whisper of Light,* & *Circle of Light*
by Jennifer DeLucy
The Hanaford Park series: *Eve of Samhain* & *Pleasures Untold* by Lisa Sanchez
*Immortal Awakening* by KC Randall
The Seraphim series: *Crushed Seraphim* & *Bittersweet Seraphim*
by Debra Anastasia
*The Guardian's Wild Child* by Feather Stone
*Grave Refrain* by Sarah M. Glover
*Divinity* by Patricia Leever
Blood Vine series: *Blood Vine* & *Blood Entangled* by Amber Belldene
*Divine Temptation* by Nicki Elson
*Love in the Time of the Dead* by Tera Shanley

＊—ய—＋Historical Romance＊—ய—＋

*Cat O' Nine Tails* by Patricia Leever
*Burning Embers* by Hannah Fielding
*Good Ground* by Tracy Winegar